"YOU CAN'T DENY IT."

Luc sighed at her ear. "You *are* my business, Paula."

Her eyes filled with such a strong need to trust that Luc's heart turned over. Something he hadn't felt in all the time since his failure stirred in him. He lowered his head, taking her parted lips.

Paula was hungry for that simple affection, but soon hungry passion inflamed them both. His thighs were pressed against hers, his fingers making circles on her breasts. Hot pleasure shot deeply through her; with it came pain. Blinding kisses from a colleague could only mean trouble, and Paula shuddered as the tears fell.

"My God, what's wrong?" Luc pulled back. "I would never hurt you, Paula. I really mean to be your friend. Your eyes plead for that...."

Stricken, she looked at him. Despite his offer, it was Luc who seemed to desperately need something....

Dear Reader:

We are very excited to announce a change to Harlequin Superromances effective with the February releases, title numbers 150–153. As you know, romance publishing is never static, but is always growing and innovative. After extensive market research, we have decided to slightly shorten the length of the four Superromances published each month, guaranteeing a faster-paced story.

You will still receive that "something extra" in plot and character development that has made these longer romance novels so popular. A strong well-written love story will remain at the heart of a Harlequin Superromance, but with the tighter format, drama will be heightened from start to finish.

Our authors are delighted with and challenged by this change, and they have been busy writing some wonderful new stories for you. Enjoy!

Laurie Bauman

Laurie Bauman,
Superromance Senior Editor

Lucy Snow

GARDEN OF LIONS

Harlequin Books

TORONTO • NEW YORK • LONDON
AMSTERDAM • PARIS • SYDNEY • HAMBURG
STOCKHOLM • ATHENS • TOKYO • MILAN

Published March 1985

First printing January 1985

ISBN 0-373-70155-1

Printed in Canada

For P.C.D.E.
in homage to Charlotte Brontë.

PROLOGUE

IN BRUSSELS IT RAINS one day out of every two, or so Paula Emanuel had been told. After twenty hours' travel, the fact that she was nearly soaked to the bone was just one more irritant to add to a list that included tired, confused and maybe just plain scared. Still, as the taxi deposited her in front of Le Berceau, she took a deep breath, squared her slender shoulders, jutted out her chin and screwed up her courage. The huge old school with its myriad lighted windows loomed above her in the darkness, and glancing at her watch, she could just make out that it was six-thirty. *Please don't be gone yet. Please don't.*

Lugging the heavy suitcases that contained practically all she owned, she ascended the wide stone staircase. A discreet brass plaque bearing the French words for Academy of Fine Arts hung over a doorbell. Paula put down her bags and tentatively pressed the bell. No response.

"That probably hasn't worked in a hundred years," said a chipper young voice behind her, and Paula turned to see a pretty teenage girl carrying an oversize sketchbook beneath one arm. "You don't need to ring. Just go on in."

Though she had no difficulty understanding the girl's French, Paula noted the same—to her—strange accent as the taxi driver's. It made her feel shy about her own accent. "Surely school can't still be in session?" she asked the girl.

"No—the last class ends at four. But some people stay around for activities and rehearsals, that sort of thing...." Apparently noticing that Paula was wilting from the combined effects of long travel and heavy baggage, the student asked, "Can I help you carry something?"

Grateful, Paula nodded, and the student, who announced her name as Kathelijne, picked up one of the suitcases and escorted her into the lobby of Le Berceau. Glancing up, Paula noticed the nineteenth-century austerity of wood-paneled walls and high ceilings, but there was a warmth to the place that appealed immediately.

"Some people think this place is a palace, and some think it's a jail," remarked Kathelijne. Not waiting for a comment from Paula, she went on, "Where did you come from? Who was it you wanted to see?"

"I had a four-thirty appointment to see Madame Saint-Pierre. I suppose it's too late for her to have waited, but I came directly from the airport, hoping there'd be someone here who could at least give her a message that I've arrived. I flew out of Montreal late last night, but there was a delay and—"

"Saint-Pierre?" Kathelijne's pert nose wrinkled; her expression seesawed between puzzlement and disgust. "Saint-Pierre isn't here anymore."

"As I said, I didn't expect she would be. Perhaps if you can just show me to her office, I can leave a note for her, and she and I can meet tomorrow."

"I don't think you quite understand, miss. Saint-Pierre is gone for good. They say she retired, but everybody knows she really got fired."

"Fired?" The idea was so impossible that Paula thought she'd misunderstood the girl. Maybe the word meant something different in Belgian French. "She can't have been fired. I had an appointment to see her. I've come all this way—"

"Look, miss," Kathelijne said with alarm, "why don't you just sit down for a minute or two, and I'll get somebody to help you. Madame Légère is sometimes still here until late. I'll run over to her office and tell her there's a foreign visitor. It'll only take a minute. Why don't you just sit here and wait?"

Together they carried Paula's bags a short distance to one of the long oak benches that lined the walls of the large open area in which they'd stood. Leaving her sketchbook on the bench beside Paula, Kathelijne trotted off across the marble floor, abandoning Paula to her own thoughts.

If Saint-Pierre had been fired, it probably meant she herself was out of a job. Specifically, out of a job that she'd come all the way across the Atlantic to accept. She was so tired she didn't have the energy to panic—not yet. Relaxing her weary shoulders, Paula closed her eyes for a brief moment. It was just impossible that she'd come all this way for nothing. . . .

Her thoughts were interrupted by the sound of young people laughing, and opening her eyes, she saw a group of students cross the wide lobby and head for the front door. She studied them for a moment, trying to pick out differences between these Belgian youngsters and the Canadians she'd devoted her professional energies to until now. There was about the boys and girls a decidedly foreign look, but at that moment Paula was capable of only the most superficial comparisons. With noisy laughter the students left, letting the heavy door slam behind them. That sound echoed in the stillness, and without warning Paula felt a return of the jabbing fear that had been her companion all the way to Belgium. *What have I gotten myself into this time?* There was no answer to that question, just as there had been no answer for all those tormenting weeks.

She closed her eyes again. When she felt the slight pressure of a hand on her shoulder she jumped.

"*Pardon, mademoiselle.* I didn't meant to startle you." It was Kathelijne, bearing evidence by her smile that her mission had been a success. "Madame Légère is still here, and she'd be happy to see you. She would have come out herself, but she was waiting for an important phone call. She told me to put your bags in the front reception room. I'll show you to her office, then I'll come back for the bags."

"Thanks." Paula sighed with relief, even though she knew this interview might turn out to be nothing but an invitation for her to return to Canada—without a job. She took a moment to glance in her compact mirror, fluffing out her auburn curls. She wished there was something she could do to soften the lines of fatigue that crinkled the corners of her green eyes. Slipping the compact back into her purse, she prepared to follow Kathelijne. She was so grateful not to be turned away entirely that it took her a minute to realize she hadn't even asked who it was she was being taken to. Again the fear jabbed at her, but she swallowed the lump in her throat.

"Madame Légère is the new principal," Kathelijne supplied in a very businesslike manner. The girl couldn't be more than fifteen, but her obvious intelligence made her appear older. "Actually, she's been here for many years. Most people felt she should have been made principal long before this, but then, Saint-Pierre was from Paris. There was a time when everybody thought foreign workers were the best. Thank goodness that's changing now."

Great, Paula thought sarcastically. Not only did she have a job offer from a principal who'd just been fired, she'd also arrived at a time when foreign staff was waning in popularity! If she hadn't been so exhausted, she probably would have turned right around and headed back to the airport. Fear was dissolving into anger, and Paula Emanuel had a short temper.

"Here we are, miss. *Bonne chance*—good luck!" With those words the helpful student hurried off, leaving Paula at the open door to an office that was considerably more modern than the long, oak-paneled hallway. Glancing in, she saw a very well-dressed, middle-aged woman seated at a desk facing her, but the woman didn't see Paula. She was staring at the phone with a look of profound disappointment on her face. Her carefully manicured hand was still poised over the receiver. Feeling that she'd intruded on a private moment, Paula made a small shuffling sound, at which the woman immediately raised her eyes. A formal but not unfriendly smile quickly replaced any sign of distress.

"*Bienvenue*—welcome," Madame Légère said, motioning to a chair in front of her desk. "What can we do for you?"

Paula cringed inwardly at the question. She hadn't expected the sort of greeting the principal would have used on someone asking for a contribution to charity. Paula reached into her purse and extracted a much-creased letter. "I came at the request of the school," she said, adding, "I've just arrived from Montreal."

"You must be exhausted," said the principal in the smooth tones she no doubt offered on occasions when such sentiments were appropriate. She really seemed quite polished, and her poise was beginning to make Paula feel at a disadvantage. "Let me get you some tea." She took Paula's letter but dropped it on her desk blotter as she rose and moved toward a small cabinet behind her desk. Slowly, with the ease of fine manners, the woman poured two steaming cups from a delicate china pot. Paula gratefully accepted one from her steady hand and sat down. She was eager to get to business.

"This letter contains a job offer. I—"

"A job offer?" The slim fingers picked up and unfolded the single typed sheet. After carefully reading it, the woman frowned deeply. "Oh, dear!" For the first time Paula caught a note of genuine concern in the cultured voice.

"Is there some problem?" Paula asked, knowing by now that of course there was.

"My dear," Madame Légère said, looking straight into Paula's eyes, "have you really come all the way from Montreal on the strength of this letter?"

"Not the letter alone, of course." Paula was trying hard not to sound defensive—or worse—as if she was begging. "Naturally there was quite a bit of negotiation beforehand. Dr. Graham and Madame Saint-Pierre—"

"Miss Emanuel, I'm very sorry to inconvenience you, especially since you've evidently had a very strenuous journey, but I have never heard of this Dr. Graham, nor of the special project that, according to this letter, he discussed with Saint-Pierre. I must tell you Saint-Pierre was terminated as principal a short time ago. Any arrangements she made have most likely been canceled. And in any case, if the current administration of the school wanted to continue one of her projects, it would have to be approved by the board of directors. That would take some time. The board meets only once a month, and their most-recent meeting was just last Friday. I'm sorry, but I . . . ."

Madame Légère hesitated. Paula, stunned at this desperate turn of events, thought the woman must surely be reconsidering what she'd just said, must surely realize she couldn't simply turn her out as though she'd come from down the block instead of thousands of miles away.

But it soon became apparent that Madame Légère

wasn't thinking about Paula at all. She was listening, listening very intently to a faint noise that Paula almost immediately recognized as the distant slamming of the school's front door. A series of sharp, fast footsteps on the marble floor followed. Clearly someone was striding directly toward this office.

And Madame Légère knew who that someone was, for at the sound of the first two or three steps, her expression changed, only for an instant, to one of surprised pleasure. Paula noted that expression with dismay, for it meant further delay in settling the matter of the job offer. If she hadn't been dazed by fatigue that grew more debilitating by the moment, Paula would have been in a state of pure panic.

"Please, *madame*," she began, but as though she hadn't even heard her, the woman once again let the important letter fall to her desk.

"Excuse me, Miss Emanuel," she said, rising at the exact moment when the footsteps stopped outside her door. She brushed Paula's arm in her haste to get to the threshold. "Luc," she said, her cultivated voice singing with pleasure, "you've come. You changed your mind. I thought by your phone call—"

The principal didn't get to finish her sentence. In a burst of impatient anger Paula stood up, and turning, declared, "I've been traveling for twenty hours to get here—"

The man Madame Légère spoke to wasn't paying attention to the principal at all. He was staring piercingly into Paula's eyes. At first she saw only that his own eyes were a strange shade of blue that danced with a violet light. Before she had a chance to decide whether the unusual color was remarkably attractive or really quite ugly, the man reached up and put on the dark-rimmed glasses he'd apparently just taken off. They must have fogged up in the cold January air. The

glasses effectively hid any expression his eyes might
hold.

There followed a moment of absolute silence, but in
that moment Paula took in the man's rumpled black
raincoat, of no recognizable style. A full, untrimmed
beard covered most of his face. The wild mane of his
hair, no doubt tousled by the wind and rain of the
unpleasant evening, needed more than a trim. It was
straight and black, though streaked at the temples with
a touch of gray that gleamed silver under the bright
fluorescent light. Perhaps it was because he'd interrupted at such a crucial moment that Paula found him
less than attractive. Yet a wiry energy seemed to infuse
the man. He was of average height; still, as he stood
poised in the doorway he appeared to tower over Madame Légère. Actually, the woman was nearly as tall.
Paula couldn't dispel the uncanny perception that the
man seemed to vibrate, and she continued to stare at
him, not realizing she was.

All she cared about was settling the matter of her
job. She thought it quite disgusting that the principal
would allow her boyfriend to interfere with business,
even if school was finished for the day. Insolently
Paula swept her eyes down the whole length of the
man. When her gaze reached his shoes, she saw they
were very wet, as if he'd been walking for some time in
the rain. Unaccountably, a little spear of pity stabbed
her heart. She shook the feeling away, glanced back up
toward the blue-violet eyes but could see nothing
behind the glasses.

"Who is this?" he asked. His voice wasn't deep, but
it was low and soft. A voice of secrets.

"Come in Luc. Sit down. Take off your coat." Madame Légère was suddenly very animated. She moved
to her desk, taking a seat behind it, clearly intending
for Luc to take one of the two chairs near the desk. He

remained standing. So did Paula, even though she was about ready to fall off her feet.

"Twenty hours?" he asked, turning his attention on Paula. She realized he had overheard her from the doorway. "And where have you come from to take so long in getting here?" There was a note of mockery in his voice. Paula didn't like it—or him—at all.

"Canada."

"Canada," he repeated, rolling the word on his tongue as he would some strange and savory morsel. He moved toward her, not very close, but close enough for her to catch the scent of cool rain and musk. She blinked.

"You are obviously quite exhausted. Sit down." He moved closer and actually had the nerve to give Paula's shoulder a little push so that she had no choice but to take one of the chairs. The man's touch had been very slight, but it made her angry. Who was he, anyway?

"Look," she said, keeping her voice steady despite her habitual shyness, "I came here at the express request of this school. It's not my fault that you've changed management. I demand—"

"Who *is* this?" Luc repeated, speaking to Madame Légère with new impatience in his voice, though Paula couldn't tell whether it was directed at her or at the woman who now handed Luc the letter Paula had given her.

"Apparently this is one more of Saint-Pierre's loose ends," the principal said with a sigh. "Nonetheless, Miss Emanuel is right. We do owe her some consideration. Perhaps we can find a place for her to stay until we can help her make arrangements to fly back to Canada. Would that suit you, miss?"

"No it would *not* suit me," Paula began, her anger now obvious. "I demand—"

"Be quiet. I'm trying to read."

Paula was stunned into silence by the effrontery of the man. He'd stated his case with total familiarity, the way one would to a near acquaintance—an intimate acquaintance, even. But she couldn't argue. He appeared to be studying the letter carefully, and as he read he sat down, not taking his eyes off the page. Paula saw that his body, though not large, was very lithe. She could tell just by the easy way he lowered himself into the chair that his legs were supple and strong. He finished reading, but she couldn't tell what, if any, effect the letter had on him. Nor did she know who he was or why he should be reading her papers. She was about to protest when he asked, "Have you any other documents?"

It was *madame* who protested. "Luc, this is out of our hands. It's a matter for the board. You know they're not meeting for another month—"

"Marie," Luc interrupted, "have some pity. This poor woman—"

"Just a minute," Paula broke in, the curtness of her voice stopping him dead. "I don't want pity. I want it understood that regardless of who's in charge right now, this job offer should stand. It wasn't the principal who promised the job, but the board itself. Look at that letter. It's on the letterhead of the school, not the principal. I have a right—"

"Americans are always speaking of their rights. . . ." There was a touch of amusement in the man's tone that nearly drove Paula around the bend.

"I'm *Canadian*!"

He shrugged as though to say, "Same difference."

Suddenly Paula's throat ached with her need to cry, but she had to fight to keep the tears back. *Oh, please God, no,* she begged silently. All she needed was to burst into tears. That would finish things just fine. She took a deep breath; she kept her eyes lowered for a long moment. An embarrassing silence hung in the room.

When she was sufficiently collected she raised her eyes. The first thing she saw was this Luc person's face. He was leaning toward her. His eyes were still somewhat hidden, but around his mouth there played a very small, very soft smile that was not at all mocking. "Have you any other documents?" he repeated.

Sighing, she reached into her handbag and produced a sheaf of letters and papers. Some of them were from the last agency for which she'd worked; some of them were from Le Berceau. And one was from the department of the Belgian government responsible for the affairs of foreign workers. All of them were in perfect order.

Luc spread them on the desk in front of him. Silently Paula and Marie Légère watched him. By rights, Paula should demand to know why her fate was clearly in his hands. Was he a member of the board? Judging from his appearance, that didn't seem likely. But then, just because board members at other places where she'd worked had been elderly men in charcoal-gray, pin-striped suits didn't mean this dark man in the rumpled raincoat didn't have a power far beyond that suggested by his clothes.

While the man read, Marie made fresh tea. Her ministrations were polite, but Paula wasn't surprised to detect a growing impatience. It was rapidly becoming late even for dinner, not to mention the fact that the school had probably been deserted for some time now. It really wasn't fair to keep the principal so long after the close of the day. Paula wished she'd thought better of her plan to come directly to the school. She cursed herself for not having gone to a hotel and gotten a good night's sleep before attempting to straighten out this mess. Of course, she hadn't known— She handed her teacup to Marie, beginning, "I'm really sorry to detain you—"

"Quiet!"

Both Paula and Marie glanced at Luc, then sat back and waited the few minutes longer it took him to reach a conclusion about Paula's papers. She had already decided his verdict would be of no interest to her until she at least found out whether he was a member of the board.

"Okay," he said, surprising her with that single English word; their conversation till then had been conducted in French. "I can see what's going on here. You are a protégée of Dr. Graham?"

"No. Not a protégée. I worked with him, and he recommended me for the current opening—"

"There is no opening." Marie interrupted, obviously irritated.

"Just a minute, Marie," Luc said. Turning back to Paula, he went on. "You and Dr. Graham were involved in a pilot project in the Montreal schools designed to combat truancy and absenteeism, am I right?"

"Yes."

"Why do you assume we have those problems at our school?"

"I assume nothing, *Monsieur... Monsieur....*"

"LeBlanc."

"Monsieur LeBlanc. The project Dr. Graham proposed for this school was based on his work with students in Canada in fine-arts academies. He found that while the problems of those pupils didn't always result in truancy, they did often seriously hamper the growth of creative young people. Until now, school psychologists have mostly had time only for testing and referral, not for counseling. It was Dr. Graham's idea that the counseling of a sensitive psychologist, dedicated exclusively to arts students, might prevent some of the common problems.''

''You call yourself a psychologist? According to these records, you're just a social worker....'' At those words, he flicked her papers derisively, sending the blood rushing to Paula's pale cheeks.

''And what are you, *monsieur*?'' she asked, not trying to hide her anger.

Even through his glasses, she could see his eyes widen at the question. If her insolence surprised him it was too bad. He didn't seem to mind exercising his insolence on her. She expected a curt answer, or at least an officious one. To her surprise, his face assumed an expression almost of defeat, and in his soft voice he said, ''I, *mademoiselle*, am a writing teacher....''

''Luc! Please....'' Marie Légère rose from her seat, but Luc LeBlanc motioned her to sit down again, and reluctantly she complied.

''You can see, if you've really studied these papers,'' Paula went on, ''that I have many years' experience dealing with young people in Montreal. I've collaborated with Dr. Graham for more than three years. His work is well documented. But perhaps a writing teacher wouldn't—''

''I'm well aware of his work,'' Luc stated, but before Paula had a chance to react to that revelation, he added, ''and in general, I consider it a waste of time.''

''But—''

''Don't mistake me, miss. I'm not so simple as to reject something just because I personally disagree with it. The point here is not the validity of Dr. Graham's theories. The point is whether the board did specifically agree to implement Dr. Graham's program.''

''The letters prove—''

''The letters prove only that the subject came up for

discussion, except for this final letter. And though it is
certainly true the stationery is that of the school, the
signature *is* the principal's. I should tell you that part
of the reason Madame Saint-Pierre was asked to leave,
is that she made it a fairly regular practice to assume
responsibilities that were not clearly hers to assume. It
is perfectly possible that Madame Saint-Pierre was a
personal friend of Dr. Graham's, and that Dr. Graham was a personal friend of yours. Favors are often
exchanged, right?''

He was so exactly right that Paula bent her head to
hide her eyes. It was true that there were personal
reasons for this appointment. But that didn't alter two
facts. The first was that she was eminently qualified
for the job. The second was that the job offer was
legitimate. She really didn't know how to convince
these people, though. She was far too tired to handle
this properly now. There was only one thing to do.

''I'm sorry to have disturbed the two of you,'' she
said simply, raising her eyes not to the man who called
himself a writing teacher, but to the woman who was
really in charge. Marie Légère nodded, her face showing a little compassion now. ''I can see I've made a
mistake coming here at a time when your work is finished for the day. I'll take this matter up with the
board when I can. In the meantime, if you'd be so kind
as to recommend a hotel nearby. . .?'' Without waiting for an answer, she stretched her hand toward the
desk with the intention of retrieving her papers, but
before her fingers closed on the documents, she felt the
cool weight of Luc LeBlanc's hand. Surprised, she
looked up at him, and she could plainly see that he was
scrutinizing her with total disregard for her privacy.
She burned in discomfort under that gaze, but she
didn't move, not even when she heard Marie Légère
clear her throat in annoyance.

"You are an honest person, aren't you?" he said to Paula. "Not very open, I'd say, but very honest. Also, you are full of fire. I think there are a few little artistes around here who could benefit by spending some time with a foreigner who's not afraid to fight for her rights. I myself tire of trying to get some spunk into some of them. Why not share the task? Relax, miss. You can have your job."

He released her hand, but not the hold on her eyes. For a second he continued to stare at her as if she were an object he'd like to investigate at his leisure. His intense, imperious curiosity bothered her, even though he'd just done her an enormous favor. Or had he?

"Please, Luc, the board...." Marie Légère protested, and Paula feared her battle was not nearly won.

But Monsieur LeBlanc stood and leaned over the desk until his face was quite close to the principal's. There was a smile in his voice; Paula couldn't see his expression.

"Marie, you know the board will do anything you ask...."

And the smile Marie offered Luc in response told Paula the woman would do anything *he* asked.

CHAPTER ONE

Luc LeBlanc lifted a glossy but already much-read magazine, thumbed through it quickly, then impatiently tossed it down onto the cluttered table beside the couch. Even if he did have nothing better to do with his time, he hated spending so much as an extra minute in the doctor's waiting room.

"It shouldn't be too much longer now, Luc," the receptionist said, and Luc smiled up at her as politely as he could manage. He didn't mind her calling him by his first name, even though he was sure she didn't address other patients that way. Heaven knew he'd spent enough time in that office that anyone who worked there had the right to call him Luc.

It was the woman's voice that bothered him. It was always so softly seductive, and it matched the sweet smile she offered and the frequently lowered eyelids that revealed long sooty lashes contrasting with the pink perfection of her young skin. He hadn't forgotten what prettiness was in a woman. And he was still fully capable of recognizing flirtation when he saw it. He just couldn't respond. He wanted to tell the young woman once and for all that she was wasting her time. Totally. Instead he picked up another magazine, a weekly news journal.

At first his eyes scanned the usual ads cursorily. He noted with mild interest a few articles written by people whose names were well familiar to him. Moens's article on the recent talks in Cairo repeated what the man had told Luc in person not three weeks earlier. Moens had always had a lot of foresight, in Luc's opinion, and the two of them often made a game of second-guessing world leaders. Moens was convinced that journalists were the only people who really knew what was going on most of the time. Luc thought the man arrogant but not entirely wrong.

Almost unwillingly he turned to the pages usually devoted to coverage of events in Central and South America. For a long time he'd stopped himself from scanning any photos for the faces of men and women he'd known or worked with. But he couldn't seem to break the habit of reading the articles, even though what he read often infuriated him.

"Put that down and get in here, LeBlanc."

Startled, but only for an instant, Luc looked up into the smiling face of Dr. Marc Fortin. For three years now Marc had been as much friend as physician, and he was one of the few whose attempts at humor never failed to get at least a smile from Luc. Fortin was a rough, large, tremendously skilled man. Luc respected him not only for his work but for his attitude, which was that life was a battle, not a voyage to be enjoyed with ease; it was more honorable to fight with dignity.

Closing the magazine, Luc did as he was told.

"I'm getting good and tired of seeing you in here, you know that, Luc?"

"Then stop forcing me to make appointments, Marc," Luc answered with a smile.

"And wound my receptionist's heart? She's convinced you're going to break down sooner or later and ask her for a date."

"Did she tell you that?"

"No. But I'm a doctor—used to diagnosing from observation...."

"Well, she's way off base."

"Someday a lady's going to come along who's not 'off base,' my friend."

"Marc, we've been through all this before."

"But there's nothing—"

"I don't want to hear it, Doctor." There was anger in his voice, but Luc couldn't help it. He'd had to put up with well-meaning people trying to run his life for a few years now, and sometimes the strain got to him. There were whole days when he kept to himself, but that was no solution, either. He was used to dealing with the loneliness. What he couldn't handle was the sense that things were happening without him. And when he holed up in his apartment, that feeling was intensified beyond bearing.

"I'm sorry, Marc," he said when the silence had become ominous. "I guess I'm just frustrated over all the time I've been wasting. I haven't worked since the fall—"

"You were overworking, Luc, and I just wasn't going to let you do it. Your blood pressure was sky-high, and the graft—"

"I've done everything you said, Marc: followed the exercise regimen, stuck to the high-protein diet, got plenty of sleep—too much, in fact. I was ready to go back in January."

"You were not."

"But I am now. If you tell me the results of that last battery of tests are anything but totally negative, I'm going to—"

"Save the threats, LeBlanc. The tests were negative. Everything is normal. Everything."

"So I can go back to the school?"

"You can go back to doing anything you've ever done before. I sincerely hope, though, that you'll take it easy."

"Well, things'll be a little hectic for me at first,"

Luc said, trying to hide his relish at the thought of getting back into action.

"How so?"

"It's March. I've missed two months of the new year, and I've got to get the kids caught up."

"Excuse me if I'm wrong, but I was under the impression that you weren't the only teacher in the school...."

Luc laughingly conceded the doctor's point. No, he wasn't the only teacher. Still, Marie would be much relieved to have him back on staff, and he looked forward to helping her out with her heavy load of administrative responsibilities. He wondered if the Canadian had helped at all. He'd almost asked Marie a number of times how things were working out with that one, but something had stopped him. Maybe he didn't want to know if the foreigner wasn't doing well. She seemed like such a lost soul, despite her freshness and her fire. How he would hate to have to send her back if she wasn't doing a good job. He felt, in fact, he knew he was responsible for her having stayed. Her credentials had been in order, but something else had made him jump to her defense. Something he really didn't understand himself. Maybe he *had* still been ill in January!

"So this is a parting of the ways, then, Marc?"

"As far as I'm concerned, the case is closed." The gruff heartiness of the doctor's pronouncement gave way to a sigh, almost inaudible but not missed by Luc.

"Marc, I owe you a lot. When you started working on me I was a wreck."

"Are you talking about your car or your body?"

"You know I don't own a car. Marc, I owe you sincere thanks. You've been more than a doctor. You've—" He really couldn't say anything else. He held out his hand and felt Marc Fortin's powerful grip.

His life had been in this man's hands more than once, and Luc had no intention of ever forgetting that fact. "I'll see you for dinner some night soon."

"And I'll see you in print."

Luc managed a smile. Another old argument. The man simply would not give up.

"Don't hold your breath, Doctor," he answered, releasing Marc's hand and heading toward the door. He turned back before he exited and nodded goodbye. He could tell by the expression on the doctor's face that Fortin was about to offer some quip in return, but he bested the other man with his hasty exit. No doubt their one-upmanship would now be carried out socially. Luc had every intention of seeing the doctor again, even if Marc seemed to think he knew more about Luc's future than Luc did himself.

When he stepped outside Luc saw that the morning rain had given way to weak but welcome sunlight. The air was cool, fresh. And he felt pretty fresh himself. It would take him a day or two to get ready to go back to work. He'd have to buy a few new shirts—of course he'd get started right away going over his notes for the classes Marie would no doubt want him to teach. For certain he'd take on the advanced course, and maybe one or two of the survey—

"Flowers today, sir?"

He'd been so absorbed in his own thoughts that he hadn't noticed the flower seller at the corner. Her cheery Dutch had greeted him for the past six months or so. She was very young, with cheeks as rosy as any flower on her laden stand. Often he bought a few blooms from her, not because he had any need for flowers, but because he was always afraid she wouldn't be able to sell everything. She reached for a yellow rose, knowing that was usually his preference. A thought crossed his mind, and he shook his head.

"Something different today," he said in French. She didn't understand, so he had to point. With careful fingers she extracted the blooms from their little tub of water and wrapped them in green tissue.

OUTSIDE THE WINDOW of Paula's office, the garden of Le Berceau seemed about to awaken to the first fresh breezes of March. *How quickly the time has gone,* she reflected as she gazed toward trees whose uppermost branches bore the hint of buds. Deliberately she kept her back to the student she was in the process of counseling, giving him time to recover from the angry outburst that had stopped the day's session dead.

Her eyes swept over the enclosed space that she imagined would soon be full of color, though there were as yet no flowers outside. *There are flowers inside,* she thought with a smile, looking at a small crystal vase full of white violets that sat on the polished wooden sill. Some unknown friend had sent them, and though at first it had bothered her that she couldn't find out who, she was now grateful for the little gift. It promised something good to come, even if that something was only the inevitable spring.

"I'm sorry, miss," the young man said, his voice still shaky, "but I can't help it. He doesn't understand anything I'm trying to do. I had to fight for two years to get to come here. He wanted me to go to the private school he and my grandfather went to."

"That's in the past, Karel," Paula said, turning toward the room and walking back to her desk. She sat on the edge, her slender legs stretched out beneath her camel's hair skirt. "We have to think about the present. About present problems."

"There isn't any problem...."

"I think you know there is, Karel. If your father is as displeased with your March report as he was with the December one, he's going to withdraw you from this school."

"He's just picking on me because of the way I dress. When I first came here my reports were even worse than they are now. He just doesn't like the fact that I dress the way all my friends do."

Paula had often had to deal with the problem of dress among students, and she usually tried to do so in a roundabout way. To directly confront the young people always resulted in resistance. She wished she could tell Karel that she quite agreed with his father—spiked hair, combat boots, chains, army pants and a T-shirt torn in six places made a rather poor impression on teachers. But her position here was even more difficult than it had been in Montreal. In her last school the pupils had been obliged to wear uniforms in class, so that only their after-school attire had offended parents. The policy at Le Berceau was to foster creativity at all times, and that included dress for class.

"Have you spoken with your dad about this?"

"My father, the distinguished Monsieur Foubert, is not someone you speak with. He's someone you listen to."

Not wanting to get back on the track that had led to the outburst only moments earlier, Paula diverted the conversation slightly.

"Karel—" she moved to the chair behind her desk and opened a file folder as she sat "—your report for December was quite a bit different from the ones that went before, or so it seems. I notice that the report for October, and the one for last June, as well, received commendations from the principal. Do you think you'd like to talk about some of the things that have happened since October that could account for a change like that? Has your relationship with your father gotten worse in that time?"

Karel was silent and brooding for a few moments, his shoulders hunched, and Paula watched him with sympathy. He seemed to bear such a burden despite the fact that he was from a wealthy banking family that spared no expense to provide everything he wanted. When he answered, his words were not in French but in Dutch. Paula was quickly learning that in Belgium, as in her own country, two cultures had for centuries lived side by side in a sometimes uneasy peace. She hadn't yet learned any Dutch, though.

"I'm sorry," she said. "I don't know what you said."

"It's an old saying," Karel answered, resuming in French. "It means 'worst can't get worse.' I think it just about describes the way things are between my father and me."

"We don't need to assume that will never change," Paula said encouragingly. "So if nothing was different at home, then perhaps there was some change here at the school? Some change in your courses or your teachers?"

"I don't know. I can't remember."

She knew he was deliberately being evasive. "Try to remember, Karel. There's no logical reason why a pupil's grades should fall dramatically from one period to the next if everything else remains the same. Did the work suddenly become harder? I realize the third year of a course can be quite a bit more challenging—"

"Challenging? That's a laugh!" Bitterness edged the spat-out words.

"I was told," Paula said carefully, trying to draw the boy out, "that the writing course here is the most challenging of all—even more so than dance, drama, sculpture, architecture...."

"Was, not is. Not anymore. You should see the stupid stuff they expect us to do now. Did you ever try to write a thousand words on your goals in life? I'm sixteen years old. I don't think I know my goals in life yet. It used to be that we were told we had to understand more about the world first, that writing was a way of investigating things. Not now. They don't know what they're doing."

"Who are they?" Paula asked softly.

"Madame R—"

"No," Paula interrupted. "No names, okay? Remember how we talked about objectivity and privacy? Don't tell me their names. Just tell me in general who you mean."

"I mean the totally boring team that has taken over the writing department in Monsieur—I mean in the absence of the regular department head."

"When did this occur?"

"He—the department head—has been away since the first week of November."

"Since about the time your grades took a dive? He must have had quite an influence on you."

"Of course he did," Karel said impatiently. "It was because of him that I wanted to come to this school. It was because of him that my father let me come. He's a famous writer—or at least he was. My father is very impressed with that sort of thing. I was afraid at first that *monsieur* would be a disappointment. I have a hard time trusting anybody that makes a big impression on my dad. But *monsieur*—the teacher, I mean— wasn't a disappointment at all. Not at all."

"Why did he leave?"

"He got sick."

Paula thought about that for a moment. In her years of dealing with young people, it had never ceased to amaze her how closely they attached themselves to role models. She often wondered if teachers realized how much of an effect their personalities had on the pupils they taught. The best ones certainly seemed to. Unaccountably, her mind wandered to Bret Graham. How eagerly she had accepted his tutelage! When she'd first gone to work for him, she had been twenty-eight with five years of agency work behind her. Though she had certainly never been accused of overconfidence, she hadn't guessed that she still had as much to learn as Bret could teach her. If only she'd confined her lessons to work. . . .

"Miss?"

"Oh, I'm sorry, Karel." How she hated to be caught daydreaming in the middle of a session! Not only was it totally unprofessional, it also wreaked havoc with the trust she was trying to inspire in her student client. She tried to cover up.

"I was just thinking of someone whose teaching influenced me a great deal," she said smoothly. "It seems to me the best teachers go on teaching you even when they can't be with you."

"What does that mean?"

"Well, what a good instructor does is show you a certain way of looking at the world. For instance, your present teachers ask you to look at the world in terms of goals—things to get or to get done. For some students, that may be an inspiring way to think. For you it isn't. You know another way, the way this person you so admire taught you. What was the word you used?"

"Investigating?"

"Right. For him the world was full not of things to get done but of things to try to understand. I can certainly appreciate that attitude personally. I admire you for choosing a role model like him."

"What's a role model?"

"Someone to look up to. Someone to try to be like."

"I'd definitely like to be like him."

"Well, what do you suppose his attitude would be toward your forgetting what he's taught you just because he isn't around?"

Karel didn't have to answer that one. Paula could see he got the point.

"He told me I have a great deal of promise," the young man said after a lengthy silence. His serious expression touched Paula's heart. If there was one thing she didn't like about her job, it was that she had to keep from showing how she felt about these kids. If she'd followed Bret Graham's teachings to the letter, she'd have kept herself from feeling at all. Fortunately or unfortunately, she didn't have to worry about that anymore.

"But of course," Karel continued, again pulling her away from her musings, "that's what my father says all the time, too. 'You show a great deal of promise, lad....'" The teenager sat ramrod straight and assumed what was intended to be a mature and serious expression for that bit of mimicry. Paula didn't try to hide her amusement.

"The thing to remember," she said, "is—" Her words were interrupted by a muffled knock at the outer door of the office. She shared the double space with the woman in charge of keeping records on the students. The outer door was almost never closed.

"I wonder why someone is knocking," Paula said. "Isn't Madame Martel at her desk?"

"Oh, I forgot to mention," Karel responded, "she said she had to leave for an hour or so. She told me to tell you that your final appointment is canceled."

"Then who...?" There was a short series of footsteps. Again the imperious knock, this time on the door to Paula's own office. Angrily she glanced at her watch. "You still have seven minutes, Karel. Maybe if we just ignore that, it'll go away." She looked up at the student and was surprised to see on his face a more-animated expression than she'd noted in some time. "What is it?" she asked, a little annoyed. "Were you expecting someone?"

"No, not exactly. It's just that I thought I recognized—"

Before he could finish his sentence, there was one further loud rap, then the door fairly burst open to reveal an imposing though not tall figure poised on the threshold with one hand still on the doorknob.

"What is the meaning of this?" Paula stood up, not waiting to hear the man's excuse for his intrusion. "What do you think you're doing?"

The man glanced briefly at Paula but seemed to look right through her. The expression on his face didn't change. It was one of determination, as though he'd been looking for someone and could attend to nothing else until he found him.

The one he sought, it turned out, was Karel, for the moment the man's eyes took in the boy, he smiled so warmly that Paula was halted from expressing her strong displeasure at the breach of professional etiquette.

"Monsieur!" Karel cried, unmistakable joy in his voice. He dashed over to the man and stuck out his hand. The intruder grasped it, soon pulling the student into a brief embrace. "You came back." Karel couldn't hide his fervor. "I can't believe it. This is great! I heard a rumor you were coming back in January. When you didn't...."

"I tried," the man said, shrugging. "I didn't even get as far as the classroom when my doctor nabbed me and sentenced me to a couple more months away from this paradise...." He gestured in mock disgust with a sweeping motion of his hand, taking in the whole of Le

Berceau. "But it looks like I'm here to stay now, so you had better prepare to shape up. What's this? You look like a blond porcupine." With a little laugh the man lifted his hand, pretending to be pricked by the sharp points of the boy's stiffened hair.

"Don't you like it? It's punk."

"It's a trick to irritate your father, isn't it?"

Paula would never have stated such a fact point-blank. She'd been working slowly with Karel to bring him to connect his appearance with the rebelliousness that was his basic problem. She had feared he would reject the idea, but now she watched in surprise as the boy laughed and freely admitted, "Guess you could say that."

Despite this man's easy ways with the student, Paula was obligated to point out that he had no right to be in her office during a private session. "Karel and I aren't quite finished," she said, keeping her tone professional but pleasant. "If you'd like to wait outside, he'll be done in a few minutes."

"Oh, miss," Karel declared, "I couldn't possibly concentrate any more today. We were almost finished, anyway, and I've been waiting for Monsieur Luc for...."

Monsieur Luc...of course. How could she not have recognized him? Her gaze slid past the bright asking eyes of the boy and took in those of the man. She saw there a teasing gleam. He hadn't forgot *her*; she could see that at once. She could see, too, that his wild hair was a good deal shorter now. In the light of her office, softer than the harsh fluorescent of their first meeting, the dark strands shone sleek and thick. Again she glimpsed the darts of silver gray at the temples, though now she realized the man was quite young, perhaps a little younger than her own thirty-two years. Something told her those gray hairs had come not from age but from. . . . No matter. That was none of her business.

He no longer wore a beard as he had the night he'd acted as her benefactor, the night his intercession had swayed Marie Légère in her favor. Without it his jaw was strong, squarish and solid, his mouth and chin firmly set, perhaps reflecting stubbornness. Stubbornness, she thought, or something else, something deeper and more personal.

"I'm sorry," she said as much to Luc as to Karel. "The session isn't over. If you've waited this long, Karel, you can wait a little longer. We've talked about impatience before. We've also talked about the privacy of our meetings. . . ." She shot what she hoped was a significant glance in Luc's direction. "In order to get the full benefit of these sessions, it's necessary that each one goes the full time."

"Surely a few minutes one way or the other can't make any difference?" Luc's voice was insinuating. He clearly found Paula's adherence to the rules too strict—even petty. "Come on, Karel, we've got a lot of catching up to do," he said casually. Without waiting for further word from Paula, he swung his arm around the student's shoulders, turning him in the direction of the door.

"Just a minute!" Paula made no effort to hide the sudden anger that filled her. This was her private office and her session. Even if Luc had been—or was still—some sort of administrator at the school, that didn't give him the right to interfere. Nor did he have any right to act as though she had no authority in the situation. "We are *not* finished." Even she was surprised at the strength of her voice.

Monsieur Luc turned. Sometime between their first meeting and this one, he'd stopped wearing his heavy-rimmed glasses. She could clearly see his strange, blue-violet eyes, especially since he was staring at her. And his expression was without a doubt defiant. She looked directly at him, though it cost her a little quiver of apprehension to do so. She would not drop her eyes, would not succumb to the boldness of his look—or of his stance, for he stood planted before her, his legs slightly spread. Once more she had the uncomfortable feeling that it was impossible for him to stand totally still; power seemed to run through him all the time.

In the end it was she who first lowered her gaze, though only enough for her to see that his sense of style hadn't improved much in his two-month absence. He wore a pair of much-washed denims that hugged his wiry legs in a threadbare fashion. Tucked into the jeans was a black T-shirt, hiding the contours of his chest. He wasn't a large man, only a few inches taller than Paula's five foot five, but something about him—that air of barely contained energy, perhaps—made him seem more of a presence than stature alone could have accounted for.

Over the T-shirt he had pulled on a loose gray cardigan that had definitely seen better days. Large pockets, evidently empty now, bulged as if they often held more than originally intended. Though scrupulously clean, the sweater was frayed at the cuffs. One elbow was worn to transparent thinness; the other was worn away. Something about this garment infuriated Paula even more. In the very back of her mind the thought tickled that this man could really be quite handsome if his manner and his dress were a little less, well, eccentric. Whatever, his clothing seemed to prove his stubbornness, as if he meant to say, "This is how I choose to dress, and if you don't like it, that's your tough luck."

What Luc did say was, "Have you completed your inspection?"

Without missing a beat, though her heart missed at least one, Paula raised her steady green eyes to his face. "It's a little difficult," she said in her best professional tone, "to criticize students for dress that displays rebelliousness when some members of the staff are obviously equally guilty."

She was rarely so courageous as to speak out in that way, and she soon realized she shouldn't have. Because Monsieur Luc LeBlanc began an inspection of his own. Paula felt his lowered eyes on her slender ankles, her well-shaped legs. A strange heat began to rise in her, and she wasn't sure whether it was caused by embarrassment or rage. She felt the violet gaze ascend to the slimness of her thighs, her hips; the camel's hair skirt scant barrier to this rude exploration that ended just under the shallow V of her fawn-colored silk blouse. His eyes lingered there, seeming to outline her soft curves. And she suddenly knew it was rage she felt. She was certain he was about to smirk or make some obnoxious crack that would reveal him to be the type of macho bore who usually pulled that kind of routine.

He didn't smirk. He didn't even smile. From his eyes shone such a piercing intelligence that Paula felt he'd somehow figured out a dark secret about her, one she didn't know herself. Never before had she experienced that sensation, and though she kept her gaze as steady as before, her eyes reflected her uncertainty. His soft voice filled the office, but his tone was not professional, far from it. It was a personal caress that touched her unwilling ear. "It looks to me, miss, as though you have to work very hard to hide your own rebelliousness," he said. "To hide your passion...."

She was stunned by his presumption. "I've never been accused of rebelliousness in my life," she insisted indignantly. She would have said plenty more, too, had not Karel, whose presence had been momentarily forgotten, let out a poorly suppressed giggle. Turning abruptly, Paula said, "You may go, Karel."

"But, miss, you just said we weren't finished...."

"I was wrong. We are. Please don't argue, Karel. I'll see you next week at the same time." Moving with what she hoped was her usual authority, she ushered the student to the door, even though doing so meant having to brush past Luc. Reluctantly Karel went, hesitating as though to beckon Luc to follow, but the man stood his ground.

In fact, when Paula swiveled from the door, she found to her irritation that he'd made himself quite comfortable. He was facing her, leaning on the edge of her desk, his legs extended in front of him. She glared at him for a moment before fairly stomping over to where he sat. She stood only near enough to avoid having to raise her voice. It was noticeably quavering with outrage.

"Just what did you attempt to accomplish by that little scene?" she demanded.

Implying that both her statement and her anger were a total surprise to him, Luc LeBlanc raised his eyebrows and casually, infuriatingly, crossed his arms over his chest, revealing even more dramatically the poor condition of the elbows of his sweater. If he was trying to be funny, Paula didn't get the joke.

"I've spent four whole sessions trying to get that kid to understand that the way a person dresses is no joking matter. His dress is a major factor in the difficult relations he has with his father. Monsieur Foubert is head of a huge banking-and-financial concern, so his expectations for his son aren't hard to imagine—"

"I'm well aware of who his father is," Luc interjected. "He used to be one of my biggest fans, though heaven knows why. He couldn't possibly have agreed with anything I said."

"What?" Paula queried. She didn't know what Luc was talking about. After a moment's silence, she remembered something Karel had said about a famous writer. "Who are you?" she asked. His lids drooped over his strangely blue eyes, shuttering them.

"I told you, miss, I'm the writing teacher." Something in his tone forbade further questions. Anyway, she wasn't about to be distracted by red herrings. She wasn't quite finished with what she intended to say.

"I'm really quite upset about your interrupting Karel's session," she said. "The school rules, as well as the rules of common courtesy, forbid—"

"Rules, rules, rules..." the dark man interrupted impatiently. He stood away from the desk, decreasing the distance between them. Before Paula had a chance to step back, she caught again the elusive but distinctive scent of his cologne. "Why are you so very concerned with rules?"

"This is a school. If rules aren't taught now—"

"Take it from me, miss. There's a difference between jail and school. This is not a jail."

"I'm not saying it is. All I'm saying is that you had no right to come bursting in here as though you owned the place. Didn't anyone ever tell you about privacy?"

"Didn't anyone ever tell you about having respect for students?" He offered this question with a toss of his hand. The gesture added fuel to the fire of Paula's anger.

"You seem to be accusing me of a lack of respect for Karel."

"Well..." he said almost smugly, shrugging his shoulders in a classically Gallic and totally infuriating way.

"You're the one who came in here in the middle of a session."

"The middle of a session?" His smile was slow

mockery. "You said yourself that there were only a few minutes to go."

"I'm not talking about x number of minutes. That should be obvious."

"Don't be sarcastic, *mademoiselle*. I don't need you to tell me what's obvious and what isn't." For the first time she heard genuine anger in his voice. It surprised her, but it didn't frighten her; in fact, it egged her on, giving her the strength to say what she really wanted to say.

"How dare you make reference to my private business in front of a student—and in this office to boot? It's no business of yours whether I have a hard time controlling my...my...."

"'Passion' is the word I used, miss. Maybe you think it's a word that shouldn't fall on the ears of the young." There was no anger in his voice now. But there was a coldness that Paula couldn't determine the exact nature of. His enunciated words were somehow riveting.

"You may hide from passion if you like, and you may run from it, but it is a fact of life. The young people at this school are training to be artists. Every day of their lives they are going to be faced with beauty and truth, the two most essential elements of art. If you intend to encourage them to stifle passion, you are going to rob them of their greatest tool. No one can comprehend either beauty or truth without the passion that enables the soul to respond to them."

Again a hint of smugness lit his features. He was waiting for some kind of answer, and Paula was fully prepared to give it to him. If he thought his lovely little speech had made up for or covered up his obnoxious behavior, he had another think coming. "I'm not an idiot, *monsieur*," she began, once more moving farther from him, though that did no good, since he, too, took a step. "I'm well aware of the passion of art. I'm also well aware that that's not what you were talking about. I don't think it's at all funny to make a suggestive remark to me in front of a student."

To Paula's surprise, the expression on Luc Le-Blanc's face changed to one of real concern. Gone was the smugness, the air of contention. "Surely you don't think I was being suggestive. I—I was trying to be kind."

"Kind?" That was the last word she would have expected him to offer in his defense. She didn't like the implications of it. "Why should you think kindness gives you the right to make personal remarks about me? If you think I should be grateful to you for getting me this job, Monsieur LeBlanc, you're right. It was an act of kindness, and I owe you—"

"You don't—"

"Of course I do. I don't know why you helped me. I don't yet know how to repay you. But please don't compound the debt by taking me under your wing, if that's what you have in mind. I don't need it, and I don't want it. My qualifications for this job prove that I'm well suited for it. The only way I can repay the faith you showed in me is to do a good job. And you can help me to do so by staying out of my office."

She knew how curt she sounded, but she didn't care. She wasn't about to be his protégée or anyone else's. Not this time. Not ever again. Not even when Luc LeBlanc was so incensed by her strong words that he stormed out of her office as noisily as he'd entered it.

CHAPTER TWO

"My DEAR, I realize how angry you must be, but I have to ask you to be patient with Luc. He's had his difficulties."

The principal's reception salon overlooked the small but carefully tended front grounds of the school. The ornamental gardens were fairly bare in March, but promised beauty to come. Madame Légère, whom Paula now called Marie, looked perfectly at home in the elegance of the formal room, furnished with brocaded sofas and chairs and a fine carpet that set off the delicate legs of the antique table. Dressed in black silk, the tall, middle-aged woman perched imposingly on the edge of her chair, her well-manicured fingers deft and calm as she lifted a sparkling cube of sugar with silver tongs and dropped it into Paula's tea without a splash.

"It's not a matter of my being angry." Paula accepted the tea. "It's a matter of keeping Karel's confidence. How can I convince a person that he speaks to me in utter privacy when both he and I know the door can burst open at any minute?"

"Pardon me, Paula, but you exaggerate. I'm quite sure Luc will not interrupt again. And as for Karel, he'd been waiting for Luc for some time."

"He shouldn't have told Luc to come to my office."

"I'm certain he didn't. Luc was looking all over for him. You see, the boy has been his prize pupil, and now that Luc's well enough to teach again, he's looking forward to resuming where they left off. The man is impulsive sometimes. It's necessary to forgive and forget.''

Paula was quite willing to forget about Luc Le-Blanc, though she could see that he was rapidly regaining his position as something of a fixture around Le Berceau. She'd learned a good deal about the structure of the private school in the two months since she'd been there.

Marie Légère was assisted in the administration of the academy by several department heads. Until the day before, Paula had met all but one at a reception: Wilhelm Steyaert, the professor of sculpture; Laurice LePan, the slender and lovely ballet mistress; Modest Batten, head of the school's painting section; Annette Struelens, a teacher who was also an architect of international repute; Josef LeBlanc, the music master, and others. Only the head of the writing department had been absent. Though she found their names difficult to remember—at least in part because of the mixture of French and Dutch, sometimes in the same name— Paula had thought them friendly and helpful.

She felt differently about Luc LeBlanc. Mostly confused. She understood now that he was the head of the writing department, but that didn't explain his championing of her cause. Perhaps he'd been impressed by her credentials. If his interest wasn't professional, however, it had to be personal. And she emphatically did not want that! Still, she thought she'd overreacted the day before to his comments, and now that she had had time to think things over, she was considering apologizing to him.

"Forgive and forget?" she asked with a smile. "I'll agree to that.''

"Good,'' Marie answered. "Then we can get on to discussing the files. I've had a chance to review—and to study carefully—Madame Saint-Pierre's entire correspondence with Dr. Graham. As you of course know, we've never done counseling of any kind here before, so our initial resistance is perhaps understandable.''

"It's understandable, yes, but Dr. Graham was convinced you'd change your mind once you saw results—changed work habits, better attendance.''

"Well, of course, two months isn't enough time to expect results, but I'm quite satisfied with how you've set things up. You seem to have a great deal of experience at this sort of thing.''

"I've been a school counselor for a number of years,'' Paula replied in the tone of one conducting a friendly but purely professional conversation. "Before I joined Dr. Graham, I worked in a school in one of the poorer inner-city neighborhoods of Montreal.''

"That must have been challenging,'' Marie commented with polite interest.

"A little too challenging sometimes,'' Paula replied, laughing ruefully. "The problems of the urban poor are heartrending. I got quite emotionally involved in my cases. I was near burnout when the chance to work with Dr. Graham came up.''

"You must have been grateful for the opportunity. From what I've read in the files, and also from what Luc remembers having heard about him, his reputation is beyond reproach.''

His reputation, yes. His actions, no, Paula instantly thought. What she said was, "Yes, quite.'' There was a moment's uncomfortable silence, as if Marie Légère had expected her to say more. Paula didn't mind talking about Bret Graham as long as the conversation stayed strictly in the area of his theories and practice. But it was hard for her not to think of personal things whenever talk turned to the man rather than his work.

Filling the silence, Paula went on. "Dr. Graham's theories are really quite simple. He feels that specialization is as important in psychology as it is in any other field. That's not at all startling, of course. What is rather controversial is that Bret—Dr. Graham, I mean—believes that the so-called artistic personality manifests itself at a very tender age, and in some cases it manifests characteristic problems at an early age, too. He did studies on infants, and he felt he could see definite differences in infant responses to certain stimuli, responses directly related to artistic activity at later stages. He studied as many biographies of artists as he could to try to glean facts about their early years, but of course he couldn't gain as much from that type of research as he hopes to from the careful records he and I have been keeping on our cases."

"Dr. Graham is a psychologist. You are a social worker."

Marie's statement was really a question, but Paula was confident that Bret's recommendation made it clear he felt she could handle most aspects of his work with students. The recommendation had been part of the deal between them. Calmly Paula answered.

"As Dr. Graham probably wrote to Madame Saint-Pierre, he considered my qualifications more than adequate to carry on his work. I'd been a social worker for a number of years before I met him. When I first began working with him in the schools, it was quite appropriate for me to remain so, but as our work went on I started to think I'd like to go back to university to get a doctorate in psychology. I'd begun courses when...." She hesitated, suppressing the memories her words brought back. Marie Légère appeared not to notice that tiny pause, and Paula continued, "When this opportunity to try out Dr. Graham's theories on Belgian students arose."

"Naturally Dr. Graham would want to continue his own work in Canada, so he chose you as his delegate?"

"Yes."

"And your family could spare you?" There was a hint of nosiness in the question. Paula had discovered in the past two months that Marie Légère's only real fault as an administrator was her inability to confine her curiosity to matters of business. She'd tried on other occasions to get Paula to reveal personal information. There wasn't much to tell, really, except of course for the things about Bret—things she'd promised she'd never tell anyone. As far as her family went, there wasn't a lot to say.

"As I think I mentioned," Paula said patiently, "my parents separated when I was a teenager. I lost track of my father, unfortunately. We'd never had a very satisfactory relationship. Later I learned that he'd died. My mother also died a few years ago. My only sister has her own family in Toronto. She could, as you say, spare me." There was no bitterness in Paula's voice nor in her feelings toward her family. She had always considered herself satisfied to be somewhat of a loner.

Marie remarked, "I'd thought that Quebec, like Belgium, had very large, very close families. Being a Catholic place too, it would seem—"

"Not everyone in Quebec is Catholic, of course. And all Catholics don't have large families."

"Well, when I was widowed I had only my two precious daughters. I would almost certainly have had many more...."

"You never thought of remarrying?" Paula asked in the same casual tone Marie had used.

Now that the shoe was on the other foot, Marie changed the subject. "We should be getting on with this, shouldn't we?'' she asked, reaching for the first of the files Paula offered her.

"This is the file on Karel," Paula remarked as Marie began to glance over the contents.

"Karel is a very cooperative boy, as you no doubt have discovered by now. His main problem is his relationship with his father. He's transferred a great deal of his affection to Luc—understandably, of course." Paula didn't know why that was supposed to be immediately understandable, but she didn't question Marie.

"When Luc was ill," the principal went on, "Karel's grades suffered. Now that he's back, I think some of this problem will disappear. My feeling is that Karel will someday need to be weaned of his dependence on Luc, but that will probably happen of itself." Marie glanced up with a smile. "Sometimes teachers do know a thing or two about students—even without psychologists and social workers to tell them!"

Paula nodded, graciously accepting Marie's good-natured observation. She handed her supervisor the next file. "Ah, yes," Marie said, "Kathelijne de Schutter. This young woman is a painter of exceptional talent. She's a scholarship student who comes from a very poor family, and a more dedicated, honest, honorable young woman you'd have to go far to meet. She has no problem with her work, as you may know, but she's having trouble adjusting to the difference between the world she experiences at school and the one she goes home to at night. I feel that this student, who is so bright and quick, needs only a sympathetic ear. You may not find your professional skills tasked to the full on this one."

"No," Paula replied, adding, "Kathelijne is not very different from a lot of the youngsters I dealt with in Montreal. I'm happy to offer her whatever help I can, even if it's just to listen—which, after all, might be far more beneficial than sophisticated treatments in a lot of cases.''

''I quite agree.'' Marie took several other files from Paula's hands, going through them with the brisk efficiency that characterized all her actions. Closing the last of the files, she commented, ''Margaret Johnson, as you have discovered, is a fellow Canadian. She has a problem with self-confidence that keeps her from advancing in her studies. Monsieur Josef, who works quite closely with her on her singing, is very concerned. Unlike his brother, Josef hasn't the will to force his students into doing their best. He's an excellent teacher—no mistake about that—but his methods are those of the persuader. Luc, on the other hand, simply bullies his pupils into doing what he thinks they're capable of doing. It's really quite remarkable.''

Paula thought the idea of bullying people reactionary and dictatorial. She almost said as much, but glancing at Marie's face, she saw there the usual admiration for Luc LeBlanc and his nefarious methods. It was beginning to get tiresome, this universal admiration for the dark, rude, intrusive writing teacher. Maybe Paula wouldn't apologize for yesterday, after all.

Marie handed Margaret's file back to Paula along with the others, except for one that she'd laid aside the moment her eye had fallen on the name. Paula had seen Marie separate that file and had noted the action without surprise. Nor was she at all surprised at Marie's comments. Paula was already quite familiar with this student.

''Before I say a single thing about the...work habits of this young lady,'' Marie began, ''I feel it only fair to mention that donations from her grandfather have saved this school from financial ruin more than once. As you may know, the old part of this building is thought to be the very pension in which Charlotte and Emily Brontë studied in the early 1840s, though the street was not then called the rue Ravenstein, as it is now.

"The modern addition to Le Berceau enabled us to have enough classrooms to teach the number of students necessary to keep the school going. Both the restoration of the old building and the construction of the new were made possible by a gift to the school foundation from this young lady's grandfather. I am not going to try to hide my belief that we would keep this girl on under any circumstances. I sincerely think that if she took it into her mind to burn the place down, her grandfather would merely apologize for her and build it back up again. Oh, don't frown so! I should know better than to mention such things to people in your profession. I have no fears that that will happen; I only mention it to point out exactly how the situation stands with this one...."

"This one," Paula said, being as frank as Marie had been, "is without question the most flighty, flamboyant, careless and infuriating young person I've ever had the dubious pleasure to meet. But I have to admit that I also find her incomparably pretty and irresistibly charming."

"Resist, Miss Emanuel. Resist or you'll regret it. I have had Laurice in my office in tears more than once on account of Villette van der Vloedt. In dance class she is, apparently, wonderful or terrible, totally according to whim. She's capable of technical feats that astound Laurice, but capable, as well, of a carelessness that we feel is a bad influence on the others. I know it's not part of your job to psychoanalyze pupils, but...."

"It may be possible to help Villette fulfill her potential without referring her to a psychologist or a doctor, but I'm not sure at this point. Of the five sessions I've scheduled for her, she's missed three and had to be dismissed from another before it was half over because she claimed her parents needed her for a reception. Still, Laurice insists the girl has a lot of talent—"

"I'm intrigued that a protégée of a scientist like Dr. Graham would even use that word," Marie said with a small smile. "There are teachers here who never let it pass their lips. They prefer to speak only of work, not of anything as elusive as talent."

"I believe in talent," Paula stated simply. "Remarkably enough, I believe in it more now that I've worked with Bret than I ever did before. It seemed to him, and it seems to me, that some people are born with a gift that's almost like a destiny. It's certainly possible to ignore that gift, even perhaps to destroy it, but not to deny it. I think a person with talent bears the responsibility for that talent all through life."

"I think so, too," Marie admitted, "which is probably why I continue to put up with people like our little Miss Villette. I wish you luck with her, Paula. You'll need it!"

"OF COURSE I'M TALENTED," the saucy teen replied when Paula tried to relay to her some of what she and Marie had discussed. Villette's hair was a golden fall around her rosy cheeks. Her bright blue eyes danced with merriment and mischief. Paula had a hard time looking directly at her sometimes, though she was well schooled in the importance of maintaining eye contact. It was just that something about the sixteen-year-old's boisterous good spirits made Paula smile in spite of herself. Sometimes she was forced to get up from her desk and move to the window, keeping her back to the girl as she spoke. This was her most difficult session of the week. Fortunately it was also the last for today. She stared straight at the youngster, who said, "I know LePan thinks I'm talented. She told me so. I wouldn't be surprised if she thinks I'm the best in the class."

"*I'd* be surprised, Villette. Ever since I came to Le Berceau, I've been told that at this school we don't stress the competitive aspects of art. I'd be very surprised if any teacher rated her students like so many trained white mice."

The girl giggled, but Paula kept a straight face as she went on. "The point isn't who's best or whose work is most popular. The point is to constantly be striving toward your own personal best."

Villette sighed and shifted in her chair. Her legs were extended and she slouched, but there was about her a prettiness and a girlish grace that made her every gesture happily attractive, even when, as now, she was being uncooperative. "It's the same thing, isn't it?" she said. "Personal best or just plain best. Best is best—that's what it's all about. I get tired of talking like this; it's so boring. Don't you ever get bored with it, miss?"

At the moment the real answer to that question was an emphatic yes, but of course Paula restrained herself. "If you find this boring, Villette, suppose you talk about something you feel like talking about."

"Anything?"

"Anything."

"Is this a trick?" The girl's tone was lighthearted, not at all suspicious or petulant the way students often were when Paula tried this form of free association.

"Maybe it is a trick," Paula replied, and Villette laughed aloud.

"Okay, miss." Villette was silent for a few minutes,

trying to think of a suitable, or unsuitable, topic. Surprisingly, she chose to talk about her problems in class, after all. "You know, the reason Laurice—Madame LePan—is down on me today is that I was flirting with Louis in class again."

"And why were you flirting with Louis?"

"Because he's cute, of course," Villette said almost with disgust at Paula's stupidity. Paula knew better than to respond to the provocation. She sensed Villette was about to say something more important than her impertinent remark.

After a pause the girl went on. "Louis is my friend, and I have to stick up for him. After class yesterday, a few of the guys from architecture were making fun of him for being in dance—you know...."

Paula nodded. "And you felt that to flirt with him would boost his self-confidence?"

"Yes. I was right, wasn't I? I was right to defend Louis." There was a note of defiance in the statement, but there was a kind of begging, too, as though Louis wasn't the only person whose confidence needed boosting. Sensitive to the nuance, Paula responded carefully.

"You were dead right in your theory, I'd say. Just a little off in your timing. To flirt in class is a distraction to the teacher, to the boy you're flirting with and to the others. Next time it might be better to help your friend with his self-confidence outside of class."

"He's not the only one who needs help," Villette said cryptically, and there was a hint of teasing in her voice that didn't escape Paula's notice.

"What do you mean?"

"Ah, Mademoiselle la Canadienne is getting curious," Villette said with another of her giggles. "*Who* do I mean? Isn't that what you really want to ask?"?

"Villette, I've warned you before that these sessions

are not to be used for gossip. That's one of the reasons I don't want you to use names unless it can't be avoided." Impatience made Paula's tone a little clipped. She could see that Villette's boredom with the session was leading the girl into a taunting kind of behavior that wasn't nearly as amusing to Paula. There were still several minutes to go, though, and as this was one of the few sessions for which Villette had shown up on time and during which she'd cooperated almost fully, Paula decided to be a little lenient—up to a point.

"Monsieur Luc LeBlanc, that's who I mean."

"There's no reason for us to talk about him. You're not taking his course this year, are you?"

"Everybody likes to talk about him," Villette answered, avoiding Paula's question. "Besides, you said I could talk about anything I wanted, didn't you?"

With a nod and a smile that was half defeat, half willing compliance, Paula sat back to listen to what Villette was about to say. She was quite certain it was of no real importance either to her or to the teenager.

"Everybody loves to talk about Monsieur Luc," Villette repeated. "He's really exciting. Did you know that before he started teaching here he was in combat?"

"Combat? You mean he was a soldier?" Paula asked, allowing her curiosity to be piqued.

"No, he was a foreign correspondent. You know, he wrote articles in foreign places and sent them back home to Europe."

"Thanks. I know what a foreign correspondent does."

"Oh, *La Canadienne* is a grouch!"

"And you, miss, are impertinent!" It was a scold without sting, and it resulted in a wide smile from the student.

"Listen," Villette went on with easy familiarity,

"I'll tell you something else about Luc. He got wounded. That's why he's teaching journalism now instead of writing. Some people say that the only sort of teachers you get at schools like this are people who have failed at what they're teaching others to do. But I don't think that can be true of Monsieur Luc. It's got to be true of Lumpy Langois, though."

"Villette," Paula warned, trying very hard not to laugh. "I've already asked you to please refrain from using names. I'm afraid I must insist that you not use derogatory names in these sessions, especially not names of teachers."

"It's all right, miss. I can call him 'Lumpy.' It's not him, you know. It's his work. Have you seen his 'Stoned Ode to a Clean Potato'?"

"Villette," Paula began, but she couldn't go on without laughing a little. "The name of the work is 'Stone Ode to a Lean Ovoid.'" She had to pause for a few seconds to regain control. "Lamont Langois," she went on, "is a promising sculptor in his own right and first assistant to the head of the sculpture department. Have some respect, please."

"I have respect for you, Paula. You know how to laugh."

As with so much of what the girl said or did, the compliment mixed cooperation with rebellion. "Please don't call me by my first name, Villette. You know *madame* forbids it."

"If I did everything that *madame* demands and nothing that *madame* forbids, I'd be even more bored here than I am now. That, my dear Paula, would be unbearable."

Shaking her head in exasperation, though admittedly not very deep exasperation, Paula dismissed the unruly girl. She had to admit, too, that rather than feeling tired from her session with Villette, she felt almost refreshed. *Lumpy Langois!* she thought. *How appropriate!*

PAULA SINCERELY DOUBTED she'd ever be able to figure out the color-coded Brussels buses, despite the fact that everyone had been telling her for two months that they were quite easy to use once you got the hang of them. She had, however, mastered the uncomplicated bus trip from Le Berceau to her apartment, a small place she felt very lucky to have.

Sometimes she remembered with a smile her first night in this bustling metropolis. Following quickly on his assistance in getting Marie Légère to accept her credentials, Luc LeBlanc had offered to talk his landlady into letting Paula stay in a temporarily empty apartment in the same building he lived in. Refusing an offer that she found somehow too pushy for her tastes, she'd insisted that she would stay in a nearby hotel, not realizing that certain hotels in the area boasted an elegance beyond what she could afford. She had ended up paying the equivalent of half a week's salary for a single night. And she had had to struggle with several Dutch-speaking hotel employees who were willing to be helpful but who couldn't understand her French very well at all.

Paula was finding that life in this bilingual city was as colorful as it was sometimes confusing. In her building she had as many neighbors whom she greeted with a hearty *"Goeden avond"* as with *"Bonsoir"* when she made her way up to the tenth floor and along the modern corridor that led to her place. Her arms full of fresh vegetables and other things she'd stopped to buy at a little market on her street, she struggled with her key and finally succeeded in opening the door and rushing to the kitchen table, where she dumped everything, including the day's copy of *Le Soir*. She'd passed up *Het Laatste Nieuws* and thirteen other daily papers. She guessed Brussels must have more available newspapers than any other city, and she was glad they weren't all in a language she could understand. That made it much easier to choose!

But it wasn't *Le Soir* that she sat down to read. It was the mail. She went back to get it, picking it up from the mat by the door. There was a letter from Bonnie, her sister. She opened it and scanned it briefly, smiling as she read. Despite the fact that she and Bonnie weren't particularly close, she enjoyed the occasional letter from home, and she generally savored it later. There were one or two bills. And there was a letter from Bret Graham's office.

Before she even opened it, Paula knew it was nothing but another piece of computer-printed information relating to her canceled pension fund. Even so, her hand trembled when she opened the envelope. It didn't stop trembling until long after she'd read the notice, filed it with the others and thrown the envelope away. She wondered how long it would be until she could look at that name, that address, and feel nothing—just nothing at all. She had thought she would be able to by now, but obviously she'd been wrong.

With a sigh she poured herself a glass of a very fine French wine. She had been surprised to learn that Belgians had no local wine to boast about, depending on France and Germany for their needs. That was okay with her; she liked the wines of both countries. But she hardly tasted the smooth liquid that was cool on her tongue. She sat by the tiny kitchen window and looked out on the patch of brightening lights that was her view of the huge city beneath her.

What she felt whenever she thought about Dr. Bret Graham just wouldn't go away. It was fear. Still fear. She reminded herself that she'd been right to promise him she wouldn't press her legal suit against him. She reminded herself that he had promised to get her a respectable position one that would keep her away from Montreal for at least two years and would also look good on her résumé when things blew over and she could return. He'd kept his promise.

And both of them had promised that it was all over. Nothing would or could ever start back up between them.

So why, after a total of nearly six months, counting the two she'd been in Brussels, was she still afraid? Afraid that it wasn't over, afraid that the miles weren't far enough nor the time long enough to mend the wrong and keep it from ever happening again.

CHAPTER THREE

LUC FOUND IT HARD TO BELIEVE Karel had been having so much trouble in his absence, though he trusted Marie totally and knew she wouldn't exaggerate about anything so important. When he had left in November he'd made the boy promise he wouldn't slack off, but maybe the pressures from home were greater than Luc had estimated. Nonetheless, he had full confidence in Karel's talent. It wasn't the writing that convinced him the student was exceptional, for Karel, like most young writers, was often too florid and needed editing. No, what impressed Luc was the originality of the boy's thinking and the ability to make that originality come across in words. Luc knew that style could be worked on, could to a large extent be coaxed, if not actually taught. But there was no way to teach a person to look at the world in a way no one else could look at it.

He red-penciled a number of things, then set Karel's latest essay aside and picked up the next. The student hadn't much to say that Luc hadn't read before, and he found his mind wandering. Laying down his pencil, he walked to the window of the empty classroom.

She was in the garden again. Twice he'd seen her there; both times she'd been alone. If he had any sense at all, he'd pay as little attention to her as possible. She wasn't the first North American woman he'd met, but she was certainly one of the most volatile. *You'd never know it from looking at her,* he thought. She exuded calm quietness, but he'd seen her explode. When he had thought about her stinging outburst later, what had been anger on his part changed to something else.

He was no psychologist, but he was almost certain she was hurting in some way. Not that he would know how to help even if he felt like it. Which he didn't. He wondered vaguely whether she'd have the decency to apologize for being so uncivilized about his coming to get Karel. He doubted it. Foreigners, especially ones from across the Atlantic, weren't known for their delicacy.

And yet, watching her walking slowly through the garden, he had the distinct feeling that she wasn't naturally overly aggressive. He had no time for pushy people, but he had a healthy respect for a person who could stand up for herself. She had that quality, mixed with another, an elusive vulnerability that made him want to protect her at the same time as he felt it might be best to protect himself from her. Or to stay away from her. He was confused; he didn't know.... Shrugging his shoulders, he moved away from the window and resumed his work.

SPRING CAME TO BRUSSELS more quickly than Paula remembered it ever having come to Montreal. Though she hadn't yet suffered much from homesickness, she did miss the sense of the miraculous that came with spring in a country like Canada, where it was truly cold during the long winter. At home, she reflected, there was probably still snow on the ground, whereas here at the end of March the temperature during the day often climbed to fifty and beyond.

Since she'd come Paula had established habits that lent order to her days, and if she sometimes felt lonely, that wasn't a new feeling for her. Long hours of dedication in a demanding profession had added to her own natural inclination to keep to herself, though she socialized with fellow teachers whenever the opportunity arose.

She had to admit her job at Le Berceau was less demanding than the other positions she'd held. Half of each day was spent interviewing students. Her other time was occupied in familiarizing herself with job opportunities in the students' various specialties, in learning school procedures, in paperwork and in other duties that fell to the teaching staff.

One such duty was to take charge of a student study period; that was the responsibility of different teachers on a rotating schedule. When it was her turn, Paula found she had an extra twenty minutes between her last interview and the study hour. She liked to spend the time walking in the garden and sometimes in the tree-lined alley behind it.

One afternoon, as she had done before, she opened the set of old-fashioned French doors leading to the garden. She stepped out into a small open court, near the windows of some of the classrooms and the school's dining hall; the latter also served as the study. Near the building the spring warmth was more intense, and already a number of pale flowers bloomed at the edge of the flagstone path. Breathing deeply, Paula caught the sweet scent of some unknown blossom. The freshness of the garden, even in winter, was always a pleasant surprise, for Brussels, like Montreal, was a large and heavily populated modern city; air pollution was ever present. Here in the sheltered court, it sometimes seemed to Paula that time had stopped a century earlier.

Slowly she walked through the fresh garden. Though the busy streets were not far from the walls, she could hear very little of the traffic. It was too early for the rustle of leaves, but there was a slight breeze that caught in Paula's auburn curls, then danced away to tangle in bushes beginning to green. After a little while the breeze mingled with a thread of music, nearly too soft to be heard at first, more insistent as Paula walked on.

It was a reedy, haunting melody; surely one she'd never heard before. She knew a little about music, enough to realize there was nothing Flemish or French apparent in this stirring little tune. So foreign it sounded, so exotic, not European at all, but more primitive. She couldn't tell whether the essential sadness of the song was a quality of the tune, the instrument or the player. Perhaps, she thought whimsically, her own deepest sadness was suddenly audible through someone else's breath, for clearly this was an instrument of the breath, like a flute.

Her curiosity piqued, she quickened her pace, tracing the source of the music. Her light steps made little sound as she moved past ornamental shrubs, small trees, ferns and occasional flowers that decorated the courtyard and the larger garden into which it opened. Though the music grew stronger as she approached, the tune was no more familiar.

In the farthest reaches of the garden she found the musician himself. A stone bench with a tall back rested against a high wall, the garden's boundary for more than a hundred years. A man sat with his back against one of the arms and his feet on the seat of the bench; he wore black jeans and a black leather jacket and was holding a set of bamboo pipes bound with twine. Paula recognized them as panpipes. Her eyes moved from the simple instrument to the musician's hands. She saw with a dart of some indefinable feeling that they looked startlingly sensitive against the dull sheen of the jacket's leather.

The musician didn't look up at her approach, and at

first Paula thought he must be one of Monsieur Josef LeBlanc's students. The music went on, flowing over the moss-covered wall of the garden with ease and grace, but still with that touch of sadness that made it sound like a sigh. Paula ventured closer. The man who played swayed slightly to the strains; in the light of afternoon, his black hair, ruffled by the garden breeze and by his own motion, gleamed softly. When Paula saw the few strands of gray at the temple, she realized with a start who the musician was. She thought she'd been silent, that he wouldn't have noticed her, but when she turned to leave he sensed her presence. He looked up without ceasing his song. His blue-violet eyes held a question, only for a moment. He seemed to recognize her in a much shorter time.

It had been a couple of weeks since the confrontation in her office, but she hadn't had a chance to apologize for her less than friendly words to Luc. She felt trapped. Smiling a little awkwardly, she acknowledged his nod as he brought his doleful little tune to a close and took the instrument from his lips. Absurdly, her eyes were drawn to his lower lip. He didn't smile, and realizing that he wasn't about to, she raised her eyes to his. He was studying her again with his habitual, unnerving scrutiny. Shyness filled her, but she quelled it. "Hello," she said smoothly. "The music is lovely."

"Good afternoon." Like her, he spoke in French, but she had noticed that his accent seemed a little different from that of most of the students. Still he didn't smile, but he held out his hand pleasantly, inviting her to sit beside him on the bench. Graciously she accepted, feeling at once the stone's coldness against her thighs through the weave of her light coat. She shivered only a little, but he saw.

"If it's too cold for you, you'd better go in." There

was in his voice that same combination of concern and imperiousness that she'd noticed both times she'd dealt with him. This time she realized it was that very combination that confused her about the man. She hadn't known—either time—whether he was being rude or genuinely friendly. She realized she should be grateful for his concern, yet his manner implied that concern granted him some sort of power over her; the thought rankled. Nonetheless, she was bound and determined not to argue with him again. If smooth relations meant ignoring the fact that she couldn't quite understand him, then she'd ignore the fact. He was the only member of the staff she'd had any problem with, and she wanted to end their differences.

"No," she said, "I'm fine. The music is beautiful. Those are panpipes?"

"Yes. They're from South America, from Chile, to be exact."

"You've been there?" she queried lightly in exactly the tone she would have used to a stranger at a cocktail party, indicating polite interest and nothing more. To her surprise, the secretive, shuttered look she had seen once before returned.

"No," he said rather sharply, looking away. She was 100 percent certain he was lying.

There was a moment of tense silence between them, a moment into which the noise of the streets flowed, more evident here at the back of the garden. The sound was far less pleasant than the music. Unable to think of anything to say and uncomfortable, she made a slight motion to rise, but his quiet voice stopped her. "Do you play an instrument?"

The question touched her. It was so obviously an attempt to delay her. Again she was struck by the feeling that she'd been impolite and ungrateful. She leaned toward him a little. "Monsieur Luc, I don't think I ever thanked you properly for coming to my aid that first night. I'm really sorry about the other day. I—''

"Think nothing of it, Miss Emanuel," he said in such a dismissive tone that she felt she must have mistaken his desire to detain her. He really was a very difficult man to understand. Maybe she'd offended him more than she realized. Gathering her wits, she decided to make one more attempt at friendship.

"Did your brother Josef teach you to play the pipes?" Her question sounded nervous and contrived, but she wasn't sorry for braving the query when she saw his face come alive with interest.

"No. I was taught by an exiled Chilean. But my brother did teach me to read music and also helped me to play by ear at a very early age. Josef, in his humble way, is quite the missionary of music. . . ." Now he did smile, a winning smile that drew a spontaneous grin from Paula.

"What else can you play?" she asked, meaning what other songs, but he took her question in a different sense.

"Various wind instruments, but I like best to play the old ones—especially the recorder. Don't you play anything?"

"Should I?"

"Of course," he said, but she could tell he was teasing her a little. "Everyone should know how to play music. It's part of being civilized. Haven't you yet learned that Belgium is the land of the amateur musician?"

She shook her head.

"Ah, then," he said, his voice the one he must use when he taught, because suddenly injected into it was the patience a good teacher might express, and maybe a good father, too, though she couldn't swear to a close knowledge of the last. "It would seem the Canadian needs a few lessons in Belgian living. We are, you may discover, not the world's most-famous producer of musical compositions, but we boast more numerous and enthusiastic performers per square mile than any other country in the world! Some years back they did a study and found there were three thousand brass bands in this country.''

"Do they ever play all at once?'' Paula couldn't help asking.

"I don't think so. No doubt some are Flemish and some Walloon. Dutch and French, in other words, and in this country they don't always make beautiful music together. But you were being facetious, weren't you?''

"Who, me?'' Paula asked, and was pleased to hear his low laughter. "When I asked you what else you knew how to play,'' she went on, "I meant what other songs.''

"I know other songs of the mountains, like the one I was playing. Would you like to hear another?''

"Sure,'' Paula answered with genuine interest, watching as Luc lifted the twine-bound reeds to his lips. Again the haunting music obliterated all other sound in the corner of the garden. With the smooth and unrelenting rhythm of the wings of mountain birds, the notes flew from the simple pipes. Caught in the gentle melancholy of the piece, Paula wandered with her thoughts until she was miles away from the spring garden. There was something cold and clear and forbidding in the music. It was the song of high, hard-to-reach places, the music of people whose days were spent in clean, sharp air that pierced the imagination as well as the lungs. When Luc finished the final strains seemed to hang for a moment in the sudden stillness.

"It's lovely,'' Paula said with what must have been convincing sincerity, for Luc immediately offered to play another song.

"This is not from the mountains," he said, "not from South America at all, but from Central America." He began a tune that was lilting, almost jolly, but just as Paula was beginning to appreciate the trickiness of the rhythm, Luc broke off abruptly, almost angrily.

"It sounds ridiculous to play this here," he said with a strange note in his voice.

"No, it doesn't," Paula protested, not knowing exactly what he meant. "It sounds wonderful. Why don't you—"

"Isn't it time for you to get along to the study hall?"

"What?" Paula had nearly forgotten about her monitoring duty. Glancing at her watch, she saw it was indeed time. "I do have to get going," she said, not stopping to wonder how he knew her schedule. "Thanks for the concert, Monsieur LeBlanc...."

"It wasn't a concert, and the name is Luc." His voice was almost a growl, his words once more dismissive. Not applying her usual professional detachment, Paula found his moodiness quite irritating; he seemed as mercurial as his music. She didn't have a lot of patience with pure pique. In her work, she helped people whose moods were capable of damaging their health, but her own pique prevented her from considering that that might be partly the case here. No doubt some women found dark, mysteriously sad men attractive. Not Paula. She knew better. Her own manner was less than warm as she bid him a polite but perfunctory goodbye.

Paula made her way to the study hall, and while the students quietly did their assignments she firmly turned her mind to her own tasks and got caught up on some of the paperwork that always threatened to get beyond her. It was the final period of the day. When the bell rang she was glad to be finished. She stopped by her office only long enough to pick up her purse and her coat before setting out for the bus stop. On the way she heard rapid footsteps behind her and turned to see Karel hurrying to catch up. "Hello, miss," he said in a breathless but cheerful voice.

"Hi, Karel. How are you today?"

"Fine. Except for an argument with my history teacher. She's such an *eigenwijs*!"

"An eee—"

Karel laughed at Paula's inability to repeat the word. "That's Dutch for 'know-it-all.' Listen, I can teach you some Dutch if you like. I speak it just as well as I speak French. Of course, legally Le Berceau is French only, and dad won't let me speak anything else when he's around, but my mom speaks Dutch with me."

"Does Monsieur Luc speak Dutch?" Paula asked, a little surprised at her own curiosity.

"*Mon Dieu!* I should say not! He's from the south, like Madame Légère. He's her distant cousin, in fact. Monsieur Luc is Liègeois. You know how they are."

Paula didn't know anything about the citizens of the city of Liège. She was about to ask Karel what he meant when they saw the bus coming and had to make a run for it.

"Going my way?" she asked the boy with a smile, and nodding, he hopped on the bus and found them a seat. When the conversation resumed it was Paula who spoke first. "Speaking of Monsieur Luc, I stumbled across him playing music in the garden this afternoon."

"Ah, yes. You never know where he's going to turn up, that one." Karel's voice was full of affection. Paula was beginning to get the impression that Monsieur Luc was a great favorite among the students. He hadn't been back for longer than a few weeks, but he seemed to be a popular topic of conversation.

"He plays the panpipes quite well," Karel commented, "but he plays other things much better."

Caught by the memory of how Luc's sensitive hands had caressed the slender tubes of his instrument, Paula momentarily lost the thread of the conversation. There was a brief silence before Karel went on. "He belongs to a musical group called The Brussels Chapter of the Expatriate Recorder and Other Small Instrument Players from Liège."

"What?" Paula asked, laughing. "You're kidding, aren't you?"

"Oh, no, miss. We Belgians are as serious about societies, clubs and organizations as we are about music. Monsieur Luc is very serious about this group. I've even seen him dismiss class early in order not to be late for one of their rehearsals."

"Your Monsieur Luc seems to be quite the well-rounded man," Paula remarked. "He's a combat journalist according to Villette, a dedicated musician according to you and a popular teacher by all accounts."

Karel caught the note of sarcasm in her voice. "You say that as though you don't like him," the boy commented with incredulity, as if a person would have to be blind to fail to see Luc's charms.

"Like him?" she answered a little irritably. "Why, I hardly know him, do I? He doesn't seem to have been around very much."

"He'll be around a lot now. He's quite recovered from his health problems," the boy said with satisfaction.

"I assume he has someone to take care of him. A friend or a wife—"

"No. He had a girlfriend once—a real beauty. I saw her picture often in magazines."

"An actress or model?"

"Oh, no. Monsieur Luc likes serious women."

Paula smiled at the naiveté of that remark, and Karel was quick to notice her amusement and to elaborate with the apparent intention of setting the record straight on the subject of the writing teacher. "Monsieur Luc was once in love with a fellow journalist. She was killed covering a story in the Middle East. You see, he's not the type of man to fall for just anybody. Villette says that if she had time, she'd seduce him herself, but she says the same thing about me, too," he revealed with a half grimace, half grin.

Apparently the irrepressible Miss van der Vloedt was extending her confidence-building campaign. Paula shook her head in exasperation. "Mademoiselle Villette would do well to pay as much attention to her studies as she seems to pay to everything else under the sun." Her voice was testy. The idea of Villette exerting her youthful charms on the journalism teacher bothered Paula, no doubt because the idea of students flirting with teachers was one to be discouraged at all costs. Glancing out the window, she saw she was about halfway home. Turning back to the young man, she asked, "So it's true, then, that Monsieur LeBlanc wasn't always a teacher?"

"Oh, he's a fine teacher!" Karel insisted, never seeming to miss the opportunity to heap praises on the object of his admiration. "But no, he's only been teaching for a couple of years. Before that he was a famous journalist. Maybe you never heard of him where you come from, but most people in Brussels knew about him."

"Why ever did he give it up?" Paula asked, curious despite her growing conviction that she and Monsieur LeBlanc would do well to keep out of each other's way. "Was it because of his health?"

"Sort of. It's a long story."

"I've got time," Paula remarked, not checking to see if the bus was near her stop.

"Okay, then," Karel said with a smile, "I'll tell you a little about Luc. For some time he was assigned to cover the goings-on in a small country in Central America. When he went there the government of the country was oppressive, but it was stable. There was an underground resistance movement—several factions—but they were disorganized and ineffectual."

Paula nodded, encouraging Karel to continue. She was impressed by the clarity of his explanation and wondered whether Luc had used his own experiences as a way of teaching his pupils how to speak concisely about current affairs.

"At first," Karel went on, "Monsieur Luc confined his activities to merely reporting what he saw—that, of course, was his job. He wrote for one of the Paris daily papers, but many of his articles were reprinted in Belgium and elsewhere, too, and he soon had a widespread reputation. He was often mentioned in news broadcasts and quoted in other people's articles. After a while it was apparent that his reporting was becoming more like the editorializing of an expert than the fact-finding of a regular reporter. This didn't bother the paper he worked for—they welcomed his opinions. He started to write feature articles for magazines and appeared on TV shows. Then he kind of disappeared—"

"Disappeared?"

"Well, the story didn't come out until later, but apparently Monsieur Luc got involved with the resistance movement. It wasn't known at first that he could write in Spanish, as well as French. Some people in Europe began to suspect he was working with or for the underground press in the country he'd been covering. Not a wise thing for a journalist to do."

"Nor a very safe thing."

"Oh, no, not at all," declared Karel with youthful enthusiasm. "His life was on the line all the time, not to mention his job. However, he was still sending home good material for the French-language press, so whatever they suspected, his Paris paper didn't put any pressure on him. Maybe they knew what he was up to and liked the idea of one of their writers being that involved. Whatever, there weren't any real problems until Monsieur Luc's activities inadvertently came to the attention of the ruling government, which revoked his visa."

"And it was then that he quit?"

"Of course not," Karel insisted indignantly. "He's not a coward."

"I didn't think he was," Paula replied, realizing that a coward was the very last thing she'd label the dark, difficult man. A pain, yes, but not a coward.

"He refused to leave," Karel went on. "Then he was injured somehow during a demonstration at the country's presidential palace."

"He was wounded?" Paula asked, remembering what Villette had told her.

"I don't know for sure how he was hurt, but he was almost killed. The resisters—the few of them who weren't arrested, that is—managed to get him away from the scene and look after him until he was well enough to be flown back to Europe. He was ill for a very long time. I guess there were complications."

"Did he tell you all this himself?"

"No, miss," Karel said with great seriousness. "Monsieur Luc never talks about any of this, not to anyone and not ever."

"Then how do you know about it?"

"At the time there was a lot of coverage in the papers. My dad used to like to read Monsieur Luc's Paris reports, so he sort of kept track of things."

"Is Luc all right now?"

"Finally, yes. He's missed school for rather long periods sometimes, but he swears that's over now. Villette seems to think there's still something wrong with him, something no one can talk about, but she has a bit of an imagination."

For once Paula let pass the chance to offer her personal opinion on the attitudes and behavior of Villette. She was lost in thought. "What sort of problem could it be?" she asked after a long pause.

"I don't know, miss, but most of the things I'm talking about happened a pretty long time ago. It's already been two years since Monsieur Luc came here to teach."

"He must miss his writing if he was once so committed."

"I guess so. It isn't really a loss, though, because he's a good teacher. And a fine man."

"No doubt," Paula commented, sighing and shaking her head. She looked up and saw an unfamiliar row of closely built, narrow houses along a winding old street speed by her eyes. "Oh, no! I've missed my stop!" Jumping up, she hastily said goodbye to Karel and ran for the exit.

SHE HAD LITTLE TIME to think about the things Karel had told her that night or the next day. At three-thirty that afternoon her last client left her office, but it was nearly an hour later before she herself was ready to go. Gathering her things, she opened the door to the outer office and was amazed to see someone was there. Not just someone—Luc. She felt his eyes take full measure of her, but she kept her cool. "Monsieur LeBlanc. What can I do for you?"

"I'd like to talk to you for a minute, if you can spare the time," he said, and she couldn't tell by the tone of his voice what his mood was or guess why he might be there.

"Have you been waiting long?" she asked, unable to think of anything else to say as she motioned him toward her inner office. She hated the awkwardness there always seemed to be between them.

"I've waited for half an hour. Madame Martel said you shouldn't be much longer. She left about twenty minutes ago."

"Why didn't you knock?"

"I remembered the last time I tried that and decided against it," he replied, and there was a rare teasing quality to his tone that Paula could only respond to with a smile. She sat not behind her desk but in one of the two chairs in front, offering him the other, which he declined, perching instead on the edge of her desk.

"I'm sorry about what I said that day."

"I've already accepted your apology, Paula." His voice as he said her first name for the first time was surprisingly soft. Her eyes shot up toward his, and she saw in the indigo depths a warmth she'd never noticed before. "I've come to offer an apology of my own...."

"What for?"

"For chasing you out of the garden yesterday. For intruding into your office, as accused, before that. And for letting you go two months without any sort of help. I know I should have made attempts to find out whether you'd settled in and how you were doing in your first weeks at Le Berceau. My excuse is that I was ill, but still, I'm sorry."

Paula's brow wrinkled in puzzlement. "I don't know what you mean. It wasn't up to you to look after me. I'm not even a member of your department. I thought your initial kindness was beyond the call of duty. I didn't expect—"

"Don't concern yourself, Paula. I've taken on one or two things beyond my jurisdiction in my time. I often help Marie, even when she's not fully aware that I'm doing so. This is a big place, not always easy to run, especially since she's just taken on the role of principal. I could see at once that your job offer was legitimate. I knew Saint-Pierre had had something like your program in mind. My helping you was a way of helping Marie."

"I see," Paula said, suddenly feeling very deflated without knowing why. She should have been happy to discover he hadn't been as arrogant as she'd thought.

"I came here this afternoon to set things right between us," he went on. "I should have paid more attention to you. It was unkind of me to ensure that Marie took you on, and then to disappear. I presume that's why you're angry with me . . . ?"

"I'm not angry, just confused . . . ."

"Confused?"

"Why should you be offering kindness to me?"

The question puzzled him. It took him a minute to realize she was serious. Her face was upturned, and he noticed that she had very fine lines at the corners of her mouth and her unusual eyes. He suspected she might be a little older than he, but that didn't take away from her attractiveness. She was a very pretty woman, with the kind of good looks he thought might have been called beauty in someone less sad.

Not quite realizing what he was doing, he leaned closer, then straightened so that he was standing directly in front of her. He caught the scent of her perfume. Something light and flowery, but it had a deeper, mysterious after scent. He took an extra breath before he asked her, "What kind of a world do you come from where kindness has to be earned as though it were a pension or a wage?"

She couldn't answer him. His question opened unexpected floodgates of regret in her. She remembered the day she'd left Montreal in what could only be called disgrace. There had been no one to see her off, and no one to meet her in Brussels, either. His own kindness had been the first she'd known in a long time, and instead of recognizing it as such, she had suspected him of intruding. A wave of loneliness swept over her, and she turned away from his scrutiny. He hadn't missed the expression on her pale face.

"What is it with you, Paula?" he asked, and quite without intending to, he reached out his hand and took her chin in his palm, lifting her face toward him. *"Mon Dieu,"* he said, nearly whispering, "your eyes are full of such sorrow...." Leaning closer still, he took her quivering lips with his own.

For a timeless moment she was still beneath his touch. She knew he had no right. But so welcome a warmth flooded from the moist pressure of his kiss that she found herself unable to pull away, unable to tell him that yet again he was using his concern for her as a bludgeon.

He soon realized the presumption of his kiss, or so it seemed, for he moved away slightly. "Now you will accuse me of apologizing improperly," he said with such seriousness that Paula, despite herself, began to laugh.

"Luc," she said, steadying her voice, "I think it would be best if you kept out of my office. Your behavior here tends to be, uh, inappropriate."

He looked as though he was about to interrupt, but she put up her hand and stopped him. "Nonetheless, I accept your apology. You did me a kindness that was unexpected, no matter what your motives, and I appreciate it. I have a feeling we'll make better friends than enemies. Truce?"

"Truce," he replied, taking her proffered hand. The moment his skin grazed hers, the gesture ceased to be a handshake and became something quite different. She felt the hot electricity of his touch, not just warm this time, but infused with a sensual heat that caught her off guard. She looked up into his eyes, but it was too late, too late to stop this second kiss, so different from the first. Now his mouth was powerful and demanding, his tongue dissatisfied with her closed lips as he sought and was granted entry into the soft recesses of her mouth. His kiss was hungry, the kiss of a man who wants far more than what the moment can give. Paula responded with a deep, abiding hunger of her own. Desire swelled in her, and she had a hard time fighting it down. Only her awareness of where they were finally saved her. That she of all people should be doing this at work!

"Stop!" she demanded, abruptly pulling away from him. Apology or no apology. Truce or no truce. She was about to give him a good piece of her mind. Again.

But something stopped her. It was the expression on his face. Luc looked shocked, as if the deep passion of the kiss had been more surprising and more shattering to him than it had been to her. It was almost as though he hadn't kissed her of his own volition. Wearily he covered his face with his hands, and when he dropped them moments later his eyes were shuttered, his mouth firm. "I know," he said. "I'm going. I'll save you the trouble of having to throw me out."

CHAPTER FOUR

AFTER THAT INCIDENT she tried to avoid him, not because she was angry—she wasn't, really—but because any relationship, even a casual friendship with so obviously complex a man was bound to cause complications. A new job and a new home were all she felt capable of handling right then.

But despite her determination to have no further personal encounters with Luc, it was hard to avoid seeing him in a professional capacity; he seemed to be everywhere. He apparently took his job very seriously, and though Paula had twice heard him describe himself deprecatingly as "the writing teacher," it soon became clear that his position as head of the writing program imposed heavy responsibilities. He spoke at every staff meeting. His crisp, precise presentation drew grudging admiration from Paula, unlike Marie Légère's; her courtly French was somewhat long-winded. Often Luc was quite persuasive, as well, even if his views frequently opposed those of the majority of the staff. No doubt his years as a journalist had honed his verbal powers. *If* it was true that he'd been a journalist.

It wasn't only at staff meetings that Paula came into contact with Luc. While teachers were allowed to take their meals in a small room off the main dining hall, most of them sat among the students, and Luc was no exception. He was almost always at the center of some vigorous argument or other, but though he excited the students, he remained cool. Apparently he felt a teacher's job was to stimulate discussion, for whenever things at his table were about to quiet down he interjected a word or two, and immediately the kids were back at it, sometimes even rising from their chairs or pounding the table with their fists to emphasize a point—an activity strictly against dining-hall rules, of course, but never discouraged by Luc as far as Paula could see.

One day the discussion was evidently about the right of a reporter to withhold the identity of his or her sources of information. Paula hadn't come in at the very beginning, but it didn't take her long to discover the topic. The sheer volume of the discussion, not to mention the vigor of it, made it impossible to ignore from any nearby table, and she'd taken a seat only two tables away from Luc and his coterie.

"The whole point about journalism is that it tells the truth," one young woman stated.

"So?" Luc prompted.

"So a writer has to be able to prove that what he says is true. Even if he has to reveal a source to do it."

"Nobody can prove a story is absolutely true, can they, Monsieur Luc?" one of the boys asked.

"It depends on what kind of truth we're talking about," Luc answered.

"There's only one kind of truth!" several voices insisted.

"Oh, really?" Luc said. "And which truth is that? A man standing five feet away from a murder victim may see him fall to the ground, but he may not be able to see a sniper in the bushes. Whereas a person standing behind the sniper might see the killer but not even realize a crime is being committed. So whose testimony is the truth?"

"Just because a person doesn't see the whole truth

doesn't mean it doesn't exist," the first girl pointed out.

"Then perhaps it might also be right to say that just because a person can't prove the truth of what he says, the statement isn't necessarily untrue," Luc replied.

"That's a whole different issue!" one of the other girls challenged Luc.

"It is not!" several of the students contended.

"Monsieur Luc," came the relatively calm voice of Karel, "if a reporter is relieved of the responsibility of revealing sources, doesn't that mean that dishonest people can anonymously pass off anything they want to say as the truth?"

Luc appeared to consider the question for a moment, and Paula waited as breathlessly as the young people for his response. Finally he said, "A dishonest person can manipulate facts, never saying anything untrue, but not speaking the truth, either. Ideally I feel that a reporter should always reveal sources, but from a practical point of view it's just not always possible. If the world was fair, everyone could deal honestly and openly, but we know that injustice is part of the lives of a great number of people, don't we?"

There was silence around the table, the silence of assent.

"The important thing for a journalist is to never compromise on honesty. Some people would hold back a story important to thousands of people to protect the reputation or the life of one person. Others would take the opposite view...."

"What would you do yourself, *monsieur*?" someone asked.

"I would tell the truth whether I could prove it or not."

Paula watched from a distance. Her own shyness, her newness, too, prevented her from being at the

center of a group of students the way Luc was. She had
to admit she envied him, the easy way he handled himself in casual encounters with the teenagers. Sometimes she watched him so intently that she left her
lunch nearly untouched. And once he caught her, his
violet eyes staring straight into her misty green ones
across several long wooden tables strewn with trays
and the remains of meals. In confusion she looked
away.

Luc LeBlanc had another personality besides the
one his students found so charming. He was a kind of
Jekyll-Hyde. In fact, it sometimes puzzled Paula that
his pupils cared to speak to Luc outside class at all, for
once he ascended the teacher's dais he was a terror.
Paula had first had wind of this from Villette, but she
hadn't taken the girl's comments very seriously. She
was well aware of the fact that Villette complained
heartily about any course that required her to put
together more than two consecutive sentences.

But the day that Kathelijne, a student no teacher
could ordinarily find fault with, came to Paula's office
visibly shaken from an incident with Monsieur Luc
only minutes earlier, Paula began to think the difficult
man who was so much a friend to the students outside
class was an enemy within classroom walls.

One afternoon she chanced to be passing one of his
classes, and without really meaning to eavesdrop, she
stopped beside the slightly open door. In his quiet,
clear voice, the teacher could be heard to say, "I can't
see this. This brings absolutely nothing to my eye. Do
you know what I mean?"

The student being questioned either remained silent
or else merely gestured, for Paula heard nothing.
There was a slight rustle of paper. "Here," Luc urged,
"take this and read the first sentence."

"It is thought that rainy weather prevented a good

turnout at yesterday's special sales," a voice haltingly read.

"Now," Luc said, "what sort of picture does that bring to mind?"

Silence.

"What does it tell you about the things that happened at the sale? Anything? Or does it just tell you what didn't happen?"

"Didn't, I guess...." said the pupil.

There was then the sound of footsteps, and Paula thought Luc had begun to pace the floor. For some reason, the thought brought an almost teasing smile to her face. Again she heard his voice. "Have I ever, does anyone remember, have I ever told you that news is not about what didn't happen, but what did?"

Silence.

"Have I ever, I wonder, mentioned that no crowd is important for the people who are *not* there, but only for the people who *are*? Does that ring a bell with any of you? Is it ever so slightly possible that you might have heard me say these things before?" His voice began to rise, and Paula could hear the shuffle of collective feet that she well knew signified the students were becoming uncomfortable.

"I allow myself to imagine," Luc went on, his voice changing again, "that when I say something seven or eight or nine times, there might be a little possibility that somewhere along the line someone will hear what I've said, understand it and take it to heart. I know I ask too much." There was a tinge of self-pity to his tone, and despite herself Paula's smile widened. *He should have been an actor. Such pathos! He's missed his calling.*

His voice became not louder, but more intense. "Day after day I say to myself: 'Maybe someone will pay attention to what I say.' And day after day I'm rewarded with efforts like this." Papers rustled, feet shuffled with renewed agitation. "*Tiens*, Monsieur Verhaegen," Luc went on. "I have told you and your colleagues more times than I can remember that I am *not* interested in what did *not* happen. And if *I* am not interested—I who spend countless hours reading what you people so blithely refer to as writing—if I am not interested, *monsieur*, who do you think will be? Let me repeat it one more time. Nobody does nothing. Nobody is interested in nothing. Nothing is *not* what I will tolerate from this class!"

He was good and truly angry now, but his seriousness, the note in his raspy voice, a note almost of personal hurt, affected Paula in exactly the wrong way. As though she herself were a recalcitrant student, she had to resist the intense desire to giggle at the intensity of the fiery teacher. Not wanting to give herself away, she covered her mouth with her hand and sneaked down the hall. She knew how difficult the students could be, and she reminded herself that in all honesty she couldn't find fault with the content of Luc's lesson, only the form. She thought haranguing as a teaching method had gone the way of dunce caps and switches.

Later, however, when she casually mentioned to Marie Légère that Luc's style seemed a tiny bit old-fashioned, the principal said that teachers who struck fear and remorse into the hearts of students were needed as much at present as they'd ever been!

There was one area in which even Marie Légère occasionally took Luc to task, however, and it amused Paula to watch the woman attempt to get Luc to dress more in keeping with what she considered the proper attire for teaching.

"You have such strong features, Luc—such character in the face," Marie commented one afternoon. "I'm so glad you decided against the beard and mustache. And I think it makes a better impression on the students, don't you?''

Luc nodded with total indifference. He seemed not at all offended by anything his cousin had to say about his appearance. Paula remembered someone had mentioned that Luc and Marie were distant cousins. Perhaps that was why Luc allowed Marie liberties Paula didn't think he'd allow other women.

Marie was not the only woman who could get away with commenting on Luc's clothes, Paula discovered. One afternoon she stepped through the open door of Marie's office and unwittingly found herself in the middle of an argument between the principal and Luc. She turned to leave, but Luc stayed her. ''Don't go, Miss Emanuel,'' he said, casually stepping between her and the door. ''*Madame* and I need a referee. She claims that T-shirts and jeans are improper attire for any teacher. I, on the other hand, maintain that the rules of this school allow full creativity in the matter of dress, and that the teachers as well as the students should cooperate. What's your opinion on the issue?''

His voice had a taunting quality to it. She knew that he and Marie had argued about this long before she had arrived at Le Berceau, and they didn't need her view. She had no intention of risking the displeasure of either of them by taking sides. She also had no intention of saying what she really thought, which was that as much as she hated to admit it, Luc LeBlanc looked better in his well-washed denims and dark, close-fitting T-shirts than most men looked in a suit.

''Luc, you yourself have told me not to pay too strict attention to rules,'' she said with a smile that she hoped bothered him a little, ''so I'm sure you won't try to persuade Marie by quoting the dress code....''
She noted with triumph the hint of displeasure that crossed his face, but she wasn't finished yet. ''On the

other hand," she said, "from what I understand, we teach the students that clothing is an art form like any other, an expression of individual feeling and thought. I'm sure that you, Marie, wouldn't deny anyone such basic freedom...."

Now it was Marie who looked disconcerted. Paula didn't stick around to see who won that round of play-offs. She left some papers for Marie and went back to her work. The next day Luc showed up for class in a suit. That was Friday. Monday he was wearing jeans again.

The gray sweater was another matter. Even Marie didn't seem to have the nerve to mention that.

"He wears it for good luck, of course," Karel said.

"He wears it because he knows it irritates Madame Légère," was Villette's theory.

"And why should he want to do that?" Paula asked.

"Oh, because she's after him, and she's a good ten years older than him, that's why," Villette answered with a knowing wink. "She's even older than you!" She giggled, flitting away before Paula could frame a suitable reprimand.

Why Monsieur Luc wore the gray cardigan in class remained a mystery. He was, in many respects, a creature of habit. Sometimes before school in the morning, Paula saw him jogging in the alley behind the garden. He wore shorts for his run no matter what the weather. She paid scant notice, not wanting to attract his attention and thereby get involved in another useless, confusing conversation. But she did know from the first glance at his physique in the revealing running clothes that he was a fit man. She had no doubt of his strength, and he seemed to possess remarkable agility. Even though her view of him was obscured by the thick trunks of old trees that lined the alley, she saw, when she chose to watch, that he ran swiftly and without apparent effort. His legs were muscular, his derriere tight and trim. Resolutely she turned away from thoughts of him. She didn't find him that attractive. Besides, even if he was interesting, she told herself, she'd learned her lesson. Never again would she pay the slightest bit of personal attention to a man she worked with. She'd learned her lesson the hard way—and well.

As SPRING ADVANCED Paula made use of her free time to explore the marvelous city of Brussels, a city more than a thousand years old. Proud to be called the capital of Europe, it was home to NATO headquarters, to the Common Market head offices and to more than a million people, many of whom looked to Paula remarkably like their forebears, painted by Brueghel so many years before.

Caesar had declared the Belgians the bravest people he'd found in Gaul, and the country was also noted for rich burghers, for van Eyck, for lace and chocolates, for Peter Paul Rubens, whose paintings recorded one of the country's richest eras, and who had been dazzled in later years by a May-December romance. Once called Broekzele, which meant a town built on a swamp, Brussels was now a proud city conquered ultimately by no one, though attacked over the centuries by envious foes and misguided friends.

Brussels was home, too, of forbidden treats that threatened the waistline but tempted the palate beyond bearing. On the streets were stands selling French fries, invented in Belgium. Even though she knew she shouldn't, Paula loved to indulge, dipping the crisp fries into the thick mayonnaise they came with, savoring the unusual combination of flavors. *Caricoles*, large snails served with little cups of broth, were also sold on corners. She tried them, but she liked *lammeke zoet*, a kind of herring, better.

Brussels restaurants ran the gamut from stalls on street corners to establishments of sublime elegance. Most of the ones Paula frequented were in the middle price range, but the food was excellent, and before long she was very familiar with the best local cuisine. *Witloof*, also called chicory, was Belgian endive, which was available in Montreal, too. Other dishes were more exotic, like *anguilles au vert*, eels in a green sauce with the flavor of fresh herbs. There were winkles and sprats. There were *crêpes aux pommes* and *beignets de Bruxelles*, the latter an elegant name for donuts! And there were *speculoos*, gingerbread cookies shaped like kings and queens, some two feet high and others much smaller but still highly edible. There were cheeses of all descriptions and a bewildering variety of beers, the drink Belgians were most fond of.

Often Paula ate and drank in cozy restaurants with a view out to the crowded streets with their tall, narrow, flat facades; sometimes she went to market. Brussels had numerous markets not designed only for the sale of food. There was a flower market, and every Sunday morning a bird market in the Grand'Place, the lovely square at the heart of the city. In the Place du Grand Sablon, another square, an antique-and-book market was held. There was a horse market in the Place de la Duchesse on Fridays and a daily flea market elsewhere in town.

The many *places*, museums, churches, covered shopping galleries, statues and gilded facades overwhelmed Paula at times. Whether she wandered in the oldest, narrowest streets of the Lower Town, or in the wider, more elegantly planned avenues of the Upper, she saw the mixture of the very old and the very new that seemed to characterize the country. She was rapidly growing comfortable there. Belgians never seemed afraid to try something modern, but never willing, either, to blithely discard what had gone before. Skyscrapers shared space with castles, nightclubs with *béguinages*, the habitats of holy women devoted entirely to prayer.

One day Paula took Villette with her on her travels. Villette was thrilled when she realized they were headed for the Galeries Royale Saint Hubert, because Villette was thrilled by anything that involved a good deal of money, and these stores had long dealt in some of the most lovely and costly luxuries in all of Europe.

Beneath a high glass roof stood the Galeries' stunning arcade, lined with shops on either side. They stopped first at Neuhaus, a confectionery where dozens of different kinds of bonbons, pralines and other candies were displayed among tufts of tulle and hand-wrought paper boxes and delicate lifelike silk flowers. Not even asking the price, Villette demanded the most frilly of a group of small pink oval boxes of chocolates.

"You're such a dear to treat me!" the girl exclaimed, popping one of the delicacies into her mouth. She licked her fingers and declared, "My father is being exceptionally stingy these days. I haven't a franc to my name." With that announcement she caught sight of a gold bracelet in a nearby shop and immediately began to calculate how many months' allowance she'd need in advance to buy it.

At Villette's insistence, they stopped at Manufacture Belge de Dentelles, where an elderly woman was demonstrating the time-honored craft of lace making. Her hands were bent and wrinkled, but they moved with a swift surety that produced such intricate loops, swirls and curves, that Paula was reminded of music.

Villette soon grew tired of watching. After wandering away to inspect some linens, she beckoned Paula over, showing her the fine work. "Someday," the young woman said determinedly, "I'm going to have a house full of things like this. The best. When I'm a famous dancer I'll have as much money as I want. I'll have a house like a palace. It'll be great!''

"Villette," Paula felt obliged to say, "it's the dancing itself you should be thinking about, not the money you can get out of it.''

The girl only laughed and pulled the woman along out of the arcade. They walked at a leisurely pace through the Lower Town to the little church of St. Nicholas. "This is the ballerina church," Villette announced. "I'll pray for good roles, and you can pray for a husband.''

"Don't tease!" Paula warned, but received for her troubles an admonition to hush, and Villette actually knelt to pray. The sight of the young girl's hair, a soft gold in the light of the church's candles, touched Paula's heart. She, too, knelt and prayed not for a husband, but that she might forget the troubles of her past and continue with her good intentions for the future. She almost felt like praying, too, that she could find some way of dealing with the one fellow employee of Le Berceau whose ways taxed her patience, but at the thought of Luc she pushed further prayerful feelings away and whispered to Villette that it was time to go.

Another day she took in a different sort of tourist sight. She picked up a pamphlet and read:

Antoine Joseph Wiertz was born in 1806 and died in 1865. The building in which you stand was built by the government to serve as his studio. The large paintings in the main hall, paintings he refused to sell during his lifetime, are unique in the history of Belgian art.

Thank heavens for that! Paula thought as she stood gazing at a monstrously large work depicting a scene of premature burial. Even though she shuddered, she imagined the work must have seemed far more sensational in the days before TV. She had already viewed Wiertz's treatment of the themes of hunger, execution, madness, crime, and questioned not the sincerity of the artist, but what she found to be the extreme presentation of his ideas. She'd had nearly enough, not sorry to have come yet eager to go, when she heard a hiss in her ear. "People who wish to indulge their appetite for the horrible would do better to look not at the products of the imagination, but at the world around them, where they might hope to make some improvement...."

Though she was surprised, she knew instantly who spoke. She had to delay turning to greet him because his arrogant comment had brought a smile to her face, and she knew instinctively that smile would infuriate him. He deserved to be teased, but she remembered her resolve to be professional with him. When she did swing around, she saw that his black raincoat, now impeccably cleaned and pressed, set off the indigo gleam of his undeniably compelling eyes and the thick sleekness of his jet-black hair. It didn't occur to her that less-prejudiced eyes might have found him very attractive in a lean, compact, energetic sort of way. "You don't like Wiertz?" she asked calmly.

"No, I definitely don't." Gesturing with both hands, he nearly hit another patron of the crowded gallery. Paula stepped back, giving him more room; she, too, nearly collided with a stranger. Without further words Luc took her elbow and began to lead her away. The last time he had touched her, he had been far from solicitous; his lips had been hard against the open softness of her mouth. She hadn't forgotten that, and somehow she could tell by the tense lines of his face that he hadn't forgotten, either. Nonetheless, he kept his hand on her arm for as long as it took to locate a small, unpopulated side gallery. "There," he said, releasing her. "That's better."

"Better for whom, *monsieur*?" she asked, surprised only a little by his assumption that he could pull her away from the main salon with no argument. "I was looking at the large paintings. These small ones don't interest me." She took a step to leave.

"The name is Luc." Again she felt the pressure of his hand on her arm, but her quick glance down made him pull away as though the green of her eyes was a laser slicing through him. "Once you've seen one of those you've seen them all," he said. "There's really no reason for a person of intelligence to dwell on sensationalism."

"Perhaps a person of intelligence would like to judge for themselves...."

"Herself...."

"There's no need to correct my French, *monsieur*. I come from a French-speaking country." She was irritated, even though, according to strict grammar, he was right.

"It's not only your French that bothers me, miss, it's your attitude. If you mean yourself, say yourself. I've noticed you do that at staff meetings, too. Why be so timid when it comes to stating your case?"

"The way I speak at meetings is none of your business."

"Everything that happens at Le Berceau is my business," he answered, but his tone had softened, as though he regretted the truth of the statement even as he spoke it. His manner took some of the rash heat out of Paula's feelings, but she wasn't ready to give up the argument.

"I appreciate honest criticism from a colleague when it comes to matters at work, Luc, but you can't really think you have the right to pull me away from paintings I'm viewing at my leisure."

"I didn't mean to pull you away rudely. It was crowded—too crowded to talk...."

"But I didn't want to talk! I wanted to look."

"There's nothing to look at. The pictures are mere sensationalism...." His voice began to rise in a way Paula knew would lead back into argument. *Really,* she thought, *is it too much to ask just to have a quiet afternoon away from work and colleagues?* Again she turned to walk out of the small room. Luc didn't stop her, but he did follow her, continuing the conversation. "You can't really be interested in such extreme examples of human suffering."

"How could I not be interested in any example of human suffering?" she said over her shoulder, dodging other viewers in the crowded museum in her effort to return to the contentious painting, though she really didn't want to see it again. A principle was at stake.

"These aren't real," he protested. "Not real examples of human suffering, only paintings."

"Only art, you mean?" Paula turned abruptly, nearly knocking him down. "That's a strange comment coming from a teacher at a fine-arts academy!"

"I did not say it was 'only art,' and that's not what I meant, either. Don't put words in my mouth, Miss—"

"The name is Paula," she replied with a sweetness intended to mock his earlier growl. He was not at all amused.

"I would argue against sensationalism, *Paula*," he went on, "in any artist, not just this one. The only thing necessary to alert sensitive people to the truth is to paint that truth clearly."

"I agree," she said, "but if you hate this artist so much, why are you here?"

How could he tell her he'd been headed in the opposite direction when he'd seen her enter the museum? How could he explain that impulse alone had made him turn and follow her in, holding back just long enough to make their meeting seem like chance. Well, they *had* met by chance, he thought. But not by accident. Quickly he framed a reply.

"It's a rather famous museum; I'd heard of it, but this is the first opportunity I've had to see it. I'm not sorry I came."

The thought echoed Paula's own feelings about the place, and she was about to voice her agreement when she looked up and caught Luc's eyes on her. Something told her that running into her was part of his reason for not regretting his choice of an outing for the afternoon. She saw at once that unless she discouraged him, she was going to be treated to more of his theories about art and the sensational.

"Well," she said lightly, "now that you've seen the paintings and decided you don't like them, I guess there's no reason for you to stay. At least you now know that you don't have to spend any more time on Wiertz." There was nothing cruel in her tone; she didn't mean to tease him. She'd never been the type of woman to be coy with men; she assumed he would understand she preferred to be by herself.

Yet when he commented in his soft voice, "Perhaps it was a bad idea to come here, after all," then muttered, "goodbye, Miss Emanuel," her feelings teetered between guilt and relief, coming down fairly strongly on the side of guilt. She shrugged her shoulders and made her way back to the main salon. She didn't mind dealing with him as a colleague. She grudgingly acknowledged his skill as a teacher. But she really didn't have to put up with his pretensions as an art critic!

CHAPTER FIVE

IF PAULA THOUGHT she'd seen Monsieur LeBlanc in all his guises, she soon learned she was mistaken, for later that same week she had another surprise in store. It began with a conversation she had with the principal in her salon over tea. "If only I could be in two places at once," Marie Légère said with a wry smile, "it would solve so many of my problems. I'd love to attend the musical soiree, but the board of directors of the school is having its semiannual dinner-meeting on Friday. I simply can't miss it. Luc attends things like this in my stead sometimes, but he's busy Friday, too. Mevrouw Marja van Beck is one of my dearest friends."

"She's Flemish?" Paula asked, sipping her tea.

"Quite typically so, but we are too close to let our cultural differences get in the way of our long-standing friendship. I don't want to minimize the very real troubles our so-called language problem has caused. It's true that difficulties between the Flemish and Walloons have erupted into violent confrontation over some issues, but it's also true that after an entire millennium, even the most severe conflicts can wear down to the bickering of old sisters with two pots of water and a single soup bone between them!"

Paula smiled and commented, "It's not so very different between Quebec and the rest of Canada, but I have to admit it'll take me some time to figure out exactly how things stand here. The other day I stopped a vigorous argument between two students. They were going at it in Dutch, making far too much noise in the corridor. When I reprimanded them, I expected them to stop arguing. Instead, they carried on just as vociferously as before—except they switched to French! They thought I was scolding them over which language they were using!''

"Oh," Marie said, as though suddenly struck with a good idea, "why don't you stand in for me at Marja's party? I'm sure she'd welcome you, and you'd get a chance to spend a very pleasant evening in a Flemish home. Marja's parties are famous! What do you say?''

"But I don't speak any Dutch," Paula protested.

"Don't worry. There will be French-speaking guests, and a lot of the Dutch will also know English. And you'll get to hear some lovely music.''

THOUGH SHE FELT TERRIBLY SHY about going to a party she hadn't been invited to, when the night arrived and she was dressed in a floral print that suited the warm April evening, Paula didn't try to quell a delicious sense of expectation. It took some time to reach the suburb the van Becks lived in, but as Marie had insisted on putting the taxi on her own account, Paula felt quite carefree. Then she experienced a jolt akin to stage fright when the taxi pulled up to the pillared white entrance and a liveried doorman stepped up to escort her to the door. A butler took her fine wool shawl, and before she saw where he'd disappeared with it, a stately woman of about fifty was at her side.

"Hello, I'm Marja van Beck," the woman said, continuing in nearly flawless English. "Marie told me she was sending her new school counselor, but I must admit I hadn't expected such a beauty. I've heard that Canadian women are among the most lovely in the world. It's all that fresh air, of course!'' Marja laughed gracefully but heartily, and Paula felt much more at ease.

"Ah, there you are!" Marja said, pulling toward her a pretty dark-haired young woman. "This uncontrollable sprite is my daughter Nele. Nele, Mademoiselle Emanuel from Marie's school. We'll call her Paula."

"So happy you were able to join us," Nele said, her French tinged with the familiar Dutch accent. "I adore foreign visitors. Brussels is nearly 25 percent foreign, but I don't get to meet many people from Canada. Come—" Nele nodded to her mother "—I'll introduce you to some others and get you a glass of champagne."

She spirited Paula into a huge reception room, where seventy or eighty people, many in formal evening attire, sipped champagne and balanced delicate canapés in bejeweled hands. "This is one of mother's more intimate evenings," Nele said with a laugh.

"If this is intimate, I can't imagine—" Paula began, but was interrupted by the bubbling Nele.

"Oh, only twenty or so, including you, of course, have been invited to dinner after tonight's concert. Mother often has sit-down dinners for twice that number. I always end up next to some insufferable fifth cousin. We have a huge family, not to mention my father's business associates and all our friends. Tonight is rather special because of the music." Snagging a passing waiter, Nele grabbed a glass of champagne for Paula. "I won't bother introducing you to anyone just yet. The musicians are the most interesting, and they're all in the green room waiting to enter. It's almost time. Come on." And again Paula found herself rushing in Nele's wake.

The music room, decorated in blue brocade, held eight rows of white spindly legged, velvet chairs. After leading Paula to one of them Nele disappeared, and in a few moments Paula was flanked by total strangers.

She was spared small talk, however, because it was evident the private concert was about to begin. The first musician to take his place on the stage was none other than the music master of Le Berceau, Josef LeBlanc. He sat at the harpsichord and adjusted the jacket of his conservative, but totally appropriate, dark suit. Several strangers followed, who took up other baroque instruments.

One of these was a striking man with auburn hair and the characteristic ruddy-cheeked, glowing complexion of a Flemish man in his prime. Paula noted that Marja van Beck, who had taken a seat of honor in the front row, looked at this man with a pride that could only be a mother's. Nele, sitting beside Marja, seemed far more interested in someone else, who at first wasn't visible to those in the farther rows where Paula sat. But he soon stepped onto the stage and revealed himself as no stranger.

Where will he turn up next? Paula asked herself as Luc took a seat surrounded by wind instruments, picked up an already gleaming fruitwood recorder and began to vigorously polish it with a small chamois he'd produced from somewhere. Paula didn't know which was more amazing: the fact that Luc should be there at all, or the way he looked. As for his playing, she remembered the haunting melody of the panpipes in the garden. She remembered, too, how Karel had told her that Luc belonged to some obscure musical organization with a silly name. He must be pretty good to be asked to play in a home like this one.

No, she decided, his appearance here was probably less of a surprise than his grooming, for she'd never seen him look as he looked this evening. His three-piece suit was dove gray. The collar and cuffs of his lighter gray shirt shone like silk in the bright light of the stage. His burgundy tie was a soft semiformal bow at his throat, and his hair was styled without fault, the few silver strands at the temples winging back, setting off the strong planes of his face. Apparently he was wearing contact lenses. He was scanning the music on the stand before him, and she knew he couldn't see that far without his glasses. He never neglected to wear them when he was reading some long and uninteresting item from the newspaper at staff meetings. His talkativeness had increased with his renewed familiarity with his colleagues, she had noted.

Paula could see even from that distance that Nele van Beck was quite taken by the vision before her. The young woman even managed to catch Luc's attention and elicit a warm smile from him. As for Paula, it killed her to admit it, but she conceded that there was no other word but handsome to apply to Luc, his compact but lean and powerful body set off by his suit. His hands were careful but confident as he readied his instruments. When he lifted an old-fashioned hautbois, an oboe, to his mouth, Paula, following his motions with attentive eyes, saw again the sensuousness of the lips that had twice demanded a taste of her own. Suddenly she felt a hard dart of longing, and with embarrassment realized she was blushing. Fortunately no one who knew her was near to see. She concentrated on the music now beginning to flow from the small orchestra. There was no doubt about it, she was soon forced to decide, Luc was a fine musician. But as for being attractive, only his clothes made him seem so. Of that she was convinced.

A sumptuous dinner was served in the crystal-chandeliered dining room later, but Paula didn't eat much. She found herself seated next to the handsome, and as it turned out, very urbane, auburn-haired man she'd seen on stage. She had been right. He was Marja's son, Pieter van Beck, a doctor.

Though she was afraid she'd have nothing to say to him, she discovered she was wrong, for he began a lively conversation almost the minute they sat down.

"You are no doubt a foreigner?" he asked, training his hazel eyes on her. There was a suaveness about him that was immediately apparent. Paula found it unnerving, but she was grateful he had taken the initiative in the table talk.

"Is it so obvious?" she asked with a smile.

"Yes, but in the most charming way. I heard you speak and noted your accent, but I think I would have known even without that. You look Canadian."

"No one has ever said that before," Paula replied with a light laugh, "though I have been told once or twice that I look American."

"Do you find that insulting?"

"I'm not insulted to be taken for an American. I'm only hurt that my own nationality seems to get lost in the shuffle."

"That's impossible! Canada is a fascinating country."

"Have you been there?"

"Several times. I've made a study of it, too. There are several ways in which it's like Belgium—a country surrounded by more-powerful nations, a country of more than one culture."

"Yes. But I must say that despite the similarities between my country and yours, it's a little hard for me to judge exactly what the rift is between the Flemish and the Walloons—except, of course, for the language."

"The language question is the most obvious, but the differences go far deeper than the fact that the northern provinces speak Dutch and the southern provinces French. The attitude toward religion, for example."

"Religion?"

"Yes. Traditionally we Flemish are devout Catholics."

"In Canada it's the French who are most likely to be Catholic."

"Yes," the doctor answered, "but the French—the Walloons—have an anticlerical streak. Actually, it's sometimes difficult to separate things like this from personality traits. The Flemish tend to be conservative—what you might call the strong, silent types. Tenacious, obstinate, down-to-earth. They work hard. They love pleasure—the paintings of Brueghel don't lie!"

"No," Paula said. "Just listening to you talk brings scenes of village parties to mind!"

"And children! We van Becks, for instance, are a huge family, so many cousins you couldn't count them."

"And the Walloons are different?"

"In many ways. They align themselves to France and its culture far more vigorously than we do to Holland. In my opinion, though, they're unique, uniquely Belgian. Like us, they're stubborn, but whereas we are obstinate, they are headstrong. A legitimate distinction...."

"Yes, I think so, too." Paula was reminded of Luc's antics in the museum. Headstrong.

"Walloons are quick, witty, spontaneous. Sometimes caustic and skeptical, too."

"An uneasy mix?"

"Always. Yet we've gone on together for hundreds upon hundreds of years."

Paula considered what Pieter had just told her as a domestic took away her porcelain soup bowl; she had only tasted a spoonful. The lemony broth had been delicious, but something about the proximity of this man was making her less hungry than she should be considering the late hour.

"I suppose it's like marriage," Paula remarked lightly. "Sometimes the couples who seemed least suited at the outset manage to stick it out, whereas those who seemed perfect for each other flounder."

"Are you married?" Pieter van Beck asked with a directness that caught Paula off guard.

"N-no. I'm not."

"Not for lack of chances, I'm sure," the doctor smoothly surmised. "A lovely woman like you must have had plenty of opportunities."

"I—I've been busy with my career." She knew she sounded awkward and silly, but she couldn't bear to speak about her personal life to a complete stranger, especially a stranger as suave as this one. Unless she missed her guess, the good doctor was practiced in the art of persuasion, or seduction. That might be too strong a word, but it did occur to her. "Are you a general practitioner?" she added, desperate to change the subject.

Dr. van Beck was silent for a moment, as though considering how best to frame a response to her question. Yet when he answered he was disarmingly frank. "No. There's not as much money in that as there is in what I do. I'm an orthopedic surgeon. I sometimes treat the dance students at Le Berceau as a special favor to Marie, but of course my private practice is much more lucrative."

In Canada, people seemed more comfortable carrying on a casual conversation about their sex lives than their finances, so Paula was a little surprised by this openness. But Pieter had more to say on the subject of salaries.

"I am always amazed at the dedication of the teachers at Marie's school. I understand you're one of them?"

"Not exactly. I'm a counselor. Why are you amazed, doctor?"

"Pieter," he corrected, touching her hand where it lay on the spotless linen of the table. Fortunately the next course arrived, and Paula was able to avoid his lingering touch by lifting up one of a half-dozen pieces of silver before her.

"As I was saying," he went on, "the teachers at the school are, for the most part, young and active. Any one of them could make a fortune in his or her profession, yet they are all content to slave away teaching for pennies. Commendable, of course, but I certainly wouldn't be able to be so generous." Without waiting for a reply, he turned to his dinner.

His table manners were elegant, but he was unquestionably a man of strong appetite. He ate with barely concealed gusto, and suddenly Paula realized the main reason why she felt so uneasy in his presence. He was undeniably an attractive man, but his smooth charm, his healthy good looks, even his husky stature reminded her of her former boss. The thought took away any appetite Paula might have had, though she made an attempt to eat some of the beautifully prepared fish.

"Judging by your silence, it seems I've offended you somehow," Dr. van Beck commented at length.

"Oh, no. Not at all." It wasn't his fault that he resembled Bret Graham, Paula reminded herself.

"Perhaps you find us too bourgeois for your taste?"

"Bourgeois? What do you mean by the term, exactly?"

"Too interested in the material aspect of things—in money."

"I do sometimes find the values here slightly different from my own. . . ."

"You mean *my* values." He laughed.

"That could be. But surely a good surgeon is entitled to be paid for his work."

"We Flemish, as I said, believe in hard work. And

in money. It was the merchants of Flanders who, some maintain, were the first to engage in modern commerce. Naturally the wise man expects a fair return for his labors—labors of the mind, as well as the body. You may accuse us of being materialistic—''

''But I don't!''

''Now, little Canadian, don't rile yourself,'' and he laughed again, his large hand coming down on top of her head as if to comfort a child. ''I find your views refreshing. I sometimes think you Canadians are more innocent in many ways than your American cousins. I like that. I like you. Oh, no. Now I've really upset you. You're blushing. How utterly wonderful!''

She was intensely uncomfortable. The doctor was hale and congenial, but his forwardness and his physicality were highly unwelcome. *Please,* she wanted to insist, *please leave me alone.* Despite his good looks and his affability, she couldn't tolerate his easy way and his free touch because, like Bret's, it carried the assumption that any woman would be pleased to be touched by him.

Apparently he sensed her discomfort. He leaned away from her, and his tone became almost professional, even though his question was personal. ''You really are a long way from home, aren't you?''

''Yes.''

''And without friends just yet?''

''Yes, but....''

''As a doctor, I know that illness can be caused by loneliness very easily. Heart trouble.''

''Heart trouble?'' Paula repeated, puzzled.

Pieter van Beck grinned. ''My English is less than perfect, isn't it? I mean not *hartkwaal*, but *hartzeer*.''

''I'm afraid I don't—''

''My dear, people who are lonely suffer not from a heart condition but from heartache. That's a fair translation—and a fair description of the situation of a number of foreign workers. But it can be treated."

"Surely nobody prescribes pills for heartache, doctor," she joked, feeling a little more at ease.

"Not pills, but I do have something. Two tickets for a concert tomorrow evening at the Palais des Beaux Arts. Have you been there yet?"

She shook her head.

"Can I persuade you to join me? Please don't refuse out of hand. I'd love to show you the *palais*. As you may know, it's considered the hub of cultural activity in Brussels. The architect was Victor Horta, hailed as the first exponent of Art Nouveau. He had a tremendous influence on the architecture of this city, which is known as the birthplace of that style. Unfortunately, many examples of it here have gone the way of other buildings, destroyed by the wrecker's ball."

Paula appreciated the information but not the invitation. The last thing she wanted to do was to date, especially someone who reminded her of Bret. Dr. van Beck was probably a very nice man, but she just couldn't.

"It's very kind of you, but I'm not—not available." She hoped he would settle for that.

"Of course you are. You're just shy. Eat your dinner. By dessert I will have talked you into the concert...."

He turned again to his food. The main course had arrived. Paula had never seen a more succulent-looking piece of meat, but she had no appetite for it. All she could think of was how much she didn't want to go out with Pieter van Beck. She felt the old fear rise up.

She still lived with the pain of her mistake. Sometimes in sleep she dreamed about the day Bret's wife had found out about their affair. About her own shame, even though she'd already told Bret she couldn't continue with him even if it meant losing her job.

The more friendly Pieter got during the meal, the more he reminded her of Bret. She actually glanced down the long table more than once to where Luc was sitting beside Nele. Paula tried to get his attention, hoping against hope that she could send him some sort of mental request for relief, if not release. If only Luc would offer to take her home!

Apparently Nele was as aggressive a conversationalist as her brother. She kept Luc quite occupied, so occupied in fact that Paula only caught his eye once, and when she did she saw him glaring at her as though she had once again offended him somehow. She smiled weakly, but at that moment Nele spoke again, and Luc turned away.

Fortunately Dr. van Beck must have realized he was being overbearing. He didn't mention the concert again. He turned away from personal subjects and included the people on his right and Paula's left in the talk, ending the embarrassing moments. The evening continued quite congenially. When it was over, Paula remembered nothing unpleasant about it at all except for that one brief glance of pure irritation that Luc had shot her way.

CHAPTER SIX

"I KNOW MADAME WORRIES about my home life," dark-haired Kathelijne said with a sigh, "but she doesn't have to. My brother hasn't been around in a long time, and I don't think he's coming back. When he's gone there's a lot less trouble. My father doesn't get so mad, and my mother goes to work almost every day. I know it sounds awful, but there's just nothing more I can think of to say about that. It seems okay to me—at least it's better than it was."

Paula had spent several previous sessions talking to Kathelijne about her wayward brother. She took the girl's comment to mean she was ready to move on to something else. "You don't have to talk about your family now if you don't want to, Kathelijne," Paula said gently. Her sessions with the sensitive and intelligent young artist were always the week's best. She found herself actually looking forward to them.

"Is it okay if I talk about my work, then?"

"It's better than okay." Paula smiled. "It's what I'd hoped you would talk about. Are you still excited about the portrait of Monsieur Josef?"

"Oh, yes!" Kathelijne's bright face became even more animated at the sound of the teacher's name. Though he wasn't her own mentor, the music teacher was a favorite of the girl's. Paula suspected she had a giant crush on the man, which seemed healthy enough. "But there's something else...."

"Yes?"

"Well, the other day we had a postmortem on one of our projects, and we started discussing the commercial value of our work—whether we could sell it and that. Some people said they didn't care whether they ever sold anything, but I think that's wrong."

"In what way?"

"Look, miss," Kathelijne said, leaning forward intently. "Lots of students here won't ever have to work very hard for a living or make very many compromises, anyway. A few are really exceptionally talented. They *will* sell their works just as they are. Others come from rich families. And one or two say they'll just marry for money. It sounds old-fashioned, I know, but they mean it. For me, I've got to earn money. It's okay now that I'm still on scholarship, but I won't be in school forever. I like to paint a certain way, but I'm practical, as well. If I have to change that for money, I guess—well, I guess I'll just have to. But it seems wrong somehow."

"The concern you're expressing comes a little early, Kathelijne. You're only in your second year. You'll have time to worry about things like this later. But you're quite right. Every artist has to come to grips with the need to cultivate a professional attitude."

"It seems to me that all I ever hear around here is that we should 'cultivate a professional attitude,'" the girl said with uncharacteristic cynicism. "It would be nice if someone stopped for a minute to tell us how to do it, or even what it is."

"Haven't you discussed this in any of your classes?"

"No—not exactly."

"Well," Paula said, hesitating a moment to carefully frame her thoughts, "for me a professional attitude comes from learning to recognize your talent, then dedicating yourself to learning and doing all you have to in order to live up to the full potential of that talent. I suppose that means something quite different to each artist. It's a very personal thing. If you like, we can talk about this today. Then maybe you can bring in some specific examples of problems in this area for next week's session. I'll do the same. No doubt something will come up."

As it turned out, the matter came up sooner than Paula expected. The very next day, she picked up her daily batch of memos and found a missive from Marie. It requested that all staff "heed the attached," which turned out to be a bright green half sheet of paper, a memo from the writing department. Monsieur LeBlanc was asking for cooperation in yet another project to, as the memo said, almost in Kathelijne's words, "assist students in cultivating a professional attitude." Luc never had any trouble convincing Marie to foster his unending schemes. So he had given up writing, had he? That would be hard to prove, judging from the volume of written material that left his office, most of it directed to other staff members, all of whom had better things to do with their time than help him. Though, to be honest, nobody ever seemed to complain.

Paula glanced over his memo. She was already familiar with this pet project of Luc's. As the memo, admittedly quite an eloquent one, argued, for not the first time that month, every teacher had the responsibility to "participate in the revitalization of student journalism." That was nothing more than a fancy way of saying Luc wanted the school newspaper, noted for its sporadic appearance, to come out not only regularly, but once a week. Considering the fact that even his senior students, young men and women who planned to have careers in journalism, found his writing assignments too difficult, how could he possibly expect other students to work on the paper in their spare time? The whole thing was silly, in her opinion.

His memo spoke of "professionalizing the paper," and ended with a demand that every teacher should let him know, in writing, how they intended to contribute to this project. The principal's circulation of the memo lent a certain official air, making it imperative that Paula answer. Still bothered by his unfriendly behavior at the van Becks' the previous Friday, Paula picked up her pen.

I intend to contribute to this project in one way only. I intend to define the "professional attitude" it claims to foster. To have a professional attitude is to do your own job on your own time using your own resources and leaving other professionals to do their duties without interruption.

She signed the memo with her usual rather modest signature, dropped it in the Out basket on Ms Martel's desk and promptly forgot all about it.

THE DINING HALL, so noisy at lunch, was a haven of supervised silence late each afternoon. Paula arrived to take charge of final study period. She welcomed the hour of quiet when it was her turn to monitor. Most days she ended up with so much paperwork that she had to take some home. She wondered how other staff managed. Teachers who had essays to correct must find themselves with very little spare time. She was sitting at the head of a long table full of students, thinking just that, when the door to the hall opened far too noisily, revealing Luc resplendent in his gray cardigan, a sheaf of papers under his arm. On top of the pile was one bright green half sheet that Paula suddenly realized she'd seen not long before.

Teachers were never assigned study hall together, a fact well-known to the students. A ripple of whispers could be heard along the length of the two tables occupied by pupils, but Paula silenced it with a stern glance. Talking was strictly forbidden.

To her dismay, Paula soon understood that monitoring students was the last thought on Monsieur Luc's mind. In fact, it seemed he wasn't interested in them at all, for he made straight for Paula. The closer he came, the more she began to regret her flippant reply to his memo. She heard his sharp footsteps echo on the marble floor, but she kept her eye on her papers. Then the sound of the footsteps stopped directly behind her chair and the bright green slip of paper was thrust beneath her nose, held in a hand she could see was tense with anger. The lines of her own handwriting on the memo blurred a little, whether because his hand trembled or because her eyes clouded, she wasn't sure.

"I do not find this response to an honest plea for assistance either humorous or illuminating. I don't see how a person can presume to write about professionalism when they show no sign of it themselves."

"Herself," Paula said softly, and saw him give the memo an angry little shake. Both of them whispered, but in the quiet made intense by the fact that the students were suddenly all ears, the whispering sounded almost like shouting. Not wanting to aggravate him further, she hastily added a rather toneless, "I'm sorry."

He hesitated for a moment; then seemed to accept her apology at face value. The green paper disappeared from under her nose. Though she had no intention of turning to confirm the notion, she thought she could feel the tense energy drain out of him as he remained close to the back of her chair. "Very well, then," he said. Again there was silence and stillness

behind her. She fully expected him to leave as he had
entered—with too much noise.

He didn't. "If *mademoiselle* doesn't mind..." he
said, clearly addressing the student sitting next to
Paula. In an instant Paula realized he had asked the
girl to relinquish her chair so that he could sit there,
and in that same instant she felt both embarrassment
and shyness. She didn't want to sit close to him. Why
couldn't he just leave her alone? Maybe Nele van Beck
liked to have him elbow to elbow and thigh to thigh at
the table, but not Paula. He always turned up when
she least needed him, and he had turned away the one
time she had needed him. Thinking quickly, she said,
"Of course I don't mind giving you my seat," pretending he had asked her to move, not the student. Her
voice was light as she picked up her papers with the intention of heading toward the next table of students,
where there were five or six vacant chairs. She could
monitor study just as well from that spot.

She didn't reach her destination. It had been foolish
to try so transparent a ploy with him. His hand shot
out, grabbing her own, and though his touch was gentle and in no way less than polite, his eyes blazed with a
fury that made Paula flinch. "So," he said, his whisper becoming too loud and harsh to be called a whisper
at all, "so this table isn't big enough for Miss Emanuel
to share with a fellow teacher? So you need more
room, do you? Well, let's see what we can do to ac-
commodate our little foreign psychologist."

The contempt with which he spat out the words
rankled, but a strange curiosity filled her. There was
something about this man that made Paula's reaction
to him different from what she'd felt with other men.
It was as though his most passionate actions hid rather
than revealed his feelings. She could almost read his
thoughts despite the false signals he sent out. Some-

how she knew he wasn't really violently angry. He was deeply hurt.

But he had no excuse to be. He should, she felt, cure himself of his horrible habit of overreacting to everything. Defiantly she said nothing and merely waited to see what he was up to.

"Ladies and gentlemen," he said, raising his voice for the benefit of the students, who were now gaping wide-eyed at this little scene. "It seems our Canadian here—no doubt used to wide open spaces—needs more room for her very important work. Let's oblige her, shall we? Get up, every one of you." Gesticulating brusquely, he moved from student to student until everyone at the first table was standing. "Over there, over there!" he cried, dropping all pretense of keeping his voice under control. "I want everyone to sit at the next table. Miss Emanuel needs more room."

At first it appeared that the students were frightened by his outburst, but they had come to expect a certain unpredictability from him, and it wasn't hard to see they soon found this very amusing, much more amusing, at least, than attending to their schoolwork. With a clattering of books and pencils and a shuffling of a great deal of paper, they made a stab at settling down as Monsieur Luc continued to demand that they do. Meanwhile Paula could see by their faces that they were trying as hard as humanly possible not to laugh. A strong desire to giggle rose in her own throat. Really, Luc was making a total fool of himself. Again a perverse twinge of curiosity mixed with some other feeling she didn't bother to try to name, and she stood rooted to the spot.

When he had completely emptied the first table and crammed the second, despite the fact that the large dining hall held many other empty tables, Luc strode defiantly back to her. "If you want to keep your distance, Miss Emanuel, you may do so now," he said, plucking a file folder from her hands and plunking it down with a slap on the polished wood at the head of the table.

She stared at him. The most sensible thing would have been to walk out of the room, and she nearly did, except the students began to twitter. She shot them a withering glance, which had the immediate effect of silencing them and reminding Paula she was in charge. With a dignity she feared might really be comic in these strained—and strange—circumstances, she took the seat the writing teacher was gesturing at. Perhaps now that he had humiliated her, he would leave. She had no doubt she'd find a way to get even with him in the future.

Once more he surprised her. Walking the entire length of the long wooden table, he took the opposite chair at the foot and slammed down his pile of papers.

She reminded herself of several things in the course of the long minutes during which they sat face-to-face, trapped at opposite ends of the long empty table by pique and pride. She reminded herself that the best way to react when someone else was being irrational was to remain calm at all costs. She reminded herself that she had worked at Le Berceau for approximately four months, whereas Monsieur Luc LeBlanc, resident pest, agitator, intruder and general pain, had been employed by the school for more than two years. He was head of a department. He was a relative of the principal. He was a native of Belgium, whereas she was a foreign worker. She reminded herself, too, that it was quite possible that he had once been a noted journalist, though she had never heard of him before coming to the school. But then nobody had heard of *her* before she came to Belgium.

Finally Paula decided she would sit quietly until the

end of study. She would then go directly to Marie and complain about Luc's treatment. In the meantime, she would get even with Luc in the only way possible: by pretending that what he had done was not bothering her at all. In fact, the joke was beginning to wear thin. She had found his actions curious and amusing at first, but she was growing angrier as the tense minutes passed. It had occurred to her that this display in front of the students was unprofessional not only of Luc but of her.

The students themselves were in a mood Paula knew was not in the least conducive to study. They giggled; they whispered. Once one of the bolder ones said something out loud, but he was silenced by a stony glare from Luc.

Fine, Paula thought. *Let him do the disciplining. He's the one who disturbed them all in the first place.* Her eyes returned to her papers as the writing teacher's eyes returned to his piles of essays. He made a great show of switching the papers from one pile to another as though he was accomplishing a good deal. Paula, too, pretended to work assiduously, but she was getting nothing done. She felt it was unfair to the students to work on their reports under the circumstances, so she put them away and took out a glossy psychology magazine. That elicited a surprised and displeased glance from the other end of the table. Paula resisted the intense urge to stick out her tongue at her captor. Surely as a teacher of communication arts, the tyrant must realize any professional worth her salt would keep abreast of the latest in her field.

However, Paula couldn't keep her eyes on the magazine long enough to read a single sentence. Really, this was all too ridiculous! In order to see the clock, which was mounted on the wall over the door directly behind Luc, she had to risk looking in his direction, something she was loath to do, but did, anyway. When she had first sat down at his insistence, she had noticed it was three thirty-five. She figured that by now it must be past four. Braving a glimpse over the dark, lowered head, she noted with chagrin that it was only three forty-seven. Only twelve minutes gone and more than a half hour to go! How would she stand it?

By being bound and determined not to let him get my goat, she decided, diving into her magazine with a vengeance. She actually managed to get interested in one of the articles. In fact, she was so absorbed in her reading that when the door unexpectedly opened five minutes later, Paula jumped. There on the threshold was Marie Légère. In her company was the president of the board of directors. And on her face was a look that could have killed.

Obviously making a quick attempt to gather her wits, Marie graciously excused herself to the president and approached Paula. Anxious to give the impression that nothing unusual was happening, Marie kept her voice at a normal level, audible to all. "This is your afternoon on duty, isn't it, Miss Emanuel?"

"Yes, *madame*," Paula answered, rising.

"Is there some reason why Monsieur LeBlanc appears to be monitoring study, then?"

"I think you would have to ask him, *madame*," Paula replied coolly. She'd be darned if she was going to get into trouble over his antics.

"Miss Emanuel is executing her duties perfectly," Luc said gallantly, getting to his feet with a lithe quickness that made Paula want to push him back down. His voice was dark with barely controlled emotion, but nobody seemed to notice except Paula.

"Would one of you care to explain the unusual seating arrangement?" Marie asked icily.

Paula remained resolutely silent, even though Luc

glanced at her, giving her the opportunity to speak first, as any gentleman would. *You talk, you rat.* She bowed her head silently as though to graciously give the floor to him.

"The students felt they'd like to leave a table for the staff to use exclusively—" Luc began.

"Like hell!" Paula clearly heard the shocking phrase come from Villette, followed by a volley of not very well stifled giggles.

"You have something to add to this discussion, do you, Mademoiselle van der Vloedt?" the principal said in her sternest voice. "If so, would you please be so kind as to speak loudly enough for all of us to hear?"

"I beg your pardon, Madame Légère. I have nothing to say," Villette replied, a deep blush staining her pretty cheeks. Paula noticed the dignified director smile warmly at the girl.

"I'd like to speak to you in my office, please, Paula," Marie announced. "Luc, I'd appreciate it if you would relieve her of her monitoring duties for now. By the way," the principal said, addressing the students in her most awesome tone, "study will continue for one half hour longer today. You are not dismissed until five o'clock." That bit of information caused many simultaneous low groans, but again a warning glance from Luc silenced the pupils.

"Please bring your things with you, Paula. I'll wait for you in the office."

She did as she was told, not really alarmed by Marie's tone. She was sure she could convince the principal that the whole incident was Luc's fault. Of course Luc would instantly be forgiven by his cousin. Sighing, she gathered her things and walked toward the door. She had to pass Luc, and she walked by him without even looking. But as she passed his chair, he reached out and very lightly touched her hand. In a tone full of feeling, he said in a low, soft, voice, "It is often the opinion of Belgians that foreigners are without good manners. I have also been told that Canadians possess a certain coldness of heart. That is a great pity in a people otherwise so attractive. Good afternoon, miss."

She didn't look at him. She gave her hand the tiniest tug. Keeping her head lowered, she walked slowly toward the door, not letting him see how his words had stung her heart, nor how hot, sudden tears stung her eyes.

CHAPTER SEVEN

LUC TOSSED AND TURNED, pulling the blanket up to his chin, then kicking it away. Hovering in the uncomfortable state between waking and sleep, he vaguely recalled the evening. He'd walked for hours after school, had had nothing but a beer for supper and had stumbled home in a state of near exhaustion. Too dozy to finish the pile of essays that seemed to be taking forever to correct, he'd fallen dead asleep at his desk. Once he'd thought he heard the doorbell, but he couldn't have roused himself in time to answer. Or had he dreamed the ringing?

He turned again, and came fully, painfully awake. Switching on the light beside his bed, he reached for his watch and saw that it was three in the morning, two hours since he'd forced himself to leave the desk, undress, shower and get into bed.

It serves you right to toss and turn, LeBlanc. You acted like a total idiot! It wasn't the first time that night that he'd chided himself for the scene in the study hall. In fact, it was nearer to the hundredth. How could he have let Paula Emanuel provoke him so? He should have taken her memo to be nothing other than an awkward joke. Maybe he would even have thought it funny if he hadn't been so angered by her behavior at Marja's. She'd let van Beck pat her on the head as though she were some little girl instead of an intelligent woman. The doctor was a womanizer, everyone knew that. Luc longed to ask Paula whether van Beck had invited her out. Of course it was none of his business.

None of your business at all. He switched off the light with one brusque motion and turned his face into the pillow. But the minute he closed his eyes, the image floated onto the screen of his inner vision. The image of her lowered head, her hair curling softly on her slender neck. He knew she'd been trying to hide her face, trying to compose herself before she had to face Marie and the president of the board. He knew, too, that he'd made her cry, and he felt awful. He wouldn't be surprised if she hated him.

He pushed the covers away and turned on his back. He crossed his arms over his closed eyes. Unlike a lot of other women—even his cousin Marie sometimes—Paula never flirted with him. She must find him totally unattractive. He knew that was just as well, but it hurt him to believe it, and the hurt was so strong that he didn't stop to realize what that pain might mean.

He had made her cry. Just what she needed. Thousands of miles from home, surrounded by foreigners, possibly pursued by that van Beck, and certainly pursued by something else, some trouble that never seemed to leave those amazing green eyes. How could he have made her cry?

He found the covers again and yanked them up to his chest. He had to apologize. That was all there was to it. He began to think of ways. In the process, he drifted off to sleep.

It was just turning light when he woke up, but it wasn't the rising sun that roused him, it was the sound of the bell again. Alarmed, he got up, threw on his robe and ran to the door.

Luc stared with amazement at the dejected figure in the hallway. "Karel! What are you doing here at this time of the morning?"

"I'm sorry, Luc. I'm sorry if I woke you, but I have to talk to you."

"It's all right. No problem. Come in. Whatever's wrong?" He ushered the young man into his living room, appalled at his pallor and the unmistakable evidence of tears on his face.

As though he suddenly remembered he'd been crying and that this man was the last person he wanted to know, Karel hastily wiped his eyes with the sleeve of his denim jacket. The action touched Luc's heart because it made the boy look so very like a child. Luc pretended he hadn't noticed.

"Sit down," he said, "and I'll heat some coffee." He left Karel alone for the few minutes it took the brew to warm up, using the time to splash some water on his face. He glanced into the mirror over the kitchen sink, not surprised to see circles the size of pie pans under his eyes.

The coffee was black, strong and laced with chicory, Belgian style. Karel accepted it gratefully. "I've been out all night," he admitted. "My father's going to have a fit." Defiance mingled with fear in his voice.

"Why did you do it?"

"Because he and I had another damn fight."

"Fight?"

"Argument."

"Karel—"

"He doesn't respect me, Luc! He treats me like an infant, and I can't stand it. I'm not two years old, unable to make any decision on my own. I don't want to do what he wants me to do. It's as simple as that."

"What is it this time?"

"University studies again. I told him I don't want to apply. I told him you can't teach a person to be a writer, so there's no need for me to get a degree. But he won't listen. He thinks writing is some game—some impossible dream."

"Being a writer is an impossible dream," Luc said.

Karel stared at him for a moment; he looked as if the rug had just been pulled out from under his feet. Then an idea dawned, and he smiled. "But even impossible dreams come true sometimes—right, Luc?"

"Sure, Karel. If you're strong enough to force them to. Listen, part of being a writer is sticking to your guns. You realize that, I know. That doesn't mean you can go through life ignoring all resistance. It's just not possible. You've got to learn how to deal with other people's expectations. Not only as a writer but as a person."

"You're the last person I'd expect to live according to the expectations of somebody else," Karel insisted.

"I know you think that, and I appreciate your faith in me, but things are never as simple as they seem...."

"Don't tell me you think I should give in to my father?"

"I only think you two still have a lot of talking to do. Not to mention the fact that you've probably scared him stiff with this disappearing act."

"I doubt anything would scare him."

"You're too smart to think like that. You have to call him. Now."

"Luc, please—"

"You have to talk with him. You two have got to learn to listen to each other before there's real trouble. I'm going to cook you some breakfast. While you're waiting you can use the phone. You know where it is."

PAULA, TOO, HAD SPENT a sleepless night, waking up the next morning with a splitting headache. She missed her regular bus by three minutes and ended up standing on the corner in the persistent drizzle for a quarter of an hour. By the time she got to Le Berceau she was convinced she was about to have one of those days.

When she arrived she found the door closed, which meant that Angèle Martel was late, as well. Paula walked through to her own office and unlocked the door. The first thing her eye fell on was a white object on the dark green blotter of her desk. On closer inspection this proved to be a bouquet of tiny, perfectly formed pure white violets in a cone of paper lace decorated with a slim pink satin ribbon. In astonishment she lifted them to her nose and detected the barely perceptible scent of musk. How? Who? The door had been securely locked. Perhaps she'd left it unlocked the night before, but she doubted that, since her office held confidential records and she was very careful. Even if she had left the door unlocked, that would explain only half the mystery.

Her puzzlement at this invasion of her privacy, combined with her pleasure in the gift only added to her confusion. She had no further time to contemplate the mystery, though. Angèle was coming in, and Marie Légère's voice drifted in after her. "Oh, Paula, you've arrived. *Dieu merci!*"

Paula turned to see Marie more upset than she'd ever seen her. "What is it?" she asked in consternation.

"Karel has been away the whole night. His father is in the salon in a complete state. He insists something dreadful must have happened. He's with the police, and they want to question you."

"Me?" Paula asked in alarm.

"They know he's had private sessions with you, and Monsieur Foubert wants to see the file. . . . "

"The file is confidential. I can't—"

"Please, Paula. Just get the file and bring it along. You needn't show him everything that's in it. Just answer a few questions."

There was such urgency in the woman's voice that Paula couldn't refuse. She'd have to think of some way to protect Karel's rights, but on the other hand, if she could help find him.... She knelt on the carpeted floor near the large file cabinet to retrieve his file from one of the bottom drawers. As she stood up again, she didn't notice that she'd dropped her bouquet in her haste. Nor did she realize that her heel caught it as she walked away, crushing the paper-lace cone.

The scene in the salon was not nearly as bad as Paula had expected, for the missing boy had come to school, after all. When she entered the room the police officer was gone. Marie stood with Monsieur Foubert as the banker listened to his son's story. Karel was fighting so hard to hold back tears that hearing his choked voice almost made Paula cry.

"I was sorry, father; I was sorry that we argued after dinner. I only left to go for a walk. Then a bus came along, and I just felt like hopping on, so I did. I ended up near Monsieur Luc's place."

"Monsieur LeBlanc, you mean, boy?" the banker asked.

"Yes, father. But he wasn't home. I waited for him for a long time, but he didn't come. Then I started to feel really depressed. I didn't know what time it was. I started to walk, and I just kept on. I got to the park, and I just sat there—"

"You sat in the park all night? Really, son, I find it hard to believe—"

"I'm not lying, if that's what you think." There was defiance in the boy's tone and stance, but still he fought back tears. Paula knew it would be very unlike Karel to lie.

Perhaps Monsieur Foubert did, too, for he softened, placing his hand on his son's trembling shoulder. "Then what happened?" he asked in low tones.

"It started to get light, so I went back to Luc's. It was very early—before six—but he didn't mind that

I'd wakened him up. He gave me some breakfast, and we talked for a long time. I called home several times, but the line was busy...."

"Because we were using it to try to find you—" The man's voice broke a little at those words. Marie glanced at Paula. Both women realized it would be best to leave father and son alone. Quietly they made their exit.

"Where's Luc now?" Paula asked Marie, curious despite the fact that she didn't particularly want to see him.

"In his classroom teaching. He looked awful this morning—such circles under his eyes...." She added, "You don't look very well yourself. I hope you're not upset about yesterday afternoon. I don't blame *you*. You know that."

"I know, Marie. You're very patient, and I appreciate it."

"It's not just patience, Paula. Before you came, things like this morning's crisis fell on my shoulders. Now I have you to mollify Monsieur Foubert. He's going to call you later to discuss Karel."

"Fine," Paula answered, though she didn't know how she was going to fit yet another appointment into the week's busy schedule.

It wasn't until she was headed back to her office that Paula remembered the violets and realized she must have dropped them on the rug. The bell ending first class had just rung. The corridors were clogged with students, and it was slow going. When she finally made it to the inner office, she saw at once that the flowers weren't where she must have left them. She glanced around the office, even looking into the wastebasket. "Angèle," she began, walking to the door, "was anyone here in my office while I was with Marie?"

"No, not that I know of. But I wasn't here the whole time. I had to collect the attendance records. Why? Is something missing?"

"No," Paula answered with a sigh. "It's nothing." Not knowing what else to do, she dismissed the mystery of the flowers, closing her door and sitting down at her desk to get to work. But her head was pounding, and she felt she needed air. She stood up again, opened the door, then resumed her seat.

She lost track of time as she pored over Karel's file, trying to think of the best way to answer the questions she knew his father would soon be asking. After that, she worked on the forms she hadn't done the night before. She thought it must be near lunchtime when she looked up, sensing someone in the doorway, Angèle, no doubt. She saw with a start that it was not Angèle.

Luc LeBlanc, his hair a little disheveled from his running his fingers through it, was standing with his legs spread, his feet squarely planted in her doorway. Though he wore his glasses, she could see that his eyes were full of profound disappointment. He wore his usual gray sweater, but beneath it a stylish shirt and matching tie were visible, as well as trim trousers that in no way resembled faded jeans. He looked, Paula thought, quite continental, almost handsome. He looked pretty angry, too. And before she even said a word of greeting to him, she found out why. Her eyes scanned his face, then dropped to his hand when a slight movement of his fingers caught her eye.

Her heart fell when she realized he was clutching the wilted bouquet of sweet white violets.

"You really are a cold, unkind woman," he said. "You mock me. You didn't need to discard my gift. If I offended you so much yesterday that you won't accept my apology, you could at least have had the courage to tell me to my face. You are a—"

"But I didn't—I had no idea—"

"You mock me," he repeated, unwilling to listen to

anything she had to say. She stood up, but his hand formed a fist, crushing quite completely the little bouquet. He threw it back to the floor where he had found it and stalked out of the office.

Oh Lord, no. Tears sprang to Paula's eyes. Slowly she walked over to where the flowers lay, a bruised mass of petals. With trembling fingers she reached for them. She noticed again the deep odor of musk, stronger than before, and knew it wasn't from the flowers, but from Luc's skin. She hadn't rejected his gift. She didn't reject it now. She held it to her nose and then, with a shrug of futility, slipped the ruined flowers into the pocket of her skirt.

"There you are, old thing! What are you doing down there—praying for me again? You'd better get up. Don't waste your time!"

Bright as the tinkling of tiny cymbals and as inappropriate to her own mood came Villette's laughing voice. Composing herself as quickly as she could, Paula got up and turned toward the girl.

"Hey!" Villette said, almost expressing concern but not quite able to dampen her high spirits. "What's the matter? Let's get out of here. You look as though you need some lunch. We're half an hour late, but I can still wrangle some food out of Louis. He's on lunch duty today. I'll be good to him and let him do us a favor. Come on. You were supposed to meet me for lunch, and you forgot. I forgive you. I know old people forget easily."

For once she didn't feel up to scolding Villette. In fact, Paula almost felt happy that the girl had rescued her. Her lunch with Villette turned out to be the cheeriest part of a day that seemed to be getting worse. Paula ate some soup. The rest of the lunch—sandwiches, pastries and fruit—was eaten by the student. "I don't know how you can eat double shares of things," Paula admonished. "Didn't anyone ever tell you you're a dance student? Dancers are supposed to be slim."

"I am slim," Villette said, popping a cherry tart into her round mouth. Paula had to admit that was true—for now. "And I'm going to stay that way, don't worry. I can see what you're thinking, but I run around too much to get fat. What was Monsieur Luc doing in your office?"

Changing the subject with stunning rapidity was one of Villette's tricks for catching people off guard. "He wasn't in my office this morning," Paula lied with perfect equanimity. "He must have been just passing when you saw him."

"Oh, you're a tricky one, old thing." Villette laughed. "I bet he came to apologize for the perfectly silly way he acted yesterday afternoon. He's sure having a bad day today. I suppose you heard all about Karel? Sometimes I feel sorry for Monsieur Luc. Well, miss, did you forgive Luc or not? Which is it?"

"None of your business, miss," Paula answered, and for the time being, anyway, the rosy mouth of Villette van der Vloedt was silenced quite effectively.

FROM BAD TO WORSE to worst. As soon as she got back to her office the expected call from Monsieur Foubert came through. Paula was touched by what she interpreted as real caring on this man's part for his son. As with so many parents, it wasn't a lack of love but a lack of understanding that kept him from Karel. She made an appointment to talk to the banker in person later in the week, but he wasn't yet ready to end the conversation. In fact, they talked for a whole hour, and by the time the call was over Paula was hopelessly behind schedule.

"I'm sorry to have kept you waiting, Margaret,"

Paula said, ushering the young singer into her office.
"I hope I haven't made you miss a lesson."

"Monsieur Josef rescheduled it," Margaret replied,
her voice nearly inaudible. Paula could see she'd been
crying. Another crisis. She led the girl toward one of
the chairs and closed the door. Of all her student
clients, Margaret was the shyest and most difficult to
reach. Paula felt a special sympathy for her because
she herself had suffered the burden of shyness for a
good number of years, and it still crept up on her even
though she knew ways of fighting it.

"What is it, Margaret? What's happened?"

"I've been practicing all month for my recital," the
girl began. "Today we went over the Handel song
and—and...."

"Yes?"

"And I just couldn't sing it! I kept forgetting the
words—my Italian just wouldn't come. Then I lost the
melody altogether. It was awful. I'm never going to be
able to do it, miss!" She wrung her pale hands. Unlike
the other students, Margaret Johnson spoke English in
Paula's sessions, though she was obliged to use French
elsewhere in the school.

"Margaret," she said softly, "I think it's wasteful
for you to worry so. There are still several weeks until
the recital. You've got lots of time to work on the
Italian words to that one song. And I have it from a
very good source that you're well prepared for everything else on the program."

"Did Monsieur Josef say so?" Margaret asked with
more animation than she'd yet shown.

Breaking her own rules about names, Paula replied,
"Monsieur Josef said so."

The student sat back a little, obviously relieved. In a
more conversational tone she said, "It's just that I'm
always so afraid."

"Afraid of what, Margaret?"

"Everything," the girl answered almost under her breath. Then she raised her voice. "I'm most afraid of being too nervous to work. I get so nervous I can hardly breathe every time there's an audience, even if it's only one or two people. Some days I sing so well in practice—and in my private lessons, too—that I feel really proud of myself. But as soon as there's someone else listening, I just freeze up inside. It's as if somebody had his fingers squeezing my throat."

"A number of performance students tell me the same thing, though they use other images. One of the piano students told me he feels as though his fingers are suddenly weighted with lead every time he looks up and sees people listening to him. It's stage fright, Margaret. It's something performers always suffer. You have to learn ways of getting past it. The best way is to keep practicing until you're so sure of your technique that nothing can faze you. Another is to make nervousness work to your advantage."

"How can I do that?"

"Ask Monsieur Josef. He'll tell you that being nervous gives a performer a certain edge. I don't know why that seems to be the case, but nervousness is a kind of energy, and energy is what singing and dancing and acting—what all art—is about. You have to learn to harness that energy and use it to make your performance exciting."

"I guess that's one more thing I'm going to have to practice—how not to be afraid. I don't know for sure if I believe a person can learn that."

"A person can learn almost anything," Paula replied in her most reassuring voice, and was rewarded with Margaret's bright smile.

LATER, WHEN HER WORK for the day was finally done and Paula had left the school to the cleaning staff, her reassuring words to Margaret came back to taunt her. So a person can learn anything, she thought, slipping on her light sweater and stepping out into the lingering sunshine of the May evening. If that was the case, why couldn't she learn how to deal with Luc LeBlanc? This was the second day in a row that she was going home upset over something that had happened with him.

Avoiding him did no good; he seemed to seek her out despite her best efforts to stay away. Simply being friendly did no good; that generally resulted in his starting in on some ridiculous conversation that ended in an argument. And arguing did the least good of all.

As she made her way to the bus stop she felt too tired, too defeated, even to enjoy the warm spring air. Once on the bus she fell asleep, and all thoughts of Luc were obliterated. After some moments of merciful blankness, she awoke with a start at the stop before her own and hurriedly made her way to the door.

Refreshed by that brief accidental nap, she was happy to find that her persistent headache was gone at last. She stopped at a bakery at the corner of her street and stocked up on crusty rolls. With the spring onions and radishes she'd bought at the market and the smooth cream cheese she kept on hand, she'd soon have a sandwich supper that had become one of her favorites since she'd discovered this typically Belgian combination.

She never got around to making that sandwich. The moment she stepped over the threshold of her apartment she saw the letter, and she knew at once it was no business form this time. The envelope was hand addressed in a script she thought she'd recognize even if she was blind.

That he should write now after all these months of silence! For one instant Paula almost convinced herself enough time had gone by, that she could pick up this letter and read it the way one casually reads a letter from a friend. She knew that that was a lie, just as she knew it was also a lie to think the feeling that shot through her now was only apprehension. Deep inside there was also just the tiniest stirring of hope, the same damning, dangerous hope that the sight, even the thought of Breton Graham had always stirred in Paula.

With shaking fingers she bent to pick up the letter. One of the fresh crusty buns tumbled out of the bag and rolled across the floor; she didn't even notice it. She left all her parcels on the floor by the door, taking the letter into the kitchen, where she sat down heavily at the table. The rays of the evening sun fell through the window and onto the page as she read.

Dearest Paula, I know you'll ask yourself at once why it's taken me all these months to write. It's because it's taken me all this time to realize how wrong I was....

Again, hope stirred in her, but she fought it down. She wasn't going to be fooled. Not this time. She should destroy the letter, obliterate his words before they had the effect he'd so often had on her. Her courage failed her, and she read on.

I should tell you right from the start that my wife is gone. I know I told you that before, but this time it's for certain and for good. She ran off with someone from her law firm. It serves me right, Paula, but I can bear the shame of it because it leaves me free at last to make up for the harm I know I've done to you. Please, Paula, let me undo the wrong.

Too late, Bret, she thought to herself, wishing she could send her thoughts winging across the Atlantic by the sheer power of her misery. *It was too late the first time I ever set eyes on you.*

I know now that you would never have carried out the harassment suit. I know it was a desperate measure, and I forgive you for it.

Paula actually smiled at those words. How like Bret to plead in one sentence, and yet to be so insufferably arrogant in the next! And so wrong. He *had* threatened to ruin her career, and she feared he still could. She continued to read, not really surprised by what came next.

I've read every report on the project that you've sent back to Montreal, and I can see you're doing a fine job. Apparently the principal praised your work to the board of directors of your school, because I got a letter from them not long ago, thanking me for sending you and expressing their pleasure at the prospect of having you for two years. But even so, Paula, it would not be impossible for me to send someone to replace you if you really wanted to come home....

She shuddered to read the words. Another person reading this letter might take that last part to be a promise. Paula knew that on the other side of every promise of Bret's was some sort of a threat. Steeling herself, she read the last few lines.

I was wrong, Paula. I know I would never say I loved you, the way you so often said those words to me. But this could change. I can send someone else, and you can come home.
Please.

Why? she asked herself, unable to stem the tears that had begun to fall at the last word. Why couldn't she just write to him and tell him to leave her alone? Not only because of her job—no. She had handled that situation before, not in the best way, maybe, but still.

No. She couldn't make herself forget that Bret Graham held for her some fatal charm that she still, after all that had happened, felt powerless to resist. Maybe because he was the first man ever to tell her she was beautiful. Maybe because no matter how sporadic the evenings he spent with her, every one was so intimate, so fulfilling, that Paula came to feel he was the only person she could ever be that close to. He'd lied to her time and time again, but she had listened as though only truth could come from his lips. Nobody had praised her work so highly. Nobody had listened to her troubles with more intense interest. Nobody had ever touched her as he had. And nobody had ever made love with her before him.

Even now, after all the hurt and the terrible shame, she couldn't forget the afternoons they'd canceled client appointments, dismissed the receptionist and made love in his office. It seemed so sordid now, and Paula cringed to think of it. But she knew that thoughts of those days still came to her unbidden and that she let them linger just a little too long before pushing them away in disgust. If loneliness was an excuse, it was a poor one. In her dedication to her work before Bret, she had been lonely. And since? Since, she'd been desolate. But she wasn't going to give in. The price of shame was just too high. "My wife is gone," the letter said. Yes, she'd heard those words before.

Wearily Paula folded the page. She reached behind her, where on a shelf beside the tiny kitchen table she kept a covered wicker basket; she stowed a few keepsakes there. She was about to put the letter in the basket when she saw a dried bouquet of white violets, the ones from the unknown admirer of two months earlier. She remembered the other bouquet then, the ruined one that just that day she'd slipped into her pocket. Why, he must have been the one who— Paula reached in and retrieved the new bouquet, laying it carefully beside the dried one. Then she crushed Bret Graham's letter, and in a gesture so uncharacteristic that it shocked her, she threw the letter violently against the farthest wall.

The gesture brought no relief, only such a wave of sadness that she finally broke down completely. As the sun set and left her weeping in the dark kitchen, nobody, least of all Paula, knew exactly what—or whom—she was really crying about.

CHAPTER EIGHT

THAT NIGHT she slept like a rock from pure exhaustion, but the next day she again went to school with notice-able circles under her eyes.

Still, it wasn't a bad day. She did quite a bit of paperwork, had two lively sessions with students and was relieved from work for the greater part of the afternoon when the principal called an assembly of all students and staff to discuss the quickly approaching *journée de fierté*, the "day of pride," as the students called the first day of parents' weekend.

The only real problem Paula had all day was that Luc wouldn't take his eyes off her. She had first no-ticed him that morning, staring at her as she came through the lobby. He'd been standing outside his classroom, having already put on his ratty sweater. "Ready for business, I see," she had teased, not waiting to see his reaction to those first words since the day before's fiasco.

He'd also stared at her so persistently through lunch that only because she'd skipped dinner the day before did she have any appetite.

Finally, during the assembly he managed to station himself at the far end of the row in front of the one she was sitting in. He glanced back at her so often that she finally gave in to the temptation to wink at him; she suppressed a giggle when he jumped and quickly turned his head to the front. To Paula's dismay, Villette, who had insisted on sitting next to Paula, saw this exchange and giggled so loudly that Marie reprimanded her from the auditorium stage before going on to delineate, at length, her plans for the exhibits and performances for the parents.

Once the assembly was over it was time to go home. As usual, Paula went back to her office to retrieve her umbrella and briefcase. She was about to step out to say goodbye to Angèle when she heard the door of the outer office close. Surprised that the woman would leave without saying goodbye, Paula glanced out. Not only was Angèle gone, but someone else had arrived. With determination Luc locked the door of the outer office and strode toward Paula as nonchalantly as if she'd invited him in. She stood rooted to the spot, unable to think of anything to say.

"Paula," he said, his voice warmer and softer than she had ever heard it, "I want you to tell me what's wrong."

"I— Nothing's wrong." It was so patent a lie that she didn't even bother trying to convince him, although her problems were none of his business.

"You look bad today—very beautiful—but not well." He moved much closer and lifted a finger as though to touch her pale cheeks. But he thought better of that and dropped his hand. His eyes burned so blue that she thought he might try to kiss her again. She swayed imperceptibly toward him.

"Look," he said, apparently about to begin one of his harangues—it was that tone he used—"I know you consider me your enemy. No, don't shake your head. It's true. Everything that's passed between us so far has been less than pleasant. Excuse me for saying so, but that's certainly as much your fault as mine—" He held up his hand to stop the denial he knew was coming, and continued his little speech before she could get a word in edgewise. "Nonetheless, you're a foreigner, unfamiliar with our ways and a little at sea here, I know, so you deserve some special consideration.''

"You're too generous," she said sarcastically, aware that his matter-of-fact tone disappointed her for some reason.

"You really must mock me. You can't help it, I know." There was genuine hurt in his voice now, and she found she couldn't stand the pain it unaccountably caused her. She remembered his words from the day before. He'd accused her of mocking him then, too. The memory of how he'd looked with the violets clenched in his fist pierced her with remorse.

"I'm sorry, Luc," she said, her voice unsteady.

"No, no please," he replied hastily. "Don't. Don't ever feel you have to apologize to me. It's I who should apologize to you."

Though up until that moment she could have compiled quite a list of reasons, Paula found herself asking, "Apologize? What for?"

"For distracting you that day at the Musée Wiertz. For losing my temper in the study hall the day before yesterday. And for being so rude about the flowers. They were meant to be a peace offering, but—"

"I'm s—"

"No," he interrupted, again raising his imperious finger, this time not pulling it away, but letting it rest on her parted lips. A dart of pure desire shot through Paula, but she resisted it with all her might.

"There it is again," Luc said, his voice a husky whisper. "There is that look of a wounded animal fearful of being struck. Don't fear me, Paula. I'm the last person in the world to strike you or anyone else. All day I've seen that look in you. I came to ask you whether a glass of wine shared with a colleague might not help you get your mind off whatever it is that puts that look in your eyes. What do you say? There's a small café not far from here. Can I interest you in some wine?''

She said yes.

She said no when, after the wine, he offered to order her dinner, though conversation with him turned out to be easy, much easier than arguing with him, so easy in fact that when he took her home via public transit she asked him whether he would like to come in for a sandwich.

''Do you trust me?'' he asked, stopping in front of the door to her place. There was no teasing in his voice and none in hers when she answered, sincerely, yes. But he couldn't restrain himself from commenting, ''A little wine works miracles sometimes.''

''Miracles?'' Paula asked, unlocking the door and showing him in.

''Yes. The enemies call a truce. The lion lies down with the lamb.'' He hadn't meant the sexual innuendo, but they both caught it, and to Paula's amusement, it was he who blushed a deep shade of red. There followed a moment's tense silence, and she asked herself whether she'd been crazy to ask him in. She gestured toward the living room, inviting him to take a seat beside a shelf of books. She thought he might like to read while she fixed the sandwiches. When she brought them in she found him absorbed in a book of French Canadian verse, which he put aside while they enjoyed their snack in companionable silence.

When they finished he took up the book again. ''Listen,'' he said, ''this is lovely. . . .'' He read her a few lines of verse, a poem she knew very well. She noticed that though his accent was not the same as that of the man who'd written the poem, a famous Quebecois *chansonnier*, Luc's soft voice caressed the words as though it had been created expressly to recite a poet's feelings.

"Eyes are windows, love,
    but mine are blind.
Ice shutters them,
    and your indifference
is a world of winter...."

"I'm not familiar with the poets of your country," he said apologetically. "There's so much you could teach me."

There was in his words a certain tension, implying more than was immediately apparent. To break the awkward silence, Paula asked casually, "Sometimes you wear your glasses to read and sometimes not. Why?"

"Why do you care?" he asked teasingly.

"Because you have very unusual eyes."

"You find them unattractive?"

"Quite the contrary. I find them very attractive. I've never seen—" She didn't finish. His face had broken into such a smile at her slight compliment that she felt too touched to continue. It seemed to take very little to please him, and she wondered suddenly whether that might mean he was as lonely as she was. *It's none of your business,* her inner voice reminded her.

"Sometimes I wear contact lenses," he said, "and sometimes I forget. You?"

"No. No, I don't wear contacts."

"I didn't think so. You're a little nearsighted, though."

"How can you tell? Don't tell me you're an ophthalmologist, as well as a teacher, journalist and musician." The minute the words were out, she regretted them. She didn't know why, but she couldn't bear the thought of being accused of mocking him again.

He was an intelligent man, obviously missing nothing, for he scrutinized her sharply, looking for any hint of sarcasm. Finding none, he answered. "Your eyes have a certain mistiness that slightly myopic eyes often show."

"So you've made a study of lots of people's eyes, then?" she said, letting her taunting voice hide the deep pleasure she felt, knowing he'd obviously studied *her* eyes and come to the conclusion that they were unique.

"I have been," he said with deliberation, "a reporter, as you point out. Sometimes you can judge the sincerity of a man or woman just by watching the movement of his or her eyes. I think I can tell by the dilation of the pupils whether a person is lying."

"Do you think my eyes lie?"

"If to conceal is to lie, then yes."

"What do you mean?" she asked, beginning to feel uncomfortable.

"Your eyes." He leaned forward until there was only a small space between them, a small space into which wafted the haunting scent of musk. "Your eyes hide secrets; they are full of shame...."

That was too much for her. She didn't want him peering into the secrets of her life as though he held a key to her mind or her heart. Paula pushed hard on her chair and heard the harsh scrape of it against the uncarpeted floor. She stood, confused for a moment because she wanted to run, and in the small apartment there was nowhere to go. The old feeling of terror seized her, compounded by the well-remembered words of Bret's recent letter. Shame. That was the right word. Needing to at least move away from Luc, she tried to brush past, but he, too, sprang up and grabbed her, his hands gripping her arms.

"Stop it," he breathed, his lips nearly brushing her cheek. "Stop trying to run from whatever it is that pursues you. Why are you here? Who is it that puts that look of terror on your face?"

"Leave me alone." She squirmed in his arms, misjudging his strength, for she couldn't have made him release his grip by physical force. "Let go of me."

"No. Not until you tell me what's wrong. You have no other friends. I know that—"

"You're really pretty nosy, aren't you? Well, I'm not about to satisfy your curiosity."

"I'm not merely curious, Paula. I'm concerned." His voice was cold; her bitterness had stung him, but he didn't loosen his hot grip.

"Concerned about what?" she hissed at him. "Why don't you mind your own business?"

"It's taken you a long time, hasn't it?" There was a teasing, infuriating hint of laughter in his voice.

"What do you mean?"

"You've wanted to tell me from the first time you ever set eyes on me to mind my own business. I dare you to deny it."

She said nothing, turning her head sharply so that he could see only the stern lines of her close-lipped profile.

"You can't deny it," he whispered, his voice a choked sigh at her ear. "But it doesn't matter. Because you *are* my business, Paula Emanuel."

His hand came up, his fingers on her jaw, turning her face toward him. Her green eyes were filled with such a mixture of emotions—such fear and yet such a strong need to trust—that Luc felt his heart turn over in his chest. Something he hadn't experienced in all the long years since his failure stirred in him. He didn't name the feeling, but the demand it made on him was clear. He bent his head and took her parted lips with as gentle a touch as he could restrain himself to offer.

Paula felt that gentleness and responded to it instinctively, hungry for the simple affection he seemed willing to give. She lifted her hand and touched his cheek. Beneath the slightly bristling warmth of his jaw, she felt hard bone. Her hand trembled.

The gesture seemed to inflame him. His lips lost all pretense of gentle friendliness. With a pressure that drove back her head, his mouth seared against hers, robbing her of breath, of the thought of breathing. Her head reeled, but she reveled in the overwhelming warmth of his lips, of his hands that captured her face and wouldn't let go. He kissed her not only with strength, but with power. The hunger that had pierced her earlier came back with such force that there was no pushing it away, though she knew she should push him away.

What she wanted was to pull him closer, to feel the tight muscles of his thighs against her own. Reason told her to pull his hands from her face, to pull away the fingers that caressed her jaw with a circling motion that sent shivers of desire through her.

But more, she wanted those small circling movements to continue. His mouth probed hers, his tongue seeking. Against all better judgment, she opened her lips to admit the strong thrust of his kiss. Her arms rose around his neck, her hands feathering his sleek dark hair. At that touch, one of his hands made a fevered motion toward her auburn curls, brushing them from her forehead, making a space to kiss her there before his lips swept along her cheek and back to her waiting mouth.

Again a hot spasm of pleasure and longing shot through to the deepest recesses of her body, but in its wake came pain.

This kiss was foolish—foolish and stupid. Just as foolish as her kisses with Bret had been and just as certain to end in hurt, if not disaster. Luc LeBlanc was a colleague, just as Bret had been. He probably had as much power to ruin her already precarious position at the school. She felt the old familiar terror begin as a stinging awareness. There was nothing different about this kiss or this evening or this man. She would squelch the desire spiraling in her like a tornado that threatens to carry with it the debris of what it has destroyed. Things would never be any different. There would never be anything more for her than blinding, eradicating kisses that promised to wipe out terror and regret, but that led back to them instead. Wasn't that what all this was about—her shame, her exile, the letter from Bret that still lay crumpled where she'd thrown it the night before? A shudder passed through her, which Luc took for passion, not a wave of tears. He held her close, increased the ardor of his kiss—until her salty tears reached his lips.

Abruptly he pulled back. "My God, I'm sorry! I haven't hurt you? I didn't mean—"

She shook her head, but she couldn't stop the tears. With brusque tenderness his thumbs stroked her wet, flushed cheeks. "Paula. . . ." He sighed. "Please."

But the sobbing wouldn't stop. Not even when he pulled her to him again, not in passion but in kindness. Dazed by this display of unexpected caring, this last assault on her already battered emotions, Paula was helpless in his arms. He held her, letting her tears flow, saying nothing when the hot moistness of them penetrated the front of his shirt. After a little while he urged her to sit, and he produced a large linen handkerchief that soon grew damp. He couldn't wipe all her tears away.

"Listen to me, Paula," he said, taking her trembling shoulders in his strong grip. "Listen to me. I had no intention of hurting you, not tonight and not before, either. I really mean to be your friend. You have to take me seriously. I didn't come to your office today to attack you. I came to help. I saw you watching me all day.

Your eyes, even across the distance of the dining hall, were pleading with me...."

Wordlessly she shook her head. He was wrong. She hadn't been pleading. She hadn't asked him for anything, and she wasn't asking now.

"No. Don't shake your head. I know what you want of me, and I'm willing to give it. More willing to give than you are to ask. Take my friendship. You need it. You need me."

Her stricken eyes sought his. She saw that his face was contorted with emotion. Despite his offer, it was he who seemed to desperately need something. She didn't have the energy to shake her head again, to shake him off. She dropped her eyes and felt once more the strong finger lifting her face to his. The blue gaze burned with a violet flame at its depths, and somehow she knew this was a man she could trust. Wearily she smiled.

He didn't smile back, but the harsh lines of his face relaxed, and he nodded curtly as though to say, "There, that's settled, then."

LATER IT WOULD SEEM that she'd told him everything about her past, and in one fell swoop, and with very few tears.

"Begin at the beginning," Luc coaxed, but she found it hard to do what she so often convinced others to do in her job. To talk about herself was difficult, let alone to reveal the intimate details of her life to this insistent man who was half friend, half stranger. "Begin, Paula," he said again, and when his hand started to gently knead her shoulder, she felt some of the tension leave her. He led her to the couch and sat beside her. "So then...."

"All right. I was born in a small town about seventy miles outside of Montreal. I don't remember a whole

lot about the place itself, but I remember the relatives.''

"The relatives?'' Luc asked. Already her eyes were
soft, as though the memory warmed her. He felt a cor-
responding warmth and urged her on. "Tell me about
the relatives.''

"Well, there must have been a hundred of them, or so
it seemed to me at the time. They were my mother's people. My father had come from another part of Quebec,
from the Gaspé peninsula. *Grand-père* always called
him *l'étranger*. But in those days, nobody really treated
anybody else as a foreigner. I had so many cousins!
Bonnie—that's my sister—Bonnie and I never lacked
playmates. I guess it could only have been for four years
that I lived there, but when I think back on it, it seems
like half my life. . . . ''

Her slight smile was so sad that Luc got the feeling
days of carefree happiness hadn't been repeated very
often later in her life. "It sounds as though things
changed.''

"Yes. My father got a job in Montreal, and we
moved. My relatives promised faithfully that they'd
visit us, but they never did, except for *grand-père* and
grand-mère. I would wait with hopeful plans for
months before they arrived and grieve for the same
amount of time when they left. At first I was sad only
because I missed them. Then there was another
reason.''

"What, Paula?''

"Their visits made my mother homesick. I didn't realize it at the time, but when we first got to Montreal we
were quite poor. My mother wanted to go back to where
she would be surrounded by family instead of strangers,
where things didn't cost so much. My father saw things
differently. He felt that if he stuck it out in the city, he'd
eventually be able to earn enough to get us a good house

and good clothes, even to send us to university, which was his dream. Well, his dream came true, but at terrible cost. They fought constantly. Not a day went by without some awful battle.''

She stopped. The pain in her face was so intense that Luc was sorry he'd encouraged her to talk. He tried to understand the combination of toughness and sensitivity that seemed to mark her character, but he came to the conclusion that it wasn't the sort of thing one could analyze. ''Paula, if you don't want to go on. . . .''

She shook her head dismissively. ''Growing up in that house was like living in a minefield. I learned to step carefully. I came to regard keeping the peace as the ultimate goal of each day. I learned not to make a fuss, because I just couldn't bear to add any more conflict to our situation. The worst part was that I never felt comfortable about having friends over. I never really made friends until I went to university.''

''It sounds like such a lonely existence.''

''No. I didn't mean to be so negative. When I got to be a teenager, I used to go back to my grandparents' for the summer. And in Montreal I had the whole city at my disposal. I had Bonnie, though we're quite different and not really close. Mostly I had my books, my dreams, myself. I like being alone, being a loner.'' She looked up at Luc, surprised to see the skepticism in his eyes.

She told him about school and about the university she'd gone to, managing her master's degree from McGill on a scholarship. It didn't occur to her to ask Luc about his education. She assumed it must be as extensive as her own. She explained that she was still considering getting her Ph.D. He seemed willing to listen to anything she wanted to say, and in the face of his obvious interest, she found she wanted to say quite a bit.

''Almost from the time I got my degree I worked with

children,'' Paula said. "That was my specialization,
and I was lucky to get into it right away. Mostly I
worked with kids who were about to be sent as foster
children to families in the city.''

"And you enjoyed that?''

"In the beginning I had difficulties. My own background, as I said, had been troubled, so I felt that I
understood the kids, though many of them had been far
worse off than I'd ever been. My problem was not at all
unusual among social workers. I wanted to save every
kid from ever being hurt or confused or disappointed
again. I devoted every waking hour to my job.''

"And you loved it.''

"Yes.''

"I know how it can be,'' Luc commented, and Paula
wasn't exactly sure what he meant. His tone was wistful, as if he mourned the loss of something.

"After a while,'' she went on, "I started to feel real
frustration. I was able to loosen up a bit, to understand
that of course the problems I was dealing with wouldn't
necessarily be solved completely or at all. But the emotional cost of several years of caring too much and trying too hard was high. I was a classic case of burnout,
so-called, when Dr. Graham . . . came to take me away
from all that.''

"Didn't you miss the kids?'' Luc asked when she began to tell him about her professional life with Bret.

"When I first started to work with Bret,'' Paula said
thoughtfully, "I think all I cared about was being in a
situation where there was some hope. I guess that feeling of hopelessness is what gets to you. I'd been very
dedicated, even to the exclusion of a social life. But
after a number of years I started to feel I was facing the
same kids with the same insolvable problems. When
Bret and I started our work with gifted students, the atmosphere was entirely different.''

It wasn't very hard to talk about her work with Bret, until it came time to talk about her personal dealings with him. Paula could only do so after two glasses of wine and some pressure from Luc.

"Tell me," he demanded, taking her hand in his as they sat side by side on the couch, not otherwise touching, but not unaware of the physical tension between them. "I won't go until you do. It's taken me a long time to make you understand that I'm willing to be your friend. I don't want to come in tomorrow and see that look in your eyes again."

She pulled her hand away. She really should have told him to mind his own business. Instead she told him about Bret.

"At first, we were purely professional with each other. He had a reputation, and I was flattered to be his assistant. It wasn't until some time later that I heard he had a reputation for something else besides his work. By that time I was already hooked...."

Paula told Luc a little about the affair, but cut short any details. The hard set of Luc's jaw made her realize he didn't want to know more than the outline of this part of her story.

"But you didn't know he was married?"

"No. It seems naive, I know. But some men have a way of hiding things like that when they want to. When I finally found out I was crushed. I approached Bret. At first he denied being married at all. Then he denied being happily married. Then he asked me why it should matter whether he was married or not. I told him it mattered a great deal. To make a long story short, we made the first of a number of foolish deals. He agreed to send me to a different school. I agreed to keep seeing him, on a platonic basis, until he and his wife settled their differences one way or another. If she left him, he said, the way would be clear for us. He couldn't leave her right then, he said, because she was studying for her bar exams and he didn't want to upset her.''

There was a look of total disgust on Luc's face at that point; ignoring it, Paula went on with her story. ''Actually, for the next eighteen months things weren't bad. I got quite involved in the project, and I saw Bret only for business purposes. I felt lonely but relieved, too. Whenever Bret wasn't around I didn't think about him much. Yet after every meeting with him, I was in agony for weeks. I knew he felt the same agony. One night he came to my apartment and told me his wife had left him for good. We got back together. It. . .wasn't until a month later that I found out he'd been lying. I told him I never wanted to see him again.

''And he told me I was out of a job.'' Paula didn't want to look at Luc now. She'd heard his sharply indrawn breath and could tell he was angry. She couldn't bear to say much more. Quickly she summarized the rest of her tale. ''I went for legal advice and found I possibly had enough evidence to sue Bret for sexual harassment. I threatened to do so. To my amazement, he was utterly terrified. He begged me not to sue. He promised to let me stay on. Then, at the end of the same week, his wife found out about our affair. She threatened to leave him. That precipitated our final deal. . . .''

''And what was that?'' Luc asked, his voice clearly edged with contempt.

Instead of wanting to hide these damning facts about herself, Paula suddenly felt a strong urge to complete her confession and have done with it. Perhaps Luc would withdraw his offer of friendship. Perhaps that was best. Steadily she finished her story. ''Apparently Dr. Graham was less eager for his wife to leave him than he had led me to believe. In fact, he became frantic at the thought of actually losing her. So he had to get rid of his assistant in a way that would cause him the least embarrassment. The farther away the better. He hadn't forgotten the lawsuit, either. We both had something on each other. He could ruin my career. I could ruin his marriage, although at terrible cost to everyone involved, because the suit would have taken months—if not years—and every detail of our personal lives, including my own foolish 'deals' and my willingness in the beginning, would have been exposed. In the end we settled for a nice little two-year appointment at a well-regarded private school for the performing arts.''

"Le Berceau,'' Luc ground out.

"Le Berceau.''

"How could you?'' Luc exploded.

"Look—you encouraged me to tell you these things,'' Paula shot out. "If you didn't want to know about me, you shouldn't have asked. I won't be judged. I've been through enough with men—''

"No, Paula,'' he cut her off, his voice far softer than she'd expected. "You've been through enough with *that* man. To have forced you out of your job, your home, your country. It's inconceivable! No wonder you're such a lost soul!''

She opened her mouth to protest, but once more he took her hand and began to caress it with slow, gentle insistence, lulling her. His eyes were lowered, his jaw firm. She couldn't tell at all what he was thinking. She wouldn't have been surprised if he was trying to come up with some excuse to be done with her. When he sighed she held her breath, waiting to hear what he was about to say.

"Well,'' he began, "now it's over and you're here. Sometimes things wrongly begun turn out for the best, whereas things done with the best intentions can easily come to nothing.'' Once more he sighed, and she had the feeling he was talking about more than her own situation.

"You speak as if you knew," she ventured, "as if you'd started something that didn't work out."

He raised his eyes. They held that shuttered, hard look she'd noticed before. But seeing her own questioning eyes, his seemed to soften. "So," he said with a small smile, "now you're here, and you can start again. The past is over."

"Not completely," Paula said very quietly.

"What do you mean?"

She got up, walked over to the kitchen and retrieved the crumpled piece of paper, smoothed it out and handed it to Luc. "Yesterday," she said, steadying her voice with effort, "this came."

He took it and read it, and as he did so his face reddened, not with embarrassment, she knew, but with anger.

"So you are still involved with him?" Luc asked, his voice rigidly controlled as he glanced up from the page.

"Yes," Paula said, and watched with dismay as Luc turned away. "But only because of my job. I don't want to have anything more to do with him. But if he causes me trouble—"

"If he causes you trouble, it's your own fault," Luc spat out, abruptly turning back to her. "Stand up to him. You're doing fine at Le Berceau. Everyone says so. I was there myself when the board voted to send a letter to Montreal praising your work. Call him and tell him to leave you alone."

"I can't."

"Why?"

"Because I haven't got the courage, okay? Because he's still got the power to cause trouble for me if he wants to."

"Stand up to him," Luc insisted. "Or if you won't, let me do it."

"You? Why should you want to put yourself out like that for me?"

"Don't you know, Paula? Can't you guess?"

It was she who turned away then. She didn't want to be rescued again. She didn't want to be indebted to him as he helped her settle old accounts with Bret.

He came closer, his nearness forcing her to pay attention to what he had to say. "Let me write to him," he insisted. "I'm not a writing teacher for nothing! I'll write Dr. Bret Graham a letter that'll scare him off for good!"

Despite the seriousness of her problem, Paula had to marvel at Luc's dramatics. His black hair suffered a severe tousling from his raking fingers. His eyes flashed pure violet, and his hands were clenched. Her shoulders heaved, not with tears this time, but with a laughter she couldn't control.

"All right," he stormed, "laugh at me. I'm nothing but a fool, right? You'd rather be in the clutches of this—this bastard—than accept the sincere help of a friend. Go on, mock me as much as you like. If it makes you feel better, go right ahead. Mock me all you want—"

"Shut up, Luc," she said, completely surprising him by grabbing his shoulders. He was suddenly deathly silent beneath her touch. Gently she kissed his lips. "Thank you," she whispered.

"What?" he queried a little unsteadily.

"Thank you for helping me to laugh at myself and my problems. You're the only one who's ever been able to do that. And thank you for your offer of friendship. I accept. I accept with gratitude, but I'll take care of Bret myself."

Once more she saw that tender smile of his. Again she saw hints of a loneliness she knew was at least as deep as her own. What were friends for if not to combat loneliness? She was going to try to be as good a friend to him as he seemed to want to be to her. "So then," she said, "friends?"

"Friends," he answered. And he bent to kiss her. It was too passionate a kiss for friends; the intensity of it shook Paula to the core. But she accepted it. Nothing's perfect.

CHAPTER NINE

BEFORE PAULA KNEW IT, the end of the school year was drawing near. The last month was the busiest for students and teachers alike. Though she herself wasn't participating in the special events of the *journée de fierté*, the increased pressure parents' weekend placed on everyone else in the school was reflected in her own job. She had to spend almost all her sessions assuring the students that what they were about to exhibit or perform would indeed bring pride to Le Berceau.

On the day itself, a June Friday that dawned sunny and warm, classes were canceled so that the students could view the exhibits and the afternoon performances of their fellows. Paula, too, was eager to see the results of the intense work that had gone on during the term she'd worked at the school. Wandering from room to room, she delighted in the various displays. The visual-arts department had mounted a stunning array of portraits. Kathelijne's painting of Monsieur Josef LeBlanc hung in a place of honor. She had captured the music master perfectly, right down to his slight unmistakable resemblance to his brother Luc.

The works of the sculpture class were exhibited in the now richly blooming garden, where fragrant hawthorn vied with scented roses, honeysuckle and jasmine. As Paula walked from piece to piece, she remembered the day Villette had compared one of Monsieur Lamont Langois's works to a potato. She stifled a laugh—just in time, too. The portly professor of sculpture was suddenly standing beside her.

"Mademoiselle la Canadienne—quel plaisir!" he drooled. "What do you think of the efforts of my class?"

"Quite interesting, *monsieur*," she said evenly, though she'd been caught off guard. "They seem to capture the, uh, the essential solidity of mass." It was a fairly stupid statement, she knew, but the teacher took it as a great compliment, insisting she join him for a glass of wine in the reception salon, where Marie Légère was entertaining teachers and parents. Paula accepted the invitation because she was thirsty.

As she entered the salon she noticed Luc. He seemed to sense her presence before he saw her, raising his eyes directly toward her as she stood poised in the doorway. He smiled, but before she could respond, his attention was drawn away by one of a veritable crowd of well-dressed women who surrounded him. He was, it seemed, as great a hit with mothers as with students.

"So you are pleased with the exhibits, *mademoiselle*?" the professor at her side asked. He didn't notice the hostess serving drinks and so poured a glass for Paula himself. It was a little too full. She had to sip it before she answered

"I've only seen about half the displays so far, Monsieur Langois, but the quality is exceptional. You teachers have a lot to be proud of."

"Thank you, Miss Emanuel—Paula, if I may call you that...."

She nodded a little uneasily. "Lumpy" Langois seemed ready for a long conversation, but with unexpected luck Paula was saved by Villette, who pulled her away from the reception salon and into the lobby. "Come on, come on. Now's your chance," Villette insisted laughingly as she thrust Paula toward the room where Luc taught most of his classes. "I know you and Monsieur Luc are enemies and that you never come in here, but now that he's surrounded by adoring old ladies, you can take a look at my masterpiece.''

"Villette," Paula scolded, though not very strenuously. "A: My friendship or the lack of it with Monsieur Luc is none of your business. B: You shouldn't interrupt staff or anyone else when they're talking. C: You shouldn't refer to the mothers of fellow students as 'old ladies.' And D: As you well know, the salon is off limits to students. You weren't supposed to be in there.''

"Don't worry, old fusspot. Nobody saw me. Look. Look what I wrote.'' She pulled Paula into Luc's classroom, deserted now except for one set of parents who were perusing the exhibit of articles and other pieces Luc's students had written. "Read it," Villette insisted, picking up an essay and thrusting it into Paula's hands.

"Canada is a cold country," Paula read, "but that doesn't mean it is without warm-hearted people—What is this?'' she asked, looking up at Villette, whose bright blue mischievous eyes glowed with pride.

"It's for you. I wrote it as a surprise. We were supposed to write about someone who influenced us either positively or negatively, and I picked positively. I picked you.''

The grammar wasn't perfect, and there were one or two sentences Monsieur Luc had been lenient to leave without correcting, but nonetheless, Paula felt tears spring to her eyes at this tribute. "Thank you," she said, sincerely moved.

"Thank *you*," Villette said merrily. "I got an A on it!''

UNLIKE THE AFTERNOON performances that had featured mostly first-year students, the evening was devoted to displaying the skills of the advanced pupils, young people headed for a career in the not-too-distant future. Strictly speaking, Paula had no students and therefore no official obligation to attend the program. In fact, she wouldn't have missed it for the world.

There was an almost gala atmosphere in the school's large auditorium as parents filed in. Both men and women had dressed for the event, and Marie looked as near to beautiful as Paula had seen her, in a salmon-pink silk blouse with a sweeping drape at the front that set off the aristocratic length of her neck and the intricate coils of her shiny hair.

When everyone had been seated by students serving as ushers, an expectant silence filled the hall. The principal stepped to the podium at the side of the stage and began her opening address.

"Mesdames et Messieurs, bienvenues—welcome to Le Berceau...."

Paula listened intently for a while. Then her attention wandered, and she began to scan the crowd until her eyes found the target she had been unconsciously seeking. Involuntarily she smiled. For all his casual air at other times, Luc could certainly rise to the occasion when he had to! Not wanting to be caught looking at him, she turned her eyes back to the stage.

For days the school had buzzed with speculation as to who would draw the lot for first position on the night's program. Only that morning had it been announced that the drama department would have that singular honor. Paula was grateful for the darkness of the hall because she couldn't hide her amusement at the sound of teenage voices performing Shakespeare in Belgian French. It was charming but very exotic. At home her reaction to Shakespeare performed in a language other than English was the same as her reaction to Molière performed in anything but French. She avoided such interpretations. Yet she thoroughly enjoyed this performance, and when it was followed by an excerpt from a contemporary play by a Brussels playwright, she was too spellbound to criticize either content or technique.

To thunderous applause the drama department members took their bows. There was some scuffling while a piano was wheeled out of the wings so that the music students could begin their recital. Margaret Johnson appeared somewhere between a tiny but powerful flautist, accompanied by Monsieur Josef, and an extraordinary string quintet, which provided the finale of the segment. Her voice was lovely, and she managed Handel with skill. But Paula sincerely wondered whether people sitting farther back in the hall could hear her. For all her delicate prettiness, Margaret's face looked more tortured than appealing. At the end of the piece, Paula found herself clapping vigorously, but soon realized she was doing so more out of sympathy than appreciation.

However, there was no need to feel sorry for Villette when the dance segment got under way. Nor was there much chance that anyone could fail to take in every detail of her performance. For the most part the pieces she danced in were choreographed for four or five dancers, but the one solo she did perform met with enthusiastic applause from every part of the auditorium. Her technique was a little slovenly, but her vivacious personality projected beyond the footlights and quite captivated the audience.

Though not performance students in the usual sense, Luc's advanced pupils read their work. Karel's was the most impressive. He read from a novel in progress that might have been edited by Luc; it was quite professional. Paula stole a glance at *Monsieur*, the Writing Teacher. Dressed impeccably in his dove-gray suit, he watched Karel with unwavering intensity. In his chiseled profile, even halfway across the auditorium, Paula could read a look of pride mingled with regret, a regret she was powerless to understand.

The next morning dawned with exceptional blue brilliance. Traditionally, the second day of parents' weekend was devoted to a mother-and-daughter brunch for the girls and a father-and-son sports day for the boys. This year, after several contentious staff meetings during which Luc took the more-liberated view, it was decided to include girls in the sports events. Paula felt that leaving the boys out gave sexist overtones to the brunch, but she didn't refuse to attend. She was touched when Margaret asked her to stand in for her own mother, who was in Canada. By custom the girls wore white dresses, and though a few of the outfits showed the unmistakable influence of punk, the overall effect was of youthful freshness.

At first Paula had considered missing the sports events, but Villette had challenged, "If the brunch will be too strenuous for you, by all means rest up after it." So following the meal, she went with the girls to the locker room and changed into the shorts and top she'd brought. Then she walked out into the large enclosed grassy area at the rear of the new section of the school.

The first person she saw was Luc. He was leaning nonchalantly against the wall, his arms and legs muscled and strong beneath his white shorts and T-shirt. He wasn't looking for her. A light breeze stirred his black hair, and his indigo eyes were trained on some distant thing. He gave the impression of being trapped in one place but dreaming of another. She took a step toward him, and hearing her, he turned. Instantly his mysterious expression altered in a disturbing way. His eyes filled with a blatant desire she somehow knew he was fighting. The knowledge of his restraint eased her mind, for, after all, they were just friends. But her own look was a little wistful as she said hello. There was no time for conversation, since the kids were flooding onto the field.

A game resembling touch football was played toward the end of the afternoon. Paula let herself be talked into participating. At first she simply ran around—like a fool, she thought—but soon she was as eager to capture the ball as anyone. The minute she did she was tackled. Even pinned facedown to the soft warm grass, she knew who had tackled her. Not only by the slight scent of musk, but by the tauntingly whispered, "I've got you."

There was a banquet in the evening and a mass the next day. Paula knelt and offered a prayer before the service began. When she raised her eyes, she saw Luc not far away. As usual, he had situated himself within her vision. He was again dressed in a suit, and she saw how his dark hair curled under a bit at his nape. Something about the duskiness of those strands against his golden skin, something about the way his shoulders were hunched slightly and his head lowered in prayer filled her with such tenderness that she found herself praying he might be granted whatever it was he was asking for.

THE PARENTS' WEEKEND was pronounced a success, and everyone basked in the glow for a few days. Then the real work began, the preparation for year-end exams. Halls that had once rung with chatter and laughter grew quiet as students turned from painting to studying math, from singing to geography.

Paula had no more sessions now, but plenty of paperwork. Sometimes she wished she had something to do in the evenings to break the tedium. Unfortunately, the only people she knew were fellow teachers, and they were all much busier than she. She even considered asking Luc if he'd like to go for coffee, but he was so taken up with his year-end work that she hesitated to approach him.

Once the exams began, however, they were thrown

together in a way Paula found unsettling. Each exam was three hours long, and by rule each had to be monitored by a team of two teachers. Luc and Paula, it turned out, were one of the teams. The classrooms, though large, didn't offer unlimited space, and before long Paula realized no one could have choreographed a more-provocative dance than the one she danced with Luc.

The first day he brought a book; so did she. He stationed himself on the dais, a little like a king ascending a throne, she thought with a smile. It was the first time she'd seen him behind the teacher's desk, and she was suitably if grudgingly impressed by his unmistakable air of authority. She sat at the back of the room. He read. She read. He looked up periodically to check on the students. She did too. His eyes accidentally met hers. She turned away. Her eyes accidentally met his. He turned away. And then he turned back and held her gaze with such bold interest that she gasped, quickly swallowing the sound, not wanting to disturb the furiously scribbling students. After that his eyes were on her as often as they were on his charges.

The next day he decided to pace rather than sit, and Paula agreed with him that it would be better to get more exercise. She stood at the front of the room while he moved to the back as the students filed in and took their places at the long rows of desks.

All day he chased her. If she moved to the head of the first row, he moved to the foot of the last. If she leaned against the corner of the blackboard in front, he took up a position at the corner of the rear windows. Always opposite her. Always directly in view. Across the lowered heads of the pupils, his compact, energetic body sent its message to her. His quiet footsteps on the marble floor seemed to move always away, but she knew he was moving inexorably closer. Hour after hour they danced like two caged lions who pace in a circle, not knowing what will happen when that circle narrows, until they stand face-to-face with only the space of a breath between them.

"MON DIEU, Paula, but you are beautiful!" Before she even had a chance to say hello, he swept her into his arms and sailed off across the floor with her. "And you can dance."

"You'd be in trouble if I couldn't—grabbing me like that! What do you think you're doing? You could have been severely trampled. And it would have served you right, too!" Paula's voice was teasing but breathless. He had come out of nowhere, and now the musky scent of him was everywhere, tingeing the air with the promise of unnamed pleasure.

"We've worked so hard these past weeks," Luc said, tightening his hold on her a little. "Now it's time for fun. This dance is the last time staff will be together until the fall, so everyone tries hard to enjoy themselves."

"Himself."

"Ourselves," he taunted, staring into her eyes meaningfully. She reddened, turning her head, but he whispered in her ear, "I've neglected you, my little friend, and I intend to make amends."

Laughing at his courtly manner, she teased him, "I've never seen you in quite so gallant a mood, Monsieur Luc."

"And I've never seen you look quite so lovely." His tone was far less light than her own. In fact, his soft voice caught in his throat, and there were no words at all for a while.

The pressure of his body against hers was a sweet drug as they danced. She felt again the flowing energy in him. His strong arms held her close, far too close for the occasion, but she didn't care. Nor, apparently, did he.

When the first dance was over, he demanded another by wordlessly holding her to him so that she couldn't escape. The emerald chiffon of her skirt brushed against his legs, lean in black formal trousers, as the music resumed and once again his arms encircled her in the accepted posture of the dance. Despite the distance they maintained when they remembered the scrutiny of fellow teachers, his hand toyed with hers, his fingers suggestively sending impulses coursing through her.

When at the end of the evening he asked her back to his place for a nightcap, she couldn't refuse.

"THIS IS LES MAROLLES," Luc said at the end of the short taxi ride from Le Berceau to his neighborhood. "It's a working-class district. Not fancy, but it has lots of local color."

He led her up a narrow staircase in the old building that housed his apartment. There was an eagerness to him that Paula found half touching, half tantalizing. His hand held hers tightly as he negotiated the stairs, and he released her fingers only to unlock the door. He ushered her in, relocked the door, then turned to her. In his eyes was a question. In answer, Paula moved toward him.

His lips on hers were as hot and as hungry as they'd ever been. She felt all the power of him move into his kiss; his energy seemed to fill her, and his desire, too. For long moments she stood totally absorbed in the moist pleasure of his tongue probing, tasting, thrusting. His hands grasped her head, his fingers burrowing into the soft curls, then caressing her scalp. His mouth was so urgent that she had to pull away to draw in a stunned and shuddering breath. But only for the briefest instant. Forgetting every reason she'd ever had for fighting him, she threw her arms around him, the smooth weave of his jacket cool beneath her fingers. She pushed impatiently against the fabric, seeking the softness of his nape where his sleek hair ended and the heat of his skin began.

"Luc," she whispered each time his tongue relinquished her eager mouth. He didn't whisper her name. He communicated with his lips on her hair, her forehead, her cheek, her chin and back again to her mouth, grown even more hungry in the absence of his kiss there.

After endless but far too fleeting moments, he pulled away, leading her farther into the room. "I'll get some wine," he said, his voice husky and soft. He went through a door that led, Paula imagined, to the kitchen. She sank onto a couch covered in a South American woven spread and glanced around. The small room, which must serve as Luc's study as well as his living room, was pleasantly cluttered. There were musical instruments. There were so many books she couldn't begin to count them. With amusement she noticed a whole row of English murder mysteries and remembered that Luc had once admitted that was how he had learned what he called "your other language."

There seemed to be a large number of photographs, too, some tacked to the wall over the cluttered desk, some in frames, including a picture on the small table beside the couch. A beautiful blond woman in her late twenties had posed for a formal portrait. Beside it, also framed, was quite a different shot of the same person. The woman wore khaki fatigues and had a portable video unit slung over her shoulder. In the background was a Jeep full of soldiers bearing machine guns.

Luc came back with a bottle of French white wine and two glasses, which he filled deftly, handing one to Paula and sitting down beside her. For an awkward moment they merely looked at each other. Paula smiled self-consciously. Luc's face was unreadable as he lowered his eyes, seeming to study the sparkling liquid in his glass. After a long pause he spoke. "Paula, you'll have reason to accuse me of taking advantage of a friendship if I—if we...."

"Maybe I'm the one who'd be taking advantage, Luc," she answered, her eye inadvertently traveling to the photographs of the blond woman. Luc followed her gaze. Wordlessly he stood, took the pictures and carried them over to a high dresser, opening the top drawer and carefully putting them away. He stood for a moment with his back to her, his hands still on the drawer pull, his head bowed. After a while he lifted his head and spoke to her without turning.

"How old are you?" he asked.

"Thirty-two," she answered, wondering what he was leading up to.

"Yes," he said wearily, "and I'm thirty. No doubt by now each of us has a lot to answer for when it comes to relationships—mistakes, false starts, bad faith—no?"

"Yes," she answered, the one word holding a history of heartache.

"So, I ask myself," Luc went on, "why start again? Another relationship, another series of hopes followed by another collection of despairs. Promise and failure. Sometimes it seems to me that's all there can be between a man and a woman." He turned, came back to the couch and sat beside her, taking her hand but not looking at her. Against her skin, his felt cold. "Do you know what I mean?"

"Yes. Yes, of course I do, Luc, but...."

"But what?" he asked flatly when she hesitated.

"I can't help it," Paula went on uncertainly. "I still find myself thinking that maybe, maybe if the time was right or the person, or both.... I don't know, maybe there's still a chance...."

"For love everlasting?" The cold cynicism in his voice chilled Paula.

"Don't be sarcastic," she said, something of her old annoyance with him returning. He must have sensed the change in her, for his eyes flashed with momentary anger. Defiantly she stared at him, daring him to argue. As she kept his gaze locked with her own, she could see his eyes change from angry to tender.

"Paula," he whispered, "I don't want to. I don't want to start again, to start something that—like all the other times—will lead to heartache for both of us. And yet, I can't...I want...."

She stopped his struggle for words, leaning toward him and cupping his face with her hands. She had no answer to his doubts. They were her own. In the deep caring of friendship, she firmly kissed his closed lips. Her only intention was to stop him from revealing things he seemed reluctant to say. Yet like kindling that sets fire to large logs, her kiss blazed into quick passion. No matter what they had suffered before, Paula suddenly knew they were weak in the power of this new thing that seemed determined to have its way with them. For an eternity they reveled in a deep kiss. In exploration now tender and fevered, their hands and lips sought confirmation of feeling through warmth of flesh.

There was, Paula soon noticed, a hesitancy about Luc, despite his passion, almost a shyness that was touching in a man of his age and, she was sure, experience. It puzzled her, but in the intense pleasure of their intimacy, as his mouth opened to receive the thrust of her bold tongue, she had no time to think about that, about anything. When he slowly undid the buttons of her blouse, she gave his too-quick fingers room. But when she began to do the same—he had taken off his jacket and wore only a silky shirt with his trousers—he stayed her fingers with a motion so abrupt that she withdrew her hand, pulling a little away.

He wouldn't let her go, though. He pulled her to him,

crushing her against his chest so that her nipples hardened beneath the chiffon of her dress at the contact. He distracted her with the power of his lips and fingers and tongue, bribing her by giving her such pleasure that she quite forgot she wanted to give him pleasure, too.

When it seemed that neither had air left to breathe, he drew away a little and laughingly whispered, "So passionate, *ma Canadienne*, so very passionate. . . ."

Teasingly she responded, "Now you accuse me of too much passion. But I remember a time when you said the opposite, when you teased me mercilessly, then accused me and my countrymen of a lack of warmth."

He knew instantly what she referred to. "You treated me like a pariah, and you were sorry afterward. I know you were. . . ." There was no taunting laughter in his voice now. The memory of the ridiculous incident in the study hall was obviously not a pleasant one for him. The touch of melancholy always vaguely present in his expression intensified. Impulsively Paula lifted a finger to stroke his strong jaw.

"You're right, Luc," she said softly. His eyes were cast down, and his sooty lashes curved beneath his lowered lids. "I was sorry afterward. But I didn't want you to sit so close to me."

At those words, his eyes shot up. She took a sharp breath when she saw the pain there. Speaking steadily she went on. "I knew that if you were that near, I'd be too nervous to work."

"Nervous? How could I make anyone nervous?"

"You do it all the time," Paula answered with a smile, thinking of his effect on his students, as well. "I don't know how you did it, but when you came into the study hall, my heart started to pound."

"And now?"

"Now?"

"Does your heart pound now when I come into a room?"

Despite herself, she was embarrassed by the question. He lifted her face with his finger and planted a soft kiss on her open lips.

"Does that make your heart pound?" he asked. Still she didn't answer. "Or this?" Drawing her close with one arm, he trailed the fingers of his other hand along the low curving drape of her dress. She trembled at his touch, and he pulled her nearer, his fingers slipping beneath the cloth. "I *do* make your heart beat faster by my nearness," he whispered in throaty triumph. "I can feel it." And he closed his warm hand over her breast, sending a shooting, familiar hunger through her. She reached for him, throwing her arms around his back, feeling beneath her fingers the corded muscles under silk.

"No," she breathed hoarsely, "you are not making my heart beat. You have no effect on me at all." Her teasing was intended as enticement, and it worked. He pushed her away, but only far enough to allow his lips to pattern kisses along her jaw, her throat, the tops of her breasts, where his slow but determined hand pushed away the soft layers of fabric between her scented skin and his exploring tongue.

"Luc." She sighed. "Oh, Luc...." Her hands began explorations of their own. She let the smooth strands of his dark hair slide between her fingers. Grasping more tightly, she held his head between her palms, but she didn't disturb his motions, which filled her with the tempting promise of even-greater pleasure. She was dazed by the insistent, inflaming pressure of his mouth on her breast and then again on her own mouth. She pushed him back a little, reaching for his shirt.

Working open several buttons, Paula bent her head

to plant a kiss in the hollow of his throat. As she did so she felt his lips in her hair. She reached up to kiss his mouth, her hand still on his chest. His hand reached for hers as though to get her fingers away from his shirt; she evaded his grasp, plunging her hand beneath the cloth, finding his nipples and teasing them with roughly tender circles of her fingertips. He gave a little sigh of pleasure. Again she sought his mouth, running her tongue along his teeth before feeling the piercing invasion of his own tongue. Emboldened, she spread her hands wide, ripping open Luc's shirt, actually sending the last button flying across the little room.

"No!"

It was nearly a scream, and the savage sound of it coming from the lips she'd just kissed so passionately, combined with the abrupt way Luc shoved her aside, shocked Paula into wordlessness. With a frantic motion he grabbed both sides of the shirt and pulled it tightly across his lean stomach. Not soon enough to conceal from Paula a red scar splashed violently across his midriff.

"Luc!"

He turned from her, hiding his eyes, fumbling with the shirt, tucking it in before turning back to her. She stood motionless, unable to speak, though already her shock was giving way to compassion. Luc's eyes were full of anger, pain and apology.

"I'm sorry," he said, his voice breaking. "I'm sorry I scared you. I'm sorry you had to see—"

"But Luc, I don't care...."

"I never should have let things get this far. I shouldn't have brought you here. I'll call you a cab."

Angry that he would dismiss her so summarily, but still full of sympathy, Paula laid her hand on his shoulder. "Please, Luc. We can talk. We can't just pretend nothing happened between us tonight."

Take our fashion tote plus two exciting romance novels...

free

YOURS FREE

Two best-selling Supperromance novels and a fashion tote to carry them in.

The editors of Harlequin would like to share two of their best-loved books with you, and at the same time, send you a fashion tote bag—FREE!

You'll find plenty of compelling reading in your *free* HARLEQUIN SUPERROMANCES. And you'll find plenty of uses for your *free* Harlequin tote. Take it on shopping sprees or out-of-town trips…to the beach or to the gym…on picnics or overnighters. It's perfect for carrying everything from parcels to your Harlequin novels.

The two Harlequin novels and the fashion tote are yours to keep—**FREE**—just for sending us the postpaid card at right.

More good news! You can also look forward to a long love affair with Harlequin *at a terrific savings.* As a subscriber, you'll receive four newly published HARLEQUIN SUPERROMANCES every month, delivered right to your home up to 4 weeks before they're available in stores. Each novel, over 300 pages of exciting reading, is yours for only $2.50. You save over $1.00 per shipment off the retail price.

Begin your rendezvous with romance right now by accepting our two free novels and tote bag. Rush the attached card to us today!

Your rendezvous with romance

Watch as TV talk show Host Russ Marshall betrays
author Sara Daniel's trust and love right on television.

Never Strangers by Lynda Ward

Follow through Dr. Robin Mitchell's struggles to
convince Dr. Paul Wilcox that marriage is the ultimate
expression of love.

Reach the Splendor by Judith Duncan

Free Gifts/Savings Card

Yes, please send me my *free* tote bag and my two *free*
HARLEQUIN SUPERROMANCE novels, *Never Strangers*
and *Reach the Splendor*. Then send me 4 new HARLEQUIN
SUPERROMANCE books every month as soon as they come
off the press. I understand I will be billed only $2.50 per book
(for a total of $10.00—a saving of $1.00 off the retail price).
There are no shipping, handling or other hidden charges. There
is no minimum number of books I must purchase. In fact, I may
cancel this arrangement at any time. The tote bag and novels,
Never Strangers and *Reach the Splendor*, are mine to keep even
if I do not buy any additional books.   134 CIS KAVH

Name_____

Address_____ Apt. No._____

City_____

State_____ Zip_____

Offer limited to one per household and not valid for present
subscribers. Prices subject to change.

Mail to:
HARLEQUIN SUPERROMANCE
2504 W. Southern Avenue,
Tempe, Arizona 85282

LIMITED TIME ONLY
Mail today and get a
MYSTERY BONUS
GIFT

Take it, tote it, swing it, sling it—

You'll just love this stylish tote. Perfect for shopping, traveling and your Harlequin novels. Made of durable cotton canvas with two sturdy straps and snap closure. Topstitched. Bottom-gusseted. Natural color attractively highlighted with Harlequin diamonds in lovely shades. A $6.99 value—it's yours *free* along with two *free* HARLEQUIN SUPERROMANCES.

"What happened tonight?" he asked bitterly, shrugging her hand away. "A few kisses. Poke and grab and sigh, same as always. You'll forget about it tomorrow."

"Stop it! Stop being so sarcastic. I don't care about your—your—"

"You don't have any idea what there is to care or not care about, Paula."

"Then tell me. Give me credit for some intelligence. Talk to me."

"So you can analyze my case, Dr. Emanuel?"

"I'm not a doctor."

"Damn right. You're not my doctor."

"And you're not being reasonable." Her voice was edged with tears, but she fought hard to keep it steady. Luc, too, steadied his voice until it was like a cold, hard knife.

"Look," he said calmly, clinically, "we decided to be friends. We have been friends. I don't need to know your secrets; you don't need to know mine. Let's call it a night, shall we?"

"Damn you! Damn you, Luc LeBlanc!" Paula shouted, finally losing her temper. "Don't you talk to me like that. You pumped me. You got me to tell you about Bret, and now all of a sudden it's 'stay out of my business.' Well, I'll be happy to stay out of your business and your life and your place!"

She stomped toward the door and grabbed the handle, but she'd forgotten it was locked. She flashed back at Luc a look of pure green rage. His eyes were a closed, stony purple blue as he advanced, unlocked the door, opened it and gestured for her to leave.

"And as for your friendship," she hissed in parting, "you can just stick it!"

CHAPTER TEN

THE SCHOOL YEAR ENDED two days later. Paula didn't see Luc again before learning that he'd left for Florida. She wondered why he would choose such a destination during the summer, but she was beyond questioning the obnoxious man and his ridiculous quirks. There was a much hotter place he deserved to be. But her laughter at this weak joke soon turned to tears.

School was over. Everyone was gone, students and teachers alike. Marie took a holiday in Switzerland with her daughters. Several students accompanied their parents on trips to the mountains or the sea. Margaret Johnson went back to Canada, but Paula chose not to.

At first she welcomed the long silent days. She stayed in bed for lazy hours each morning. After lunch she walked or read. She explored the crowded streets of the Lower Town and the spacious vistas of the Upper. The time alone was relaxing, and she thought she could feel the bonds of tension loosen and drift away. She reminded herself that she'd never really had a chance to sit back and calmly consider her life since coming to Belgium. Directly after the fiasco with Bret had come all the strain of settling in a new place and working at a new job. She was proud that she'd had so few problems adjusting. There was only one problem really, but she didn't want to think about Luc.

By the end of the first week the dreams had started. It was Thursday, and for no apparent reason she was exceptionally tired. She went to bed early. It seemed she'd slept for several hours when she woke up shaking and sweating, shivering despite the warmth of the summer night. No matter how hard she tried, she couldn't recall the dream, but the terror of it lingered, preventing her from going back to sleep until well after dawn.

The next night the dream was so vivid that she spent all of Saturday trying to get it off her mind. She had dreamed about Montreal. At first she was working in the municipal agency, but she was having a hard time because her huge office was full of poorly clothed, dirty children, all of whom were calling out to her and trying to grab her skirt. She yelled to them that she couldn't help, but their crying got louder until the door burst open and a man looking very much like Bret stood on the threshold. Instantly all noise stopped. The children filed by the doctor and out the door. Bret came to Paula and embraced her, his arms rough but welcome. She looked down, then, surprised to see she was wearing only her underwear. Bret kissed her passionately. Reluctantly she responded.

They were interrupted by a knock on an outer door. They ignored it, though Paula could hear footsteps, then a knock on the inner door. The door burst open to reveal a police officer holding handcuffs. Paula ran to him, telling him over and over that she was sorry, though not knowing what for. The policeman, his face revealing profound pity, couldn't be dissuaded from duty. He reached for her as though to arrest her. Paula woke up then, her face and pillow soaked with tears.

The next day she more or less succeeded in putting the dream out of her mind. That night she went to a French Canadian movie she discovered was playing in a small theater in the heart of town. It was a comedy, and though it made her a little homesick at times, it lifted her spirits considerably. She managed to stay in a good mood for several relaxing days. Until the night of the third dream.

There was fire everywhere—flame and smoke. She tried to run, but her feet were tarred to the earth by thick black oil. Suddenly a spray of machine-gun fire rent the air, winging off a nearby building in dangerous ricochet. Instinctively she turned her head. And she saw him. He was backed up against a wall facing a line of soldiers armed with rifles poised at their shoulders, ready to shoot. His hands were tied behind his back, and he was blindfolded, but she could see by the determined set of his mouth and the proud carriage of his black head that he was not about to give in—neither to fear nor to the enemy. Paula took a step toward him but was stopped by a piece of green paper thrust in front of her face. It read, "You are the answer to Luc's memo." Puzzled by the meaning of the sentence, she shrugged her shoulders.

Her gesture was taken as a signal to proceed with the execution. The squad let loose with a loud volley of shots that turned into her own screams.

After that dream she gave in. Isolation, loneliness, disappointment over the way things had turned out with Luc, all took their toll. Paula even lost track of time, sleeping far into the day and pacing her apartment at night.

FROM HIS THIRD-STORY BALCONY, Luc stared down across the sparkling blue canal to where several tall, graceful palms threw stark shadows onto the opposite condominium's patio. Four boys, Americans, were down there, carrying on what appeared to be an intense discussion. They were too far away for Luc to make out their words, but the cadence of their speech was English. One of the boys sat on a bicycle; as he talked he wheeled it back and forth a foot or so. The rhythmic motion was almost hypnotizing, Luc thought. Or was it the unrelenting sun that made him feel so dazed? He had forgotten the power of such sun.

Sighing, he ran his fingers through his hair. He was perspiring and wouldn't be able to sit out much longer. He took a draft of the icy drink in his hand, the glass stinging cold against his skin.

He wasn't ready to go back into the room. He didn't have an answer for the men in there, men whose voices he could hear faintly through the sliding-glass doors, over the ever-present hum of the air conditioner. They were speaking Spanish.

As amazing as it seemed—as disappointing as it was— nothing had changed in more than three years. A few of the men and women had disappeared; Luc still knew enough not to ask where. The ones who remained treated him with a deference that made him nervous. But he couldn't hide from himself the tinge of pleasure he'd felt when he realized they still wanted his contribution. *Contribution,* he thought. *That's an understatement.*

Again he sipped at the drink. A woman in a bikini had joined the boys below. She was slender and very tanned, her pale blond hair a tumble down her back. He found American women a little too brash sometimes, though he liked their friendliness to strangers like him. He suspected Canadian women might be a little more reserved with foreigners. Uncomfortably Luc cleared his throat and turned away from the scene below. He looked up and let his eyes be seared by the sun in the blue noon sky until they burned with defensive moisture.

AT TIMES sleep was merciful release, but at other times Paula's thoughts were as sharp as pine needles after a summer's drought. The future seemed as bleak as the past.

It was during one of those dark moments that the phone in her apartment rang for the first time in two weeks. Listlessly she walked toward it, slowly lifting the receiver to her ear.

"Mademoiselle Paula Emanuel?" the operator asked.

"Yes?"

"Hold the line for a transatlantic call, please."

"Transatlantic?" She had a wild stab of hope. Luc was in Florida. Would he really call all the way from there to apologize? A smile teased the corners of her mouth.

"Is that you, Paula?" Even if the man hadn't been speaking English, she'd have known from the voice alone that it wasn't Luc. This was the smooth voice of a man used to cajoling people into talking about their deepest secrets. The persuasive, manipulative voice she'd sincerely hoped never to hear again.

"Bret."

"Don't hang up, darling. Please don't. I had to cancel an appointment to call you, and I won't let you hang up until you've heard me out. Okay?"

She didn't answer; he didn't care, apparently. He went right on talking.

"Listen, honey, I waited a long time for you to respond to my letter, and I thought your answer was a little cold. I mean, I didn't exactly need the travelogue of Brussels, you know? But still, you did write—and I figure that's a start."

"A start toward what Bret? It was only a note. I didn't expect you to call." *I didn't want you to call. I don't want you to call.*

"Honey, I wasn't kidding about Alicia. She's gone for good. I want you back here. Let bygones be bygones. The term's over at your school, and it would be easy for me to send someone else for the fall."

"No. Bret—"

"Don't kid me, sweetheart. You don't really want to work over there in Timbuktu. I know I've been a son of a bitch, but I'll make it up to you. Come back. I'll take you sailing down south. The Caribbean, Florida—"

"No."

"Honey, don't be stubborn. Come back, or I'll come after you. In fact, I was thinking of booking a flight to Brussels for next—"

Paula couldn't stand it anymore. She didn't slam the phone down; she just let it fall very gently into the cradle. She held her hot face in her cool hands and let the tears come. After five minutes the phone rang again. And five minutes after that. And again and again for longer than an hour. Finally it stopped. But Paula had already gone to bed.

Futilely she sought sleep. She'd let all the clocks in the house stop. She didn't know what time it was, except that it was dark. She tossed and turned for a little while, then got up, intending to take a drink in the hope that it would help her sleep. It wasn't a solution she had resorted to before, but she was more upset than she'd been at any other time in the past two miserable weeks. In the kitchen she checked her supplies. There was one bottle of white wine; a sweet local gin called *péquet* and a new, unopened bottle of apricot schnapps, a year-end gift from Karel's father. With shaking fingers she removed the cap and sniffed the clear liquid. The aroma was strong but not unpleasant, fruity and inviting.

The schnapps was much stronger than she'd expected. The liquid burned her throat all the way down, followed by soothing warmth. She carried the brimming glass to her bedroom. Sitting on the edge of her bed and sipping slowly, she hoped that the alcohol would bring the sleep she was desperate to have. *If Bret comes here....* Paula didn't want to finish the thought. He had cast her off, and now he was pursuing her. He had got her this job, and now he was taking it away. There was nothing left but to run again. Would it never stop? Tears came, but no sleep.

The schnapps had another, stranger effect. She felt a new restlessness come over her. Anxiety made her heart beat wildly, her stomach churn, her throat constrict. A wave of dizziness overtook her. The hot air in the little bedroom was suddenly stifling, and she knew she had to get outside.

Hastily she put on a sleeveless sweat shirt and jeans. She ran a brush through her tousled curls, but she didn't bother to look in the mirror. Nor did she take her purse, remembering only to shove her wallet and keys into her pocket.

In a daze she raced out of the elevator and through the building's front door, which slammed shut behind her. It was a hot night, but the air was cool on Paula's flushed face as she ran down the front walk, turning at random when she reached the end of it. She was vaguely conscious of a bell ringing somewhere; automatically she counted the strokes, finding they stopped at ten. She avoided being out alone late as a rule, but tonight she just didn't care.

Waving rather frantically, she hailed a passing cab and asked to be taken to the neighborhood of Le Berceau, knowing there was a large park nearby. It wasn't at all smart to wander there at night, but it was better than the alternative, aimless wandering in the streets.

The cabbie let her out at the park gates, and she sighed with relief to see them still unlocked. Here and there pools of light punctuated the darkness. A coolness seemed to waft toward her from the dark green boughs of illuminated trees. To her surprise, she discovered a group of people watching a performance on a small wooden stage set up beneath a large tree. Standing in the darkness at the edge of the area lit only by a stage light, she watched.

The little troupe included three mimes and four musicians. All were dressed in bright silk costumes belonging to the characters of the comedia dell'arte, a sixteenth- and seventeenth-century form of Italo-French comedy. Staring hard at the group, she blinked, then blinked again. Maybe her tired brain was playing tricks on her, but she could swear Luc was sitting on the stage, his recorder cradled in his hands as he joined in musical accompaniment to the antics of the three mimes.

The three were dressed as Pierrot, Harlequin and Columbine. Though the scene conveyed a deep sense of unreality to Paula as she watched from the shadows, she understood that the two male figures were vying for the favors of Columbine, whose hair, undoubtedly the actress's own, shone like a bright swath of gold. She was very young with a lithe but full figure clearly outlined beneath the royal-blue-and-crimson silk of her costume. She flaunted her beauty shamelessly before her rival suitors, each of whom tried to outdo the other in tricks to capture and hold her attention.

Paula gazed in fascination at the scene. Pierrot was sad, dressed all in white except for black buttons, belt and skullcap. His face was as white as his costume, but beneath his black-outlined eye a red tear was painted in the shape of a heart. When wooing he was ardent; when spurned, patient. Crumpling to the floor at Columbine's final rejection, he received a kick from her dainty, blue-satin-shod foot, at which there was a healthy round of boos from the audience.

Harlequin was a different sort of lover altogether.

Dressed in diamond-shaped patches, he was dapper, confident, cocky and bold. For him Columbine had whispered secrets that resulted in his attempting a kiss, from which she coyly turned away—but not very far.

Unwilling to give in to defeat, Pierrot jumped up and began to tussle with Harlequin, their struggle made dramatic by the accompanying music. Both men then lunged for the teasing Columbine, who evaded their embraces with maidenly trickery. Whether or not the next bit of stage action had been improvised, Paula couldn't tell, but to avoid her two suitors the winsome Columbine fairly threw herself into the lap of Luc LeBlanc, preventing further recorder playing for the time being. She gave him a modest kiss on the cheek. Luc, possibly as part of the rehearsed plot, possibly not, jumped up from his seat, grabbed the young woman and kissed her with theatrical passion. For a split second the woman responded to that kiss; Paula could tell. Then Columbine feigned shock. Her painted lips formed a naughty little ''oh'' as she gestured her surprise to the audience.

Clearly, the people gathered on the grass found this all charmingly funny. They laughed. They applauded. They sent catcalls into the fresh night air. Everybody thought the festive little performance most amusing. Everybody but Paula.

In the moment when she'd seen Luc grab the actress, she had also realized his sexual hunger was an act. Still, his grip on the woman's shoulder was forceful, wrinkling the crimson silk of her blouse. Paula noticed his muscles beneath the purple fabric of the close-fitting pantaloons. As he lowered his head to claim the commanding kiss, a lock of black hair shielded his indigo eyes, but the strong jaw, the sculpted cheek were clearly visible. The sight of him forced Paula to realize she'd been blind to find him less than strikingly handsome. He was more than a teacher, a journalist and a musician. He was simply and solely a man. Jealousy filled her. A jealousy so strong that she gasped to feel the unexpected sting.

Yet it wasn't his handsomeness that disturbed her so, it was that unbridled sexuality, devastating even in imitation. As the mimes left the stage and the musicians struck up a new tune, she watched Luc through the eyes of desire. Silently moving closer to the stage, but keeping behind the margin of light, she watched the hands that had caressed her so fleetingly. She imagined how they might feel should they seek and find the most hidden recesses of her body. She watched his lips, supple on his instrument, and remembered them on her breast. *Oh, Luc. Oh Luc, damn you!*

There was no denying she wanted him, that she'd wanted him for a good long time. She couldn't have him. He was a stubborn man and a proud one. She had made him angry too many times. And he'd made her angry, too. She leaned a little closer. Even if she was to apologize, the most she could hope for would be his agreement to resume their friendship. That was the last thing she wanted. Wistfully she looked at him, intending to turn and leave.

In the nick of time, he, too, looked up and saw her. The minute his eyes met hers, she felt all the hopeless, lonely agony of the past two weeks sweep over her again. With stunning rapidity the images of the ugly dreams came back, the anxiety, the memory of Bret's oily smoothness. She didn't want Luc to see any of that agony. He kept secrets from her; she had no intention of giving him even a hint of the state of her private life—not anymore.

She turned and ran, her steps making slight impressions on the damp grass of the dark park. Tears flew back into her disheveled hair. Without knowing where she ran—except away from Luc—she kept going, not noticing that the music following her was soon diminished by the departure of one of its players.

She was not conscious of distance, direction nor the passage of time. All she knew was that when she looked up finally, a building's dark hulk loomed above. At the exact moment when she saw where she was, footsteps sounded, much too close. Paula had slowed, but now she tried desperately to pick up speed. Too late. A hand came down heavily on her shoulder.

"All right," he said, "this is as far as you're going to run."

CHAPTER ELEVEN

BEFORE SHE HAD TIME to utter a single word, Luc's lips were on hers, devouring her with such hunger that she had to hold her tear-choked breath. His hands on her bare arms were hot with heat more intense than the sultry night's. The musky scent of him filled her nostrils and sent dizzying sensations through her body.

He had the advantage of having taken her at least a little by surprise, and he drove home that advantage and others through his determination and his thirst for the moist kisses she couldn't refuse. His hands moved to her head, grabbing her hair in handfuls, though he didn't hurt her. Her own hands pushed weakly at his shoulders before she gave in entirely to the flame that seared the whole of her. There was no power in her to push him away when every part of her only wanted him nearer.

But when he pulled away, she saw that his passion hadn't wiped away anger.

"What the hell are you doing in this neighborhood?" he demanded to know. "Don't you know what time it is? Why are you roaming the streets? Don't you have any regard for your own safety? How can you be so foolish?"

His voice was gruff, not so very different from the last time she'd heard it, the time he'd as much as thrown her out. She felt something in her give way. Blackness descended, receded, threatened again. The anxiety that had attacked her earlier returned with renewed force. *Let it come,* she thought to herself. *I don't care—*

"Paula—what's the matter?" Luc's voice was still gruff, but the arm that encircled her shoulder and steadied her felt like a lifeline, and she leaned against him. His hand brushed her cheeks gently, smoothing the tears from beneath one eye, then the other. "Paula?" he repeated, unwilling or unable to hide his concern.

For a minute she simply leaned against him, then slowly she felt her strength come back. He led her gently toward a bench beneath a streetlamp in front of the school; she had been drawn to Le Berceau. In that weak light his eyes were dark and unfathomable as he searched her face. With his back to the light, he could see her more clearly than she could see him. Obviously her appearance disturbed him.

"What's happened to you?" he asked, softness replacing his angry tone. "You look distraught, as though you hadn't slept in days. Are you ill?"

She shrugged.

"Paula, I refuse to let you go home alone. My place is much closer. I'm going to take you there. Can you walk?"

She could, but she didn't want to say yes, didn't want to go back to the scene of their argument. But when he stood and helped her up, she was steady on her feet. She took a deep breath and felt the night air enter her lungs with reviving coolness. For the first time since the scene at the park, she took a good look at Luc.

She should have found his appearance ridiculous. He had clearly been running very fast, even for him. His chest still rose and fell. He was perspiring. In his haste he had apparently begun to relinquish his silken costume, then given up on the idea. The purple pantaloons remained, but the white blouson with its wide sleeves was torn open, revealing a black T-shirt. Into the waistband of the trousers he had tucked a jesterlike cap, and at the sight of it Paula glanced up at the hair standing out a little from his head. He lifted a hand to smooth it, that motion alone marring his sudden stillness.

She stared at him. She felt again the strange energy that seemed always to be vibrating through him; it could have been coursing through her, too. This man was beautiful, she realized, a strong, handsome, stubborn, totally self-reliant man, a man of deep secrets and unspoken pride. Paula didn't admit to a growing feeling for him. But she had often misjudged him, and she would never do so again.

"I know," he said, watching her carefully. "You'd be ashamed to walk the streets with me."

"Oh, Luc! You idiot!" she cried, laughing and crying simultaneously, reaching for him. He didn't resist, taking her swiftly into his arms. She melted into the comfort of his embrace. He was so warm, so solid, so real. And she was so glad he was back.

"What do you say? Will you come back to my place? I have a very nice bottle of wine. . . ."

"All right. You can tell me about Florida," she said lightly.

"I have nothing to say about Florida," he said in a tone she took to be dismissive, though it could have been interpreted any number of ways. "You talk. You tell me what's been going on that's made you look as miserable as you do."

"Thanks a lot." She pouted with mock sarcasm. Actually she needed someone to talk to about Bret, and once she began her tale she didn't stop until the whole story was told, by which time they'd reached Luc's.

"He's exploited you, threatened you, pushed you out and now he expects to come here to rescue you?" Luc's voice was full of barely controlled rage. "You are *not* going to allow it, do you understand? You cannot possibly have so little self-respect."

"It's not a question of self-respect."

"It is! Paula, don't you understand? The man has nothing on you. You're the one who's in a position to do him harm—deserved harm, by the way. I know you don't want that. But you must stand up for yourself. You must—"

"Luc, please. I've tried. Don't think I'm not ashamed of myself. I am. I never should have started with him in the first place."

"That's immaterial. Your entire past with him is immaterial. You have got to tell him to leave you alone. He has no power over your career anymore. He can threaten you all he wants, but he can't alter the fact that the board approved your contract for next year. Paula, call him. Tell him you've had enough. Call him, or we can no longer be friends." He turned from her then, but she wouldn't be manipulated.

"You can't threaten me, Luc. You can't make me do something I don't want to do."

"Oh? Is that so?" He turned back to her, his voice cold, his eyes shuttered, but there was a low violet light shining there, the light not of anger but almost of mischief. "So I can't tell you what to do. Why is that?"

"Because—"

"Because," he interrupted, coming very close, lifting her chin with a finger and staring deep into the green of her eyes, "because I wouldn't even try, despite my haranguing. Because I respect you too much. Because I believe you wouldn't let me push you around. I can't threaten you, Paula, because I care about you. He doesn't. He never will. He's a fool, and you're much stronger than him. He'll back off if you stand up to him."

"Please, Luc, don't use your teacherly tactics on me. I've seen you persuade people before."

"Only to help them do what I knew they wanted to do all along. A technique of your own profession, I believe...."

He was right.

Paula called Montreal. She got Bret Graham out of the shower, but she wouldn't let him call back. She told him in a cold, clear, 100 percent effective voice that he was never to call her again, or to write to her, either. She told him her business with his agency was to be conducted without his personal intervention, in line with their original agreement. And she told him she never expected to see him again.

When the conversation was over, she was amazed she'd been strong enough to stick up for herself. Amazed, too, that the direct approach had worked. Suddenly the problem of Bret was solved.

"I told you to trust me," Luc said, coming from his bedroom at her announcement that the call was over. He kissed her lightly on the cheek, a brief congratulatory peck, but when she raised her eyes to his she was startled to see a look of deep hunger. "Paula," he whispered huskily. "Paula, I missed you...."

His hands cupped her face, his thumbs drawing lazy circles on her cheeks. Instinctively she leaned toward him until her thighs met the hard planes of his. She ran her hands along the tensed muscles of his upper back and felt him relax beneath her fingertips. But he tensed once more when her hands continued the motion, caressing his waist before, with a quick motion, grabbing the firm curves of his derriere, temptingly hard beneath the soft, worn denim of his jeans. He drew in a sharp breath of pleasure and surprise. And in response she began to slowly knead his flesh.

"Paula," he tried to say again and again, but every time his lips parted she thrust her tongue into his sensuous mouth. The hands that had caressed her face now descended, one hand reaching for her slender waist, the other for the deep vee of her sweat shirt.

His fingers were cool against the heat of her skin, but she didn't recoil. In fact, the contrast excited her, and she shivered with pure pleasure. Feeling her quiver, Luc made as if to withdraw his hand. She didn't let him. She caught his wrist, gently forcing him to press his fingers into her breast. He needed little prompting. Soon his avid touch wreaked havoc with her senses as he brought her to a hardened state of longing.

"Luc," she murmured.

"Paula, what is it? What do you want that I can give?" His voice was a teasing, rasping heated breeze at her ear, the spiced breeze of the tropics promising the pleasures of as yet untasted fruit.

"Luc."

With relentless desire his mouth took kiss after kiss, but he was unable to resist kissing her hair, as well, her face, the swelling curves his fingers discovered but soon relinquished to his mouth. She took what he offered as sensuality swept reason away. She felt herself falling into an abyss of distracting pleasure, a whirling vortex that pulled her with a familiar, frightening power.

"Luc," she cried, trying to make her voice firm, but the short syllable ended in a quavering sigh that Luc answered with the ministrations of his tongue, and swirling pleasure claimed her again.

He had heard that note in her voice, though, and raising his dark head, he clasped her so tightly she could feel his arms tremble with tense energy. "You are about to tell me," he breathed into her hair, "that if I am to expect your trust, I have to trust you, too. Right?"

She pulled away from him. In his eyes she again saw stubborn, lonely pride, and shame, too. Once he had told her there was shame in her eyes.

"Luc," she said, suddenly filled with a compassion so strong that she had to fight tears, "let's have some of that wine you promised. Then let's talk. You can tell me about Florida."

"Forget Florida," he said tonelessly, rising to get the wine. While he was in the kitchen, Paula's eyes strayed to where the photos of the blond woman had been. She remembered how he'd put those pictures away, as though he'd buried her before Paula's eyes. A shiver passed through her.

Luc returned with two glasses and an open bottle. In the soft light of the room's charmingly Bohemian lamps, the wine was a golden stream that he directed into etched-crystal glasses. He handed Paula one, and she couldn't help but notice that his fingers shook slightly. She took the glass and gestured for him to sit beside her on the couch. When he did, she reached up and stroked his cheek with a gentle hand. "Luc," she said softly, "the time has come."

She saw by the tightening of his jaw that he knew exactly what she meant. She feared a return of the anger that had driven her from him the last time she'd tried to get him to talk about his past, but she wasn't going to give up. She knew because of her profession, but even more because of her caring, that Luc LeBlanc had held things bottled up inside himself for a long, long time. "To truth," she said, lifting her glass.

He stared at her for what seemed an eternity, during which she held her breath. His eyes were darkly secretive, his mouth grim. He looked at her, then away. Finally, sighing and turning back, he said, "All right. To truth." He clinked his glass against hers, then drained it in several gulps, refilling it before he went on.

"Here—for what it's worth—is the truth. Plain and to the point. As you and everyone else know, I haven't always been a teacher. Three and a half years ago I was a reporter, a foreign correspondent, you might say. I was injured in the line of duty. Severely. I am a journalist, and like others of my kind I abhor riddles. The plain fact is I'm scarred. I am certainly sterile and possibly impotent, though my doctors assure me there's no physical reason for the latter...."

His voice was so straightforward, so level, that Paula feared for him. She knew from long experience that people who talked about severe traumas in toneless voices were signaling a need for help that they might not even recognize they had. Her heart went out to him, but she avoided any emotional display. After a lengthy pause he went on.

"At the time of this—this accident," he said, putting on the word a barely perceptible accent of bitterness, "I was in love with the woman whose picture you saw here last time. She wasn't in love with me. For years we'd played cat and mouse with each other. Sometimes she loved me to distraction, and I tired of her. Sometimes it was clearly the other way around. But when I got hurt she stayed at my side with a devotion that neither of us had ever guessed she was capable of." He turned his head away, and Paula saw him swallow before he took a deep breath and went on steadily.

"As much as we wanted to be together—as much as I needed her—we agreed that she shouldn't pass up an assignment she'd been waiting for pretty much since she'd begun her career. She wanted to go to the Middle East, and she finally got there. She was killed within ten days."

His sorrow was so palpable that Paula was struck dumb. He went on, his voice wavering only a little. "I've had more than three years to come to grips with these things, but sometimes—" He turned away again, and when he turned back he changed the subject.

"Paula, any woman who was foolish enough to get involved with me now would have to bear the burden of proving to me either that I'm still a man or that I'll never be one again. Alone I can bear the thought of that. A person pays the price of his courage. Though I've been told my body is healed, I may never be able to believe my mind is. I'm too considerate a man to impose on a woman the onerous task of solving this puzzle." A sarcastic smile curled his mouth, but his eyes were intense and shining.

"Too considerate?" she asked levelly, "or too cowardly?"

There was a moment of absolute quiet. If there was a sound in any other apartment, it didn't penetrate these walls. If there was laughter or singing or any other sign of life in the busy little culs-de-sac of Les Marolles, nothing reached this room. There wasn't even the sound of a breath until Luc drew his and answered. "Cowardly."

She couldn't look into his eyes, nor could she let him see the wild, hot tears in hers. She whispered, "Luc," and reached for his hand, relieved when he let her take it. "Luc, I've watched you from the first night I came to the school. You knew I used to watch, because you used to catch me at it...."

She heard the low rich sound of his laughter and was emboldened to look at him. He sat as proudly erect as usual, but his eyes studied the rug a little distance ahead of him.

"I've heard you coax music out of wood and air. I've seen you run like the wind. I've seen you inflame students who had never had an exciting idea before they started to listen to you. Why, you even taught Villette to write. That's not just an accomplishment, it's a miracle!"

Again he laughed, though his mouth remained grim, and deep sadness clouded his eyes.

"You speak of impotence, of powerlessness. Luc, you have no right. You're talking about psychological impotence, mental powerlessness. That has nothing to do with you. You're not powerless. Your students practically adore you. Marie Légère would do anything for you. Even the cleaning staff make an extra effort—"

"And what about you, Paula?" he ground out, bitter self-contempt choking him. "What does our *petite Canadienne* think of the oh-so-powerful writing teacher?"

"Luc," she said. "Luc, I love you."

His eyes flashed violet in defensive disbelief. She saw it, saw his shattering doubt, but she wasn't about to give in to timidness. She had more to say. "Luc, you affect everyone whose life you touch—with your ideas, your energy, your dedication. You have the power to make me love you, but not only that. For the first time in my life I can love without feeling like a fool. You don't have to love me back. Don't misunderstand—"

"But I—"

"Be quiet, Luc. Just be quiet." Gently she leaned toward him and kissed his cheek. Then as slowly, as patiently as possible, she loosened the buttons of his cotton shirt. He remained perfectly still as she undid the collar and planted a kiss at the hollow of his throat. She could feel his pulse racing frantically, but he said nothing, and she continued.

With caring, with a love more intense than the passion growing in her, she released each button, always fearing he would stay her hand, and knowing she must stop if he wanted it. When she opened the last button and pulled the shirt out from his jeans, she saw the redness she'd seen before. She was neither shocked nor repulsed, but she felt Luc draw in his breath in a spasm.

"Let me..." she whispered, taking his glass from his hand and putting it aside. He allowed her to remove his belt and finally his jeans and what he wore beneath, assisting her then with trembling motions that were part fear, part desire.

Paula saw nothing that shocked her. It was true he was scarred, but as she'd half expected, the scar on his midriff was the worst of it. He was unquestionably still a man in every respect, and with love, with an almost laughing elation, she set out to prove it to Luc. She touched him with a teasing lightness at first, and he was perfectly silent, perfectly still beneath her exploring fingers.

But when her touch grew so intimate that he couldn't keep himself from arching toward her hand, and when her bold fingers began to be followed in their fiery path by her tongue, Luc was no longer content to take without giving. His sure hands seized the soft fabric of her sweat shirt, pulling it up, urging it over her head while his own head was a dark, tantalizing presence, his kisses grazing her breasts.

He found the zipper of her jeans, impatient but not fumbling in undoing the fastening. He helped her out of jeans and panties, tossing them aside before drawing his hand up in a line of flame from her knee to the inner curve of her thigh. Then his hand was a warm, intimate weight against her, still for a moment before his fingers began to tease her in a way she thought would rob her of all power to pleasure him, too.

But though a dizzying, delicious sensation shot through her, Paula ran her fingers along his smooth, well-muscled thighs. Turning toward her instinctively at this tempting touch, he clasped her head, his fingers so gently but so insistently holding her scalp. His lips were only a breath removed from hers. His eyes burned with such intensity that it was an act of courage just to stare back at him. In his gaze she saw doubt give way to trust, resistance give way to compliance, lust give way to what she dared not call love. And then Luc's eyes closed and his lips took hers with breath-stealing power.

He didn't relinquish her lips as he manipulated their bodies so that she lay beneath him, his body completely covering hers, but light and energetic over her. She reached up to knead his firm, rounded buttocks, to slide her hands along his back, now shining, she imagined, with the perspiration she could feel on his hot skin. She feathered her hands across his shoulders. And then, as his tongue found even deeper, more-secret recesses of her mouth, Paula grasped the dark springiness of his hair.

She could feel the flame of his contact burn along the length of her. And after a very short while she could feel the effect her nearness was having on Luc. In that shared moment her hunger swamped even her joy, driving her to whisper, "Luc? Luc. . . ."

"Paula," he breathed in answer to her invitation. Deftly he shifted, giving her room to part her legs. Exhaling a sigh that trembled with an emotion Paula couldn't name, Luc thrust his full power into her, and she received his gift ecstatically, circling his waist with her legs.

She knew what that act of courage had cost him, and she also knew that his pleasure was as deep and real as her own. His sighs, his moans of hunger and fulfillment mingled with hers in the air of the little room. As mind-

ful of her delight, Luc brought her carefully toward
and away from the brink of ecstasy, teasing her until
she thought she would explode from pure sensation,
then easing away until she moved her body in ways
that made him know she wanted more. They continued
until there was nowhere else either could go on the
road to rapture. Together, clinging in pleasure and intimacy, they cried out their triumph over all that had
kept them—might keep them—apart.

A LITTLE WHILE LATER Paula lay in the crook of Luc's
arm. Covered with a light blanket but still on the
couch, both were silent, sipping more of the wine Luc
had poured for them. His hand played idly in her
curls, and if she glanced up Paula could just see his
chin, as stubborn and strong as ever, and his mouth
that had about it a softness she'd never seen before.
Paula felt a happiness beyond words. A long while
later Luc finally spoke. "You still haven't told me
what you were doing roaming the streets. . . ."

"I was upset about Bret's call, as I told you. And
though I hate to admit it, I guess the loneliness was beginning to get to me."

"Ah, yes," Luc said with meaning. "Loneliness."

"You still haven't told me what you were doing in
Florida," Paula said with fake casualness.

"Vacationing."

"In the middle of summer? Come on."

"Paula." He urged her to sit up so that he could
look at her. Yet the sight of her face seemed to rob him
of words for a moment. He reached out, drawing a
finger along the line of her cheek. "Beautiful Paula,
how many miracles do you hope to accomplish?"

"What?" she asked, understanding the feeling behind the words but not the words themselves.

"The day will come when some of your many ques-

tions will be answered. Unfortunately, you may not—"
He didn't finish. "Paula, I'm going to call you a cab.
I'm going to take you home. Tomorrow we'll talk. We
can be together all day. What do you say?"

She was tired with a good tiredness and not unwilling
to get home. Despite the intimacy she and Luc had
shared, she felt shy about suggesting they spend the
night together.

He called the taxi. They dressed, and he went with her
all the way to her place and had the driver wait until
he'd walked her up to her apartment. At her door he
took her in his arms for an impulsively passionate kiss,
and before he released her he whispered, "Be ready
tomorrow. I'll be here at ten."

She moved to close the door, but her eyes stayed
glued to him as he walked to the elevator. Before the
elevator doors closed, he turned and glanced at her one
more time. His eyes were shuttered, hiding his feelings,
but his lips hadn't regained their grim tightness.

As Paula got ready for bed she still glowed with a
happiness that nothing seemed capable of dampening—
not even the thought that Luc had told her very little
about his past, or about his future, either. What *had* he
been doing in Florida?

When she thought about his sexual fears and how she
had helped him begin to overcome them, she felt triumphant. But a doubt niggled at her. Perhaps impotence
wasn't his deepest fear. He wasn't a man to give up his
secrets willingly. Had they solved one problem only to
be faced by another too great to solve?

CHAPTER TWELVE

THOUGH SHE SHOWERED AND DRESSED quickly the next morning—she'd slept soundly until after nine—Paula didn't accomplish the task easily. She changed her mind about what to wear three times and her hairstyle twice.

When Luc arrived, she saw at once that he had also taken special care. His lightweight beige trousers emphasized his physique. He wore a white knit shirt and sandals that looked smartly continental. His hair was dark and shining, as always. Excitement fluttered inside her.

"Better," he declared.

"Better?"

"You look better this morning. It's a good thing I rescued you when I did. I shouldn't have waited until after the concert."

"What?" Paula asked, not understanding exactly what he was getting at. She motioned him farther into her apartment, but he wouldn't take a chair.

"I arrived back from Miami yesterday afternoon. I called several times before the concert, but you didn't answer. Finally I just had to leave for the park. I felt bad about how I'd acted before I left. I—"

"Forget it, Luc," she said, genuinely forgiving any wrong he might have done her. He seemed not to hear her.

"I should have called or written. I should have known that staying here alone in Brussels wasn't going to be good for you. . . ."

It didn't surprise her at all that he had guessed she'd be there alone, though she was sure she hadn't told him. He simply couldn't mind his own business, but for once she welcomed the invasion of her privacy.

"You know," he continued, "you wouldn't have been the first teacher to have been driven mad by Le Berceau. The old place has done in a few people in its time." He smiled wryly, but she sensed an undercurrent of seriousness.

"Would you prefer to teach somewhere else?" she asked. He was so dedicated that she had assumed he loved the school, but perhaps she was wrong.

"Prefer to teach somewhere else?" he repeated, a look in his eye that defied analysis. "No. I would prefer to walk out into this most amazing summer day. I would prefer to show you a little of Brussels. I know this city fairly well, though not, of course, as a native Bruxellois knows it. I thought maybe you'd like to have breakfast in the park?"

"Great idea!" Paula got her purse and slipped it under her arm as she led the way to the door. Luc followed, his hand at her shoulder. From the place where his fingers lay, a warm sensation spread through her. For the first time in longer than she could remember, she was looking forward to the coming hours with enthusiasm.

They walked through the colorful streets of Paula's neighborhood. Though it wasn't close to Luc's and was somewhat newer, it too had a nearby area of lush greenery. Bordering on the park was a row of narrow shops and a café whose entire front wall slid aside to allow small white tables to spill onto a flagstone patio facing the park. "How's this?" Luc asked, motioning her to a seat and accepting her nod with one of his rare heartwarming smiles.

They drank café au lait, and Paula watched as Luc

managed the separate pitchers of hot milk and coffee. Confidently he poured from both at once in the Parisian manner. When he offered her the cup of steaming creamy liquid, Paula refused. She reached for the pitchers and handled them as skillfully as he.

"Did you learn that in Paris?" Luc asked.

"No," she said with a teasing smile. "I learned it in Montreal."

"What's it like there?"

"Like itself!" Paula laughed, but she felt a twinge of homesickness. Vivid images of the faraway city flashed through her mind, and she tried to convey something of its tough beauty to Luc. "For starters, it's an island."

"Some of the best cities are built on islands," Luc said. The comment suggested he was referring to another place altogether, but Paula knew he meant for her to go on.

"There's a mountain in the middle of it, too—sort of. You'd love it. Every morning that it's not too cold, the mountain is just crawling with joggers. A lot of people there like to run before work, too."

"How do you know I run before work?"

The question caught her completely unawares, but it took her only an instant to realize what she'd revealed. Actually her blush revealed the most.

"You've been spying on me!" His teasing laughter seemed as sunny as the caressing warmth of the morning.

"It serves you right," she said. "You're a first-rate spy yourself!"

He knew she was kidding. He loved the creases at the corners of her eyes, the laugh lines that framed her mouth. *I'm going to keep you smiling, Miss Emanuel,* he thought, *for as long as I can.* Aloud he said, "Okay, what else does Montreal have?"

"Well, it has wonderful restaurants—everything from French cafés to Jewish delis, including the second-best bagels in the world."

"Second best?"

"After New York."

"You Canadians really aren't very boastful, are you?" he said affectionately.

A little unnerved by the tone of his voice, Paula went on awkwardly, "Montreal has some of the best clothing shops in the world, and we have a lovely old quarter that most North Americans think of as ancient. They flock to see it, especially in summer. Compared to Europe, though, I guess every part of Montreal is pretty young, although the streets of Vieux Montréal sometimes remind me of Paris."

"Is Quebec like France? I've never been there," Luc commented.

"Not much, if you ask me. As I said, it's like itself, like Canada, in my opinion. But of course not everyone is willing to call Quebec a part of Canada."

"You aren't a separatist?"

"No, though I think I understand some of the changes they want. But I'm Canadian. I consider Canada my country, just as you no doubt consider Belgium yours."

"I live in Belgium, it's true," Luc said, "and I was born here. But I'd never call myself Belgian. I am Liègeois. *C'est tout.*"

"But Liège is only a city. I wouldn't call myself Montréaloise!"

"Not only a city, Paula," Luc began. Prideful passion stole into his voice. *He's going to get teacherly again,* Paula thought, hiding her affectionately mocking smile behind a lace-edged linen napkin. She settled back in her seat, listening.

"Liège is both a province and a city, but it's the city

I'm talking about," Luc went on. "It isn't hard to understand how people might consider their city the center of the world—take Venice, for instance."

"But that was ages ago!"

"Liège celebrated its one-thousandth birthday in 1980. When it was founded, it too was built on islands and lagoons, of the Meuse River. Unlike Venice, however, it was famous not for commerce, but for industry, and still is to this day."

A waitress interrupted them momentarily, setting down a plate of warm rolls and a dish of strawberries and grapes.

"Industry?" Paula prompted.

"In the twelfth century coal was discovered near the city, and Liège has been a mining and steelworking town ever since. There are those who feel it's ugly. Some call it 'the burning city.' "

"But you don't consider it ugly?"

"Like any responsible person, I hate the desecration of the landscape caused by mining. And it's a terrible job. But there is, for me, a grim beauty in Liège, a quality I've never seen elsewhere. All that is good is not beautiful, and what is evil doesn't necessarily repel the eye. It would be an easier world to live in if that were so."

He became so quiet that Paula hesitated to speak. She wondered what other grimly beautiful landscapes he might have seen. The images of her fiery dream came back. She shivered, but he didn't see. His dark head was lowered, a lock of hair across his brow. *So black,* she thought, *like jet.*

"Coalheads," he commented, looking up into her eyes and startling her, because she thought he'd read her mind.

"What?"

"Coalheads, that's the nickname for people from Liège."

"Why?"

"Because of the mining, I guess. But we are hot-heads, too." He had interrupted his flow of French to use the English term. "Hothead—is that the right word?"

"It sure is!" Paula answered in English, thinking back to his outburst at the last staff meeting of the year. He had lost his temper over an issue Paula had known he'd been stewing about all term. Only the smooth-talking Marie had kept the other staff from ejecting him. "Hothead is exactly the word!"

He ignored her teasing, continuing matter-of-factly. "Of course, you, who know only Marie, Josef and me, have no way of knowing how stubborn and excitable the average Liègeois can be. We are accused of being the most volatile and passionate people in Belgium."

"You don't say?"

"But we have our redeeming qualities, as well." He gave her a sudden, exceptionally warm smile.

"I guess you do," she answered a little breathlessly. She was finding it very difficult to remember that she once thought he was impossible to get along with.

"Let me show you something," Luc said, reaching into his pocket for a key ring; an object hanging from it caught the bright sunlight. As he pulled his leg back beneath the table, his knee brushed Paula's thigh. The sudden contact sent a shiver of desire through her, and her hand trembled, nearly upsetting her cup. Luc saw and responded with a passionate look. Reaching across, he covered her hand with his. His other hand dangled before her eyes a perfectly executed charm in the shape of a pineapple not an inch long. The crystal facets sent splinters of light shooting in every direction.

"What is it?" Paula asked. Clearly the lovely pineapple had some sentimental or symbolic significance.

"The pineapple represents Liège," Luc explained.

Ever the teacher despite himself, Paula reflected, realizing he was pleased by her curiosity.

"If you come to my city, you'll see the pineapple motif everywhere. It represents the solidarity of a people who have been loyal to Liège for fifty generations. It's made of crystal, because that's another thing Liège is famous for."

"Can I look at it?" Paula held out her palm. Luc took the delicate object off the chain and passed it to her. It looked like a piece of the clearest ice, but as her fingers touched it she could feel it was warm from the heat of his hand.

DURING THE NEXT FEW WEEKS Luc took her everywhere. Sometimes she noticed he was melancholy and withdrawn, his mind clearly far away, his thoughts imprisoned in a territory he wouldn't let her enter. But often, perhaps because he was free from the pressures of teaching, he seemed an entirely different man. It occurred to her that she might have something to do with the fact that he seemed happy and relaxed, but she pushed the thought to the back of her mind. She didn't want these brief weeks to be a time of false hope about the future, not when their pasts had disillusioned them. The future had a way of becoming the past, and she wanted a purely present joy.

Still, Paula had to admit that while Luc had once seemed obstinate, he now appeared self-confidently assertive. She had once considered him maudlin and self-pitying; now she thought him sensitive. Even his voice, which conscience told her she had once called a hiss, filled her with warmth.

"I know you've explored the city yourself," he said to her one day as they finished lunch in one of the fine restaurants near the Grand'Place. "But if you like I can point out some things you may have missed.''

Full from the delicious *flamiche*, a pie of cheese and leeks, she welcomed the prospect of a walk. Without hesitation she followed him into the narrow street and toward the magnificent square itself. Though it had rained that morning, it was sunny now. The tall, lean, ornate buildings glinted gold in the sun.

''There,'' Luc said, ''is the Hôtel de Ville.'' Shielding her eyes, Paula looked up toward the town hall's delicately wrought spire. ''Greater Brussels has nineteen boroughs that we call communes. Each is essentially self-governing. It has its own mayor, police force and fire department.''

''Who's that up there by himself?'' she asked.

''On top? That's Saint Michael. He's one of the special saints of Brussels. The other patron saint is Saint Gudule. She was a maiden who was too smart to be taken in by the wiles of Satan.'' Luc winked wickedly at her, eliciting the laugh he'd evidently hoped for. ''In the *salle des mariages*—the wedding chamber—civil ceremonies are performed,'' he went on. ''They say the waiting list is several kilometers long!''

He showed her many of the details of the wonderful guild houses that stood in the Grand'Place, a continuing reminder of the Belgians' industry and talent for commerce. ''The houses are named after the guilds they once housed, and also after certain figures in their ornamentation.'' Luc pointed out Maison du Renard, house of the fox, home of the haberdashers; Maison du Chien, house of the dog, home of the hosiery makers; Maison du Sac. . . . He would have gone on and on, she knew. Never had she met a person more willing to share his knowledge. Unless of course, that information was about himself. . . .

He couldn't resist showing her what was perhaps the most-visited spot in town. ''I really hate to treat you like a typical tourist being dragged from one curiosity to another," Luc said, "but to be here and not to have seen the Mannekin Pis is like being in Paris and not seeing the Eiffel Tower. But maybe you've already met 'the oldest citizen of Brussels'?"

Paula shook her head, but she knew what he was talking about the moment they turned the corner onto the rue de l'Etuve. The charming bronze figure of a boy ejecting a stream of water, forming a fountain, met her eyes.

"He's a formidable figure, this little one," Luc said with mocking gaiety. "The statuette you see was cast in the seventeenth century, but there was an earlier one. The little guy has quite a wardrobe. You don't always see him as nature—or should I say art—intended!"

"You mean he has clothes?"

"Yes. He has hundreds of outfits, gifts from around the world. The list of donors includes at least one king, and I've heard he has the uniform of a Canadian hockey team. It might even be your team's. What's it called?"

"The Canadiens. Come to think of it, I've been to games at the Forum where they would have got more action out of that little guy than our guys!"

Another day Luc had to visit one of his best friends, a Monsieur Merit who owned a bookstore near the Place du Grand Sablon, which was a haven for lovers of antiques, including old books. Though there was little conversation in the afternoon silence of the bookstore, where the smell of old leather and paper mingled with the not unpleasant odor of dust motes dancing in the window light, there was a communion between Paula and Luc that she could feel as she felt his touch. Every once in a while she found him browsing near her, and his hand would surreptitiously graze her cheek, her hand, her waist. Her almost-solemn happiness at their shared love of books was rivaled by a different feeling. Each time she sensed him close by and drew in her breath to smell the subtle fragrance of his musk, she felt the passion that hadn't resulted in lovemaking since that first rapturous night. But it would soon. She knew it would. She couldn't rush Luc, but that was all right. She didn't have to.

WHEN PAULA WAS BY HERSELF, she still found the trams and color-coded buses outside her own neighborhood a little intimidating. But with Luc she followed his lead, hopping on and off with speed and confidence, both of them laughing in the warm air of the city in summer. Thus he led her to Anderlecht, once a town in its own right but now a suburb of Brussels, famous for the house Erasmus lived in for a time in the sixteenth century.

"I love to come here," Luc said as they crossed a small garden and entered the building, which appeared unchanged since it had been built. "When I'm here I'm unaware of the time, the season or the city."

He introduced Paula to the curator, who seemed quite content to let them roam. There were no other visitors on this sultry afternoon. In the Renaissance Room, the main hall, they admired wall coverings of tooled leather touched with gold. "I've never seen so much gilt as I've seen since coming to Brussels," Paula said with awe. "This is a golden city."

"These are golden hours...." Luc's soft voice was suggestive, his eyes misted with longing. Paula's eyes met his with a question neither seemed able to answer. Taking her arm, he led her out of the room.

They wandered around the library, where volumes of *In Praise of Folly* stood displayed. Luc drew Paula's attention to an old print showing Erasmus in

discussion with his fellow intellectual, Sir Thomas
More. Downstairs in the study, both Paula and Luc
smiled at the sight of a black hat on a hook. It was the
sort of hat the philosopher had always worn for his
portraits, and it gave them the uncanny feeling that he
was lurking somewhere in the shadows.

Luc and Paula tarried in the old building, relishing
the serenity that seemed to radiate from old objects
reverently cared for. The polished floors gleamed.
There was a scent of candles in the rooms, and where
windows opened onto the garden, the breeze wafted in
with a freshness as new as their feelings for each other.

They rode back to the center of town late in the
afternoon in contented sleepiness. When they neared
the bus stop for Luc's place, Paula was startled to find
she'd fallen asleep with her head on Luc's shoulder and
her hand held in both of his. He had wakened her
with a kiss on the top of her head, and gazing up, she
saw such tender regard in his expression that she closed
her eyes against the intense feeling that swept through
her.

"No," he whispered, "wake up. We're almost
there."

He preceded her up the stairs to his apartment, hug-
ging her to him the moment the door was closed. Still a
little sleepy, Paula welcomed his comforting embrace,
resting her head on his shoulder and feeling beneath
her hand the steady beat of his heart.

"Shall I run downstairs to one of the shops and get
us something for supper?" Luc asked, keeping his
voice low.

Paula shook her head. "I'm so tired," she protested. Without further words Luc led her to the bedroom. Like the rest of his place, it was old-fashioned
Bohemia, comfortable without much regard for more-
modern tastes. His bed was high, large, made of dark,

heavy wood and covered with a silk spread. Without warning he lifted Paula in his arms and deposited her on the silk.

He began to languorously kiss her, his lips gentle but persistent as they explored her forehead, her cheek, her lips. His fingers found the buttons of her blouse and began to undo them slowly, one by one. His hands were so unhurried, his touch so insidiously pleasing as he pulled open the material, that Paula felt herself hovering between sleep and a sensuous, teasing awareness. But when his lips caressed her breasts, her eyes shot open and her hand rose to cradle his dark head. At his nape the warm dark hair was damp, and she combed it with lazy fingers.

Through a little parting in the heavy curtains, the hazy sun of late afternoon sent a single shaft of dusky light across the bed. In that light, Paula saw Luc's physique, his compact but powerful body. She longed to see it again without the encumbrance of clothes. Pushing him away, she urged him to get undressed, which he did. Only then did she take off her blouse, her summer skirt and everything beneath.

As hot as the room was, she welcomed the warm pressure of Luc's weight on top of her. His hands cradled her head; his kisses were a moist promise of greater pleasures to come. She reveled in the thrust of his eager tongue, responding with passionate kisses.

Holding her tightly, not only with hands and arms, but pinning her down with his thighs, he rolled her so that she was over him, trading the sensation of cool silk at her back for the heat of him beneath. She gazed into his eyes and saw once more the misted look of desire. "Paula," he whispered, "do you know how beautiful you are?"

"Luc," she answered teasingly, "I'm an old woman, older than you."

"No," he said, raising a finger to stroke her cheek. "You are young and magnificently beautiful. Your eyes are like emeralds. There is a tribe in South America that believes emeralds are the love seeds the gods use to impregnate mother earth. Those that fertilized her grew into the lush greenness of the jungle, and those that didn't stayed in the earth to be found by man." For a moment, his eyes left hers. "Paula," he went on, now speaking with difficulty, "if we, if we decided to stay together, would it bother you that there would be no children?"

"No, Luc," she said simply, but when he lifted his eyes and she saw the question there, she felt obliged to explain. "At one time I wanted children a great deal, but I was very involved in my career and my relationships weren't intimate, just dating, really. Later, with Bret, having children was out of the question. Now I'm past my prime—"

"Don't say such a stupid thing."

"No, listen. Physically I'd be able to have children, but I've lost the emotional freshness—the joy, I guess you'd say—the optimism. I've seen so much suffering in my work that I've come to think it's better not to bring children into the world."

"You're wrong, Paula," Luc declared. "Your attitude is—"

"Luc," Paula interrupted playfully, "teach me about right attitudes some other time. This is the bedroom, not the classroom." She had meant her voice to be teasing, but there was a huskiness to it that wasn't lost on Luc. Again he turned, this time keeping her beneath him not only with his weight but with the seduction of his hands, his mouth.

As though knowing instinctively how to please her, his touch inflamed. Again and again, she arced toward his skillful hands or drew his head closer to intensify the burning pleasure his mouth brought to the most intimate part of her.

When they joined, it was with indescribable power and passion. The rhythms of their lovemaking, the silent, strenuous, splendid music of love vibrated in the air.

Like a blessing, the shaft of sun caressed the lovers. Now in shadow, now in light, the curves, the planes, the softness, the strength of Luc and Paula melded. They were one as darkness and light are sometimes one. Twilight...dusk...or dawn.

CHAPTER THIRTEEN

THE VACATION that had seemed endless when it first began was over far sooner than Paula wanted it to be. Autumn brought to a close the languid days of her pleasure in Luc's company, just as it brought the students back to Le Berceau. The halls rang once again with the voices of teenagers who had grown bored with summer and were eager to begin the school year, which would also bore them in due time.

But for the first few weeks all was bustle and excitement. There were new pupils, of course, a whole crop of fresh faces, some already quite beautiful, both boys and girls, and some struggling with the more-awkward aspects of adolescence. They all looked good to Paula. The past weeks had infused her with an energy that surprised her. She didn't question the source, merely accepted the fact that nothing tired her. Not the long staff meetings, at which Luc had a good deal to say, as usual. Not the endless paperwork. Not the hours it took her to plan a new phase of her work, an orientation program to make things easier for the first-year students. Combined with sessions for individual counseling of both new and old students, the increased work load put quite a burden on Paula.

Luc, too, was very busy. Again he threw himself into the school newspaper project, and student reporters were soon roaming the halls in search of stories—a procedure that seemed exactly as silly to Paula as it had before, despite the fact that she was coming to understand how much it cost Luc to devote himself to his job, because she suspected his heart wasn't in it. He was carrying his usual heavy load of courses, teaching basic communications to several classes each day, as well as handling the more specialized senior courses. He had also become involved in some outside work, though Paula found this out not from Luc himself, but from Marie. They had been discussing the new year's increase in enrollment, but talk turned to other matters.

"Of course," Marie said, "the increase makes us all look good, but it puts a burden on teachers of academic courses like math and French, and teachers who do surveys, like Luc with his communications course."

"Has Luc complained?" Paula asked, genuinely concerned.

Marie stared at her for a moment, but if she noticed any change from Paula's previous attitude, she had the discretion not to reveal the fact.

"No. Luc is as uncomplaining as ever. But I worry about him."

"Why?"

"Because he consistently bites off more than he can chew," Marie answered, her voice losing some of its usual control. "He tells me he's writing again—for one of the papers."

"Oh?" He hadn't told *her*.

"He's agreed to cover the new bylaw debate for a paper that's already taken a strong stand on the issue. The debate is over a law to curtail the activities of certain street vendors in the Lower Town. Luc, in his unceasing campaign to champion the cause of any underdog he can find, is supporting the vendors. The man simply cannot mind his own business...."

Despite the negative words, Marie's tone was far from negative, so much so that the other woman's tenderness filled Paula with an unworthy jealousy that she fought down. "You seem to care a great deal about Luc," she said frankly. "Is it his health that worries you?"

"No. Luc's health took a turn for the worse about a year ago, but he's quite recovered now."

"But still, you are concerned."

"I've known Luc since we were children in Liège. I, of course, am a little older than he and Josef, but we are cousins. We played together often when we were very young. Josef had an astounding talent for piano, and his family proudly sent him off to the academy. In some ways Liège is the most musical city in Belgium, so it was an honor for everyone involved. Luc, however, was rather uncooperative. He went off to Paris when still a young teenager. My family lost track of him then. Three years or so ago, when I learned what had happened, I encouraged him to come here. There was an opening, Josef was already here and I knew that with his credentials, Luc had a good chance at the job. He's done extremely well. His teaching at Le Berceau is good for the school—and it's the best thing for him, too."

"How is that?" Paula asked. She could see that Marie's feelings for Luc were stronger than those of a distant cousin. Maybe Marie was encouraging Luc to stay at the school for her own reasons.

"My regard for Luc is deep and long-standing," Marie said, astutely reading Paula's thoughts. "Though I lost track of him I never forgot him, and when his name began to appear in the papers often, I followed his journalistic career with increasing admiration, but increasing fear, as well.

"People tend to glamorize the work of journalists. The habit of glorifying conflict by presenting it in the guise of entertainment is bad. It becomes a trivial matter for a journalist to lose his life—just one more character blown out of an unending story with the same continuous plot. I abhor the thought of human life being wasted at all, but I abhor especially the idea of people dying simply so that other people can keep abreast of events thousands of miles away. I know courage is required to get into the fray, armed only with a tape recorder or a camera, but it's not worth it. Trade the life of an intelligent man or woman for a story—a photograph? It's insane. And when I think of the possibility of it being Luc—''

Marie was silent for a moment. Her voice had risen, but now it was low and calm. "It's easy to forget how the families of these men and women must feel. My children idolize Luc. Sometimes they speak of following in his footsteps. I discourage them. But as for Luc himself— Well, I've felt a profound sisterly regard for him for nearly a quarter of a century, from the days when I was a teenager and Luc was the smallest, dirtiest, toughest boy in the streets of Liège.''

"And you think he's going back to journalism?" Paula tried to hide the pain the thought caused her. The idea of his leaving filled her with an abrupt, strong sense of desolation.

"When he came here," Marie answered, "he swore he was done with it forever. He'd been through hell, and he was more bitter than you can imagine. Despite the amount of talking he does, Luc never reveals his deepest thoughts. I was convinced at first that he meant to stick to his renunciation of his work in Central America, but now I'm not so sure. Luc's an excellent teacher and a dedicated one, but there are days when I know he works as he does only because he took on the job and his conscience compels him to give it everything he has. If the man had to split rocks for a living, he'd do it with the utmost energy. It's his way. But he doesn't fool me. Sometimes I see him walking out there, pacing like a lion. What is he thinking? Where are his thoughts? Not here in the garden of a high school in this old city. . . .

"This assignment he's taken on is the first sign that journalism still holds an appeal for him. I don't care at all what he says or doesn't say about street vendors. What I care about is that once he gets going, there may be no stopping him. I don't want him to throw away his life in some godforsaken country half a world away."

"Nor do I," Paula said, uttering the words without revealing the depth of her fear.

THE SUMMER WEEKS with Luc had filled Paula with a tender regard for him, with a hunger that didn't abate and with a hesitant hope that the future might hold some promise. Yet as the pressures of school descended on them both they argued so vigorously and so often that it was sometimes hard to remember they were no longer sworn enemies.

"What do you mean?" she asked him one day as they started in on the second hour of a session at his apartment. He was helping her write a brochure to explain her work to parents. "How can you make me sit here writing and rewriting this thing in order to change people's minds about our program, and then accuse me of wanting to write propaganda? Why are you teaching me to manipulate people's thinking if you have such disdain for the process? That's a bit inconsistent, isn't it?"

"You know," Luc said, "I get tired of everyone accusing me of being inconsistent."

"And I get tired of you accusing me of thinking like 'everybody else.' I resent being lumped in with other people."

"Then exercise your brain a little more. Obviously I'm not accusing you of wanting to write propaganda. I'm not talking about that silly brochure."

"Silly? If you think it's so silly—"

"I'm not talking about that brochure—" Luc cut her off "—which, heaven knows, is innocent enough. I'm talking about the writing techniques involved. Obviously, intention has something to do with whether a thing is propaganda or not. If you can't understand the distinction, I'm wasting my time."

"If you think teaching me is a waste of time," Paula retorted, pushing back her chair, "I'll just leave, okay? That'll save you any further waste of your precious time." Her eyes flashed and she expected equal anger from Luc. Instead she saw the corners of his eyes crinkle mischievously.

"Are you sure you're from Montreal?" he teased.

"Yes. Quite sure. Why ask a stupid question like that?"

"Are you sure you're not from Liège?" He pushed aside papers and pens, and reaching for her, imprisoned both her hands before she could pull them away. "So quick to passion...." His thumb began to trace the lines of her palm, then his hand circled her slim wrist.

"Leave me alone."

"There's so much I could teach you about the ways of persuasion," he insisted, his voice seductive and low.

"Luc, don't...."

"Don't what?" he asked, but before she could answer his lips were on hers, his kiss more persuasive than any words he might teach her to write.

Not all their arguments ended so quickly or so satisfactorily. As in the previous year, Paula was required to attend all staff meetings. The weekly gatherings took nearly two hours, time Paula felt was wasted. She had no idea why she had to sit through long reports on supplies and procedures. Nor did she feel confident voting on issues that had to do with departments other than her own. So when a motion came up suggesting that general meetings be held only four times a year and that weekly meetings be departmental, Paula was all for it. She was considerably less shy about speaking out than she had been during her first semester at Le Berceau. When Marie, with a nod, gave her the floor, she didn't hesitate to state her case.

"Not being an 'insider' in any of the arts departments," she began, "I can offer a different perspective on this issue. It's obvious to me each department has unique problems, and it doesn't make sense for us to have to listen to details about difficulties that may never come up in our own work."

"You of all people should be aware of the problems of every department, since you deal with students from all of them," Luc declared, without having been recognized by the principal. "How can you possibly be content to try to help a student when you aren't aware of the context in which he or she is operating?"

"In order to help someone, is it really necessary for me to know—for example—how many pads of drawing paper he's gone through in the past month?" Paula asked sarcastically. "I hardly think so. As I was saying—"

"It might be very important for you to know something like that."

"I believe *I* have the floor."

"We only have supply reports once a month," Luc insisted.

"And they take up a whole hour each time. I don't know about you, Luc, but I don't have an hour to waste—not even once a month."

"Well, considering that you are so very much busier than everyone else who works here, maybe we should just excuse you from meetings entirely!"

"Now just a minute!" Paula nearly shouted.

"Please, you two," Marie interjected. "Luc, you haven't been given the go-ahead to speak. Paula, are you finished?"

She wasn't, but she was so angry that her tongue was tied. Marie, apparently misreading her silence, said, "Thank you. Luc, the floor is yours."

"We are all aware," Luc began, carefully controlling his voice, "that an arts education demands not only of the students, but of teachers, as well, attention to details that are tedious, mundane, certainly less than inspired. It is a matter of discipline, however, to apply one's full attention to even the least interesting aspects of our jobs so that we can teach our students to do likewise when it comes to disciplining themselves for the sake of their art. A writer who pays more attention to style than to content, a dancer who is self-indulgent in expression because careless in technique, a painter who is contemptuous of his tools—all of these artists have not been taught proper discipline...."

You're missing the point entirely, Paula wanted to cry out, but she was intimidated by the rapt and respectful silence.

"It is essential for us to work as a team. The weekly exchange of information, time-consuming though it is, has always been a vital part of maintaining the standards of this school. I know that with the increased enrollment, the demands on us have become greater, but I, for one, am fully prepared to meet those demands...."

In the end, Luc's side won, overwhelmingly. In Paula's opinion, he had completely manipulated the other teachers. Lumpy Langois was decidedly on Luc's side. "The man is absolutely self-sacrificing. He's an example to us all," the sculpture professor whispered to Paula during the final moments of the long meeting.

"Oh, go sit in some clay."

To which Lumpy replied, "Oh, miss! Your French is so charming—but not always accurate. Do you know what you just said? It's so amusing. You just told me to—"

Before he could finish she'd turned and stomped out of the room.

Then there was the public debate.

"Intervention is wrong under any circumstances," Luc declared during one of the lunch hours when Paula sat at his table.

"Suppose the country whose affairs are being interfered with has invited intervention?" one of the students asked.

"That's a contradiction in terms," Luc stated flatly.

"That's not necessarily true," Paula began. . . .

The discussion was so engrossing that neither Luc nor Paula finished lunch. They didn't finish the conversation, either, until after school. In fact, they argued all evening, and they were edgy for several days afterward. Paula was beginning to despair of their ever being able to patch things up, when she wandered into the teachers' lounge after classes three days after their argument and saw that Monsieur Langois was very excited about something on TV, as was Marie Légère, Laurice LePan and several other teachers. "Go to it, Luc—you tell him!" Lumpy shouted.

Peering over the shoulders of those seated around the set, she was astounded to see a close-up of Luc on the screen. He was silent; the camera was catching his reaction to someone else's speech. He looked remarkably intense. His glasses hid his blue-violet eyes, a shame, Paula thought. Angry with him though she was, she had to admit he looked quite wonderful on television. Wonderful, too, was the company he kept. Two well-known journalists, one from New York and the other from Paris, joined Luc on a panel devoted to the subject she and he had argued so violently about. She waited for him to speak, but abruptly walked away when he began. She had heard all she intended to hear from him on that topic.

Then she walked back, took a seat and listened in earnest.

"OKAY, NOW—" Paula signaled to the other teachers, who turned down the TV but hovered near to catch her voice as the phone-in segment of the show continued.

"Go ahead, please. Identify yourself," Paula heard the announcer say over the phone.

"I'm a school counselor here in Brussels," Paula began, "and I'm calling to express my support for Monsieur LeBlanc's view. As he states...."

THE NEXT DAY it was all around the school that Paula's on-the-air defense of Luc had been brilliant. Nobody knew how much it had cost her, both in the courage to speak at all and the concession of coming around to his way of thinking. Nobody knew the phone call was really an apology. Nobody, that is, except the person who unlocked her office door the next morning with a key he wasn't supposed to have and left on her desk blotter a bouquet of white violets. There was the barest hint of some familiar scent....

CHAPTER FOURTEEN

SEPTEMBER GAVE WAY to October, but the days didn't seem to grow much colder as far as Paula could tell.

Nine months, nearly ten. It seemed far longer than that since she'd left home. So much had happened. As far as her job went, she was finally independent of Bret. A few weeks after her phone call, she'd received a letter on official stationery. It stated that Dr. Graham's agency was ending its association with Paula Emanuel and her project, with the understanding that the directors of Le Berceau would be taking over the project themselves. Fancy words for two simple ideas: the school was now employing her; Bret was out of her life. Paula felt the phantoms of her past were finally quite firmly laid to rest. And in their place were the very real, living personalities of Marie Légère and Paula's colleagues, her student clients and Luc. Luc above all.

Despite its size, Le Berceau provided the cozy intimacy usually associated with much smaller private schools. That was reinforced in Paula's mind as she grew familiar with the full cycle of school events, including the special celebrations that were a traditional part of the year. Among these were the name-day parties given by the student association for teachers who were special favorites. Paula remembered a lovely tea she'd attended during the second week of her new job. At the time she hadn't quite understood that it had been a name-day party honoring Marie. Now it was October 18, feast of Saint Luke, and Luc's turn for a fete. Just about everyone in the school got involved in the upcoming affair.

"You've got to let me go, miss," Villette insisted on the morning of the big event. "They need me, and I promised."

"Villette," Paula answered as patiently as she could, "I'm disappointed that you would promise to help without checking with me first. If I don't see you this afternoon, we won't be able to discuss your report until next week. By that time your parents will have—"

"Oh, come on, miss. What difference does it make whether my father scolds me before I talk to you or after? I promised I'll do better next time, and I will. Please, Paula? I want Monsieur Luc's fete to be the best ever."

"Don't call me by my first name," Paula said automatically. After a brief pause she relented. "All right, Villette, you can skip this afternoon's session, but I want you to remember the things we talked about last week. This is your senior year. Your attitude needs a great deal of work if you hope to enter the professional world."

"Oh, great, thanks. . . ." Villette said, not paying the least bit of attention. As the blooming girl bobbed out of her office, Paula shook her head in exasperation. Villette had lost some of her childlike roundness during the summer, but she'd lost nothing of her power to charm.

Students and teachers alike, but mostly students, had planned Luc's party for weeks. The teens had set up committees to handle various aspects of the affair, and it amused Paula to see how much they enjoyed the parliamentary exactitude with which they conducted meetings. She had helped them choose a decorating scheme—crepe-paper streamers of burgundy and royal blue and a large, affectionate caricature of Luc done by one of the visual-arts students.

Along with her official contribution to Luc's fete, Paula planned a personal one, a gift she'd made herself. In fact, she'd stayed up most of the night putting the finishing details on her present, a shirt in off-white cotton with a discreet design embroidered in the same shade on the edges of the pocket, the collar and the cuffs.

Despite her lack of sleep, Paula wasn't tired at all. She was probably as excited about the impending celebration as the students, because the morning seemed to drag, and she found herself watching the clock. Finally she decided to put aside her paperwork a few minutes early and head for lunch.

Though she and Luc had decided it would be more discreet not to eat at the same table, she often saw him in the dining hall. Today he was conspicuously absent, as were all the students on the decorating committee. She knew their plan was to get everything ready in the back room, then do the actual decorating the minute the lunch crowd had dispersed.

She ended up eating lunch by herself, unusual now that many students knew her and sought her company. Afterward she took a walk in the garden.

Used to more dramatic seasonal changes, she found the garden looked very similar in autumn to how it had in the spring. Still, it was always a pleasure to stroll along the flagstone pathway. There was silence among the trees and shrubs, though in the far distance she could hear the murmur of traffic on the rue Ravenstein, and in the nearer distance, the students' lunchtime conversations, the scrape of chairs, the clink of china and silver. She walked on, coming to the stone bench and pulling her light coat around her as she sat down.

She remembered the day she'd seen Luc on that very bench, when he'd played the tune on his panpipes, then abruptly terminated it, insisting the song sounded out of place. She remembered, too—much later—him putting away the photos of the blond journalist. Clearly her death had been a great blow to Luc. For the hundredth time in recent days, Paula wondered not only what Luc had really lost, but what he still yearned to regain. His body responded ardently to her, but his mind remained the enclave of secrets. Some of the loneliness was gone from his eyes, but almost none of the defeat. Paula wanted so badly to ease his burden, but he, who talked and talked, said nothing.

Sighing, she got up and resumed her walk, making her way back to the school. Stepping inside, she caught a glimpse of Luc in the distance. He looked dapper in well-tailored slacks topped with a casual jacket similar to what some of the students wore. It was well styled and a great improvement over worn jeans and the old gray sweater. He was wearing his lenses. This bit of sterling grooming could only mean Monsieur Luc was well aware of the "secret" plans for the afternoon. It was patently impossible to hide anything from a nosy person.

That hardly mattered; he looked good to Paula. With warmth she recalled the first time she'd ever seen him. The man who had then seemed dark, rumpled and repulsive now pleased her more than any other.

Villette van der Vloedt, her hands full of streamers, came by at just that instant. Seeing Paula's face, she loudly asked, "Dreaming of your beloved?"

Really, Paula thought, *that girl is a dreadful brat!*

"WE'VE DECIDED, miss. You're the one who should bring him in. You can be tricky—you know, give him a false start or two."

She looked up over her desk into the shining faces of Karel and Kathelijne at the head of a delegation of a dozen students. "All right. I'll try. When do you want him?"

"Right away, miss. Everybody's already in the dining hall—it's time."

As usual, Luc's door was slightly ajar. She knocked lightly, and at his *"Entrez,"* pushed it open and stepped into the room.

"Paula," he said, his voice soft, "what are you doing here?" No doubt he'd been expecting one of the students. A puzzled look crossed his face, but he stifled it.

"Is there somewhere else I should be?" she teased.

"No, I guess not. I mean. . . ."

"Are you busy?" she asked, peeking at the papers on his desk on top of the dais. She caught a glimpse of the latest catalog from Monsieur Merit's bookstore before Luc moved his arm to cover what he'd been reading.

"I'm a little busy. I'm just going over a few things for my classes tomorrow."

You liar, she thought. *You're just sitting there waiting to be "surprised!"* Tauntingly she said, "In that case I guess you can't spare a minute. . . ."

He looked at her carefully, and she could see by his brightening expression that he now realized she was the emissary he was waiting for. He was so obvious she had to force herself not to laugh.

"Okay, Luc," she said, "you know why I came, and you know where to go, don't you?" He attempted ignorance for a moment longer, but clearly the ruse was up.

She preceded him to the dining hall, reaching the door first. Opening it, she stepped aside so that Luc entered to the enthusiastic shouts of "Surprise!"

Though it wasn't that particular emotion that lit Luc's face at the sight of the gathered students, his deep pleasure was cheering to all, and especially touching to Paula, who watched closely from a short distance away.

When the shouts died down, Villette ran up, and

boldly kissing Luc on the cheek, led him to a table heaped with gifts. During the next half hour or so, Luc was so gracious, so charming that not one of the students could remember the times he'd harangued them as hopeless writers of the unreadable. Nor could any teacher recall how he'd shortened the hours of his or her leisure with his long speeches and interminable memos. All grievances were forgotten as he opened his gifts and expressed heartfelt thanks.

Last of all, he opened a card from Paula. It said simply, "Come to my place for your gift." When Luc read it, he blushed. Paula reddened, too, but mercifully, he didn't look in her direction. He slipped the card into the pocket of his jacket before thanking students and teachers alike one more time.

After the gifts, Villette again took up the role of hostess, leading Luc to a huge cake elaborately decorated by the kitchen staff—all of whom were present. Luc kissed each one. There was more laughter. Toasts followed, a speech, a round of applause. . . .

Paula watched all of it as though from a great distance. There could be no doubt that Luc was a kind of hero to the people gathered in his honor. Yet something was wrong with the scene. There was about it a strange note of finality, a hint of goodbye, of farewells to come.

Or was that just her imagination? With an effort she shrugged off all negative thoughts. Despite the arguments they still occasionally had, her caring for Luc was still growing, eclipsing past love and wiping out the pain of mistake. Why not be happy with the present instead of worrying about a future that might hold happiness, after all? Why not?

With a smile she raised her glass in yet another toast. "To Luc," she whispered. "To Luc, my love."

CHAPTER FIFTEEN

IT SEEMED to take him forever. First he opened the small card on which she'd written only *"Bonne fête,"* and her name. That was worth, it turned out, several tender kisses. Then with infinite patience he undid the ribbon, the tape and the tissue.

Paula watched him intently as he saw what the parcel contained, and she breathed a sigh of relief when a look of pleasure crossed his handsome face. He lifted the shirt in both hands, letting the tissue he'd so painstakingly unwrapped fall unheeded to the floor. Clearly he hadn't expected anything so exquisite.

"Why, it's beautiful!" he exclaimed. "And someone has made it by hand!"

"Not someone."

"You?"

"Me."

"But it must have taken hours and hours!"

"Yes."

"And you had to have planned a long time ago in order to have it ready—"

"It wasn't ready until the last minute. You like it?"

"Oh, yes. It's wonderful." Without hesitation, he took off the shirt he was wearing, donning the new one with care. "It fits perfectly," he declared. "How did you know my size? You never asked."

"Maybe I learned some of your sneaky techniques for finding out other people's business."

"Ah." He laughed. "You mean the tricks of a reporter?"

"I mean the tricks of a confirmed nosy person. Are you ready for your name-day dinner?"

"All this and dinner, too?" he joked, opening his arms as though to examine the sleeves of his new shirt. Unable to resist, Paula moved toward him, knowing those arms would close around her. He kissed her long and hard, his lips as always both fulfilling and promising. "Hmm...all this and dinner, too?" he repeated.

"Come here," she said, pulling him toward a table she'd set up in her living room. It was only a card table, but covered with a white linen cloth it looked quite elegant, especially since she'd bought two fine-china plates for the occasion. She had half her mother's silver and half her grandmother's crystal; she and her sister had shared.

"I hope you'll like what we're about to have," she said. "It's going to be typically Canadian."

"Moosemeat and berries?"

"Why, how did you know?" Paula pushed him into a chair. Standing behind him, her hands on his shoulders, she couldn't resist leaning over and kissing the top of his head. His hand reached up to capture one of hers, and she felt a hot kiss on her palm.

"Whatever you want to give me, Paula, I'll take." His voice was low and husky, and he wasn't talking about food.

"Delicious," he declared after his second bowl of rich pea soup. "What's next?"

"Tortière," she announced, serving up thick slices of the meat pie. This was accompanied by fiddleheads she'd gone to great lengths and some expense to procure, and sweet yams. Luc ate with gusto, enjoying every morsel. For dessert they had vanilla ice cream with real maple syrup.

"I'll help with the dishes," he offered when they'd finished.

"Oh, no you won't," she protested, rising, intending to clear away his dessert dish. But when she got to his side of the table, he grabbed her, his arms tight around her waist as he buried his face in the warmth of her stomach. She stood still, caressing the dark richness of his hair. She could feel the gentle rhythm of his breathing. As always, the nearness of him, the scent of his hair and skin, filled her with desire.

"Luc," she whispered, "let me go. I have to do the dishes."

"I don't think so..." he replied, pulling back and looking up at her. "No, I don't think you'll be doing the dishes for a while...."

Now it was she who pulled away, but not far enough. She didn't really want to deny his insistent embrace as he stood up to hold her closer yet. Nor could she refuse the shower of hot kisses over her forehead, down her cheeks, past her parted lips to her throat. Her auburn hair was a shining tumble as she arched back to receive the tremulous touch of his mouth wherever his moist kisses cared to fall. His hands caressed her shoulders, his hold first gently massaging, then gripping, so that she could feel the strength of his fingers through the fabric of her blouse.

Her hands found again the heated skin at his nape, then descended to mold the planes of his shoulders. Her fingers felt the cotton, and under it, the pliant but unyielding muscles. How fit he was. His body vibrated with health, with a vitality that came from hours of jogging and walking, including, she knew, pacing the floor of his classroom!

As his hands descended to her waist, she lowered

hers. He was trim; not an extra ounce met her exploring touch, but as she dropped her hands farther, she cupped the pleasing roundness of his derriere, kneading boldly. This was fast becoming one of her favorite parts of his anatomy. . . .

He was bolder still, capturing her derriere with one hand while the other massaged her breast. The surprising quickness of the motion combined with the darting pleasure emanating from her sent her head reeling. She tightened her hold, drawing him hard against her. The pressure of his arousal was a new heat against her thigh as he, too, tightened the embrace.

"Luc," she whispered hoarsely, her voice a choked plea. "Oh, Luc!"

"Come on," he answered, his own voice rasping into almost a sigh. "Come with me, Paula."

She followed him the short distance to her small bedroom, switching on a low light as they entered. Its softness fell on the rosy tones of the room; it fell more harshly on the sculpted planes of Luc's face, now more strong than grim, more determined than melancholy. Luc stared back into the hazy green depths of her eyes, his look blazing pure desire. She felt herself to be burning with the brilliance of sensation and emotion, love and passion.

As if in slow motion, she moved toward him, and he opened his arms to receive the whole gift of her.

"I want you, Paula," he breathed into her ear. "I want only you, wholly—body to body, mind to mind. I want you in my arms and in my life." His kiss seared her again, and closing her eyes against the vision, against all sensation but of his touch, she returned the flaming pressures kiss for kiss.

After what seemed both a long time and no time at all, he pulled slightly away from her. Wordlessly he began to undress her. Totally trusting, she stood motionless beneath his sure hands.

With a teasing slowness that left her shivering, he undid the pearl buttons of her silky blouse and drew it inch by inch from her shoulders. Everywhere the silk touched, his fingers brushed, and everywhere his fingers brushed, his lips followed. When the blouse finally fell away, a soft heap at her feet, he ran his hands over her shoulders, let them meet over the place where her heart pounded; they separated again to hold her breasts.

Again and again Paula murmured Luc's name as he continued the languorous disrobing, until she stood naked and beautiful before him.

But she wouldn't have him remain clothed. Her fingers were as skilled as his, though a little more impatient. Her lips were as knowledgeable in the ways of pleasure, though a little too eager. Even so, before she could quite finish, he whipped off his briefs and reaching out, swept her off her feet, holding her to him for one long moment before they walked together to bed.

Stretched out beside her, Luc propped himself up on one elbow, leaving his other hand free to tease the planes of her face with a light finger. "Paula," he declared, bending down to kiss her sweetly, "you have given this all back to me—these golden moments, this intimacy...."

"Luc, I—"

He wouldn't let her speak. The finger that had grazed her flushed cheek now lay across her kiss-sensitized mouth. "No, my combatant, I want no argument just now. I want to be the one talking. I used to feel I was keeping a lonely vigil, waiting for God knows what. At times the loneliness has been unbearable. I thought I'd lost a good deal, Paula, thought I'd lost it forever. But you've given it back to me, and it's richer, stronger, more wonderful. I'm not speaking only of sex, though, you must know—"

His voice broke, and he looked away. Paula, though

she had no words at that moment, put her hand on his. He turned back to her, and his eyes shone with tears. He went on, his voice strong again. "I'm talking about love. I'm talking about myself. I love you, Paula. I love you so much that I'm glad I waited all the long years it took before you came to me. I'd wait again. I'd wait no matter how long it took...."

She wanted to cry out her own love for him, but her heart was too full. She could only throw her arms around him and feel his trembling response. She couldn't dam the tears that sprang to her eyes, and they fell freely, scalding her cheeks and Luc's skin.

Feeling them, he held her away a little, kissing her again and again but with banked fire, with restraint. "I know," he said. "Being loved by me is fit reason for a woman to weep uncontrollably. Still, it has its compensations. Unlimited free writing lessons. A willing victim to eat fiddlehead plants. Someone to help you speak proper French—"

"Oh, Luc!" Paula laughed, amazed that he could tease at such a time, but happy, oh, so happy that he could. "You are a crazy idiot! I love you, too. I love you far more than anybody in their right mind would love another person."

Despite herself, she was crying—laughing, crying, loving and being loved. He lowered her. His weight on her was further incitement to the passion that had flared between them, that had been building all the time they'd known each other.

Making up for lost hours, they loved with an energy that brought them irresistibly to ecstasy. Sometimes their motions were a heated frenzy as, bodies locked, they swayed to the imperative rhythms of their mutual desire. And sometimes there was a lazy, teasing backing off that cooled their fire for a while but soon fed a hotter flame.

When neither could bear the rising, piercing pleasure a moment longer, their bodies sang in noteless rapture, and their voices cried out, ringing from all the walls of the room.

LATE, VERY LATE, they remembered the dishes they'd left in the sink. "I can do them tomorrow," Paula insisted.

"Tomorrow's a workday, and you're going to be exhausted," Luc answered, pushing Paula toward the edge of the bed. "I wouldn't think of letting you come back to that mess. I want to help. Now. Get going."

Thinking that it would take some time to clean up and therefore it would be some time before Luc could leave, Paula agreed.

Actually, they were done quite quickly. "Well, that proves it—there's a first time for everything," Paula declared.

"Proves what?" Luc asked warily, familiar with the implied taunt in her tone.

"Proves that you and I can work well together, after all."

With unexpected seriousness Luc replied, "There's no telling what you and I will be able to do together given half a chance."

"Will we, Luc?"

"Will we what, my love?"

"Will we be given half a chance?"

He dropped his eyes, hiding his expression, but his voice was tight, his profile hard in the room's harsh light.

"I don't know, Paula. I just don't know."

FOR THE FIRST TIME he stayed the night. All during the hours of darkness he held her to him. Even in sleep she was aware of his presence; a warm, comforting, promising strength beside her in bed.

For the first time he had said he loved her. And he had told her that his happiness with her had wiped out at least some of the misery of his past. The triumph of that, the pure joy of having helped him would stay with her no matter what. But there was more than one way of interpreting his words. He had talked about the past. Paula thought of loneliness with reference to the future—her future.

Would she have to let him go? Would she have to wait in unbearable solitude for him to return? She knew the secrets of his body. She trusted totally in the sincerity of his love. Yet she knew nothing—still nothing—about what she sensed was a momentous plan.

In the morning Luc left early, in time to go back to his place before going to school. But as she closed the door on his retreating back, Paula had to fight her thoughts: that the day might come when she would say goodbye, close her door and not be able to say whether she'd ever see him again.

CHAPTER SIXTEEN

AFTER THE NIGHT of Luc's fete, everything changed. For one thing, there was no more arguing. Though she couldn't take his side on every issue, Paula found she no longer got angry when he presented an idea contrary to her own. Even staff meetings became calmer.

And she lost the urge to provoke, even to tease him. The thought of his being in discomfort, even the momentary discomfort of being the butt of a joke, was too much for her. She felt so tender toward him that she couldn't stand others to tease him, either. The innocent flirtations of the irrepressible Villette also tempted Paula to a jealousy that she fought whenever she saw the winsome girl trailing after Luc in the hallway.

Paula suspected she and Luc had probably become common knowledge around Le Berceau, despite their discretion. Still, she refrained from eating lunch at his table. Now when his eyes met hers across the dining hall, he didn't look away or stare defiantly as he once had. Now he smiled. Such a warm, loving smile that the first time Paula noticed, she blushed and dropped her eyes, causing students sitting with her to ask what she'd seen. After that, she always ended up sitting in such a way that if Luc looked up, he could see her.

He took her all over. He seemed to know every nook and cranny of the complex city that Brussels was, even though it had only been his home for a few years.

"I know Paris even better," he said with a smile

when Paula commented. "A faithful Liègeois doesn't usually have much love for Brussels, for two reasons, I think. The first is the loyalty to our own city that I've already mentioned. The second is that Brussels is the capital of Brabant, and that's essentially a Flemish province, not Walloon. There's some rivalry and some mistrust. For myself, I try to take each city on its own merits. This one has many."

Proving his statement, he introduced her to fine restaurants. Though his apartment was modest and his salary at Le Berceau could be, at best, only a little higher than her own, Luc always seemed to have money for special treats. It occurred to Paula that as a noted journalist he must have made a good deal of money, but perhaps that had been eaten up by his medical expenses. She never asked. But she did wonder.

"Luc, what is this place?" she asked one evening as he led her into a small room in a townhouse overlooking the Place Rouppe.

"In all the world, there are fewer than ten restaurants outside France that have received the honor of three Michelin stars. This is one of them...."

Small though it was, with only fifteen tables, the restaurant was lovely, and the smells were so tempting that Paula asked no further questions. They were guided by the head waiter to a secluded nook perfectly suited to an intimate dinner for two.

"This is love food," Luc joked as he helped her enjoy the appetizer, oysters in champagne. And after a main course of *carbonnade à la flamande*, browned beef simmered with onions in beer, he extended the teasing metaphor by convincing her to order a sorbet of passionfruit. Paula was sure she'd never dined in such style. She couldn't imagine when she might have the chance again, so she savored each morsel, each moment.

It wasn't the elegant restaurants, the theaters, the concert halls or the flashy Las Vegas-style nightclubs he took her to that most delighted Paula. Luc's real haunts, the places he preferred to go when he was in the mood for relaxation, were far more interesting.

One of Luc's favorites, to Paula's surprise, turned out to be a pastry shop. Custard tarts, sugar tarts, tarts filled with rice flavored with vanilla—not to mention the ubiquitous *gaufres* and *speculoos*—were a regular part of Luc's diet, though they never added a centimeter to his waistline. Despite his sometimes gruff ways, Luc's manners were impeccable, and he was at ease in the shop with its silver trays and lace doilies, not to mention the rotund Flemish proprietress. More than once she received a brusque peck from her countryman of that "other" community.

In her ramblings with Luc, Paula soon learned just how skillful the Belgians were at making and consuming their favorite drink. Luc encouraged her to try a few of the four hundred brands of beer available. He ordered local types for her, first introducing her to *geuze*, a mixture of old and new beers. To Paula, it was slightly sour, and when poured it had such a big head that she ended up with foam on her face, which Luc found immensely funny. The next time he ordered *lambic* because it had almost no head, but this she found too strong. So he made her try *faro*, a weaker brew containing cane sugar, and *kriek*, a reddish beer that tasted of cherries.

But the real pleasure of being with Luc in the pubs wasn't the drink, it was the company he kept. Luc might be a dedicated teacher during the day, but he was still a newspaperman in the evenings—at least as far as his acquaintances were concerned.

A particular friend of his—or was it enemy; Paula couldn't quite decide—was a journalist Luc never called by any other name but Moens. Moens was a tall, gaunt man with a quick mind and a razor-sharp tongue. He spoke Dutch to most people, French to Luc, and for some reason known to himself alone, English to Paula, very slightly accented, lively English.

"Your country is an example to others in many respects," Moens told her one night as she and Luc shared a beer with him in a crowded tavern. "It must take some doing to live peaceably with a neighbor who's a giant."

"As one of our statesmen once said," Paula answered, "it's a lot like sleeping with an elephant. You become adept at figuring out when it's going to turn over!"

"So the incentive to live in peace with your neighbor is great," Moens replied.

"But it's also necessary to live at peace with oneself," Luc added.

"You seem to be doing a good job of that, Le-Blanc," Moens remarked. "How else to explain how complacent you are these days."

"Don't start, Moens."

Ignoring his friend's warning, the tall man went on speaking to Paula, clearly meaning for Luc to hear. "What you have here is a man content to rest on his not inconsiderable laurels."

"Moens, I'm warning you!"

"In person you're not a very threatening man, Le-Blanc. In print, yes. In person, no."

Luc scowled, and Moens shut up, though Paula sensed that little snatch of argument was part of a larger one they must carry on continually. It occurred to her that if Luc wanted to avoid such reminders of his past, he would have avoided press people.

Not by a long shot. He seemed to know every reporter, stringer, columnist and news photographer in town—mostly the French-speaking ones, but some Flemish, too. Paula discovered that Luc obviously understood Dutch, because when addressed in that language he answered appropriately, though always in French.

He also had friends in the literary world, friends he'd met through the editor of the paper he now admitted he wrote for on a regular free-lance basis. He would say very little about this work, and Paula never saw his by-line. She didn't even know which paper he was contributing to; something in his manner told her not to ask.

Of all Luc's friends, Paula's favorites were the poets. They were a motley crew with nothing in common except the French language and their special love for it. Many of the pieces were on political themes. Paula had thumbed through a batch, reading one or two with great interest.

It was very late on a Saturday night, well past midnight, and Luc's small living room was littered with empty wineglasses, photocopies of handwritten poems, books—some closed, some left open at well-read pages. This was the aftermath of an evening spent discussing literature, politics and love. The others had left, and both Paula and Luc were struggling to get up enough energy to tidy the room.

"Are any of these poems yours?" Paula asked.

"My poetry isn't of the caliber of my friends'."

"But you've written poems?"

"One of those is mine, yes."

"Must be this one," Paula said with great seriousness. "It's definitely the worst of the lot."

Taking the paper from her hand, Luc glanced at it, and his face paled. "That is mine," he said. "Do you really think it's that bad?"

"No, silly. It's quite good. I knew it was yours—I

was just teasing. I recognized the handwriting. It's a fine poem.''

"It's nothing," Luc said dismissively, free to engage in false modesty now that he knew she didn't dislike his poem. "Just a little emotionalism, guaranteed to have an effect."

"Do you always have to have an effect?" she asked with interest.

"Yes," he answered thoughtfully, "yes I do. Life is short, and there's little time for a person to make his mark."

"Why does a person have to make a mark?"

"That's a strange question coming from someone who works at a school dedicated to young people who are learning to be artists."

"But artists don't change the world."

"Is that what you think?"

"Well, I guess the famous ones do, but—"

"Paula, Paula!" Luc's voice rose with the excitement of his convictions. "Of course an artist—every artist—changes the world. So does a journalist. So does a social worker. So does a teacher, though I sometimes think that's a secondhand sort of change. Listen, what else are people alive for if not to change for the better the things they find around them?"

"But Luc, isn't it arrogant to think you know something or can do something so special that you have the right to inflict your views and your ways on others?"

"Arrogant? Of course it's arrogant!"

"Well, then?"

"Well, what? It's a healthy arrogance. It's the arrogance of being yourself, of knowing your view of the world is important, unique. I was qualified to speak as a journalist because I was a practiced observer of life. I wrote with total confidence."

"And now you teach with total confidence."

"No, I don't."

"That's ridiculous, Luc. I've watched you. You know exactly what you're doing up on that dais."

"It may appear so, but it's not true. I'm uncertain of the most fundamental aspect of my subject."

"Which is?"

"That writing can be taught at all." He was ominously silent for a moment. They were sitting on the floor with their legs spread in front of them, their backs propped against the couch. There hadn't been enough chairs, so some people had sat on the floor during the evening's discussion. Paula and Luc had been so tired they hadn't even seen the guests to the door. That tiredness was forgotten now.

"You know," Luc said contemplatively, "by the time I was the age of my senior students, I had already been supporting myself for two or three years, and I'd been writing long before that, as long as I can remember, in fact."

"Marie said you ran off to Paris at a tender age."

"My cousin makes herself not only the repository of my history, but of all legends concerning me," Luc said with an indulgent smile. He went on. "I did leave home fairly early. Not because I was unhappy. My parents were cultivated and kind people. But I was restless, and restlessness made me a bad student and an uncooperative son. Fortunately, Josef, as you might imagine, was a model child, and his behavior took a lot of the pressure off me.

"By the age of fifteen, I found myself in Paris." He paused. "No. No, I didn't *find* myself there. I worked in a factory in Liège until I had enough money to go. I was bound and determined, and that determination made me fearless. After only a few weeks in Paris, I got a warehouse job with a book publisher. From there I moved into the circulation department of a magazine publisher—and so on—until I finally got an editorial job. It took me a few more years before I saw my by-line in print. I've always considered that to be just about the greatest day in my life—my professional life, that is."

Turning to her, he planted a soft kiss on her cheek. He cleared his throat, and with the air of a person who had started on a topic he really didn't want to pursue, he changed the subject, nonchalantly offering her more wine.

"Luc," she said softly, "forget the wine. You've never told me about your past before. Please, please tell me now."

Her eyes pleaded with him, and for the first time he felt he might be able to trust someone else with the burden of his bitterness. Not that he wanted to make her bitter, too. "Surely these old stories are going to bore you, Paula?"

"No."

Again he stared into her eyes, eyes that had lost completely the hunted look he had once been able to see so clearly. "All right," he said in his accented English, "I'll spill the beans." Reverting to French, he added, "But first, more wine." He filled their glasses with a bloodred burgundy, drew in his breath and began.

"In a short while I had become a regular reporter on one of the Paris dailies. I wasn't twenty yet. For a while I was a foreign correspondent in the Middle East, but I wasn't happy there."

"Because of the danger?"

"The physical danger? No, not particularly. It wasn't the danger that bothered me; it was the fact that the issues weren't clear-cut for me. There were times when I sympathized with both sides and times when I couldn't sympathize with either. It's commonly believed that reporters shouldn't take sides—that objectivity is the mark of the best journalists. Well, maybe that's the test of a good reporter, if you define a reporter as someone who merely records the facts. But a good journalist needs a stance. At least I do. And I couldn't take a stance in the Middle East.

"So I finagled until I ended up in Central America. I'm not going to try to tell you what it's like there...." Thoughtfully he sipped his wine. "I think I mentioned once before that I believe this world would be an easier place to live in, or at least to understand, if all that was bad was ugly and all that was good was beautiful—or if the two were segregated, at any rate.

"In Latin America I saw such fierce beauty and such dreadful ugliness that I had no trouble taking a stance. No trouble at all. I am, Paula, a lousy reporter. The facts interest me not nearly so much as the truth does. Fortunately, the chief of the Latin American bureau of the Paris paper was an understanding man. He had others in the field willing to feed him facts. He let them be reporters, and he let me be a journalist. I did fine work. I was—" He stopped, shook his head a little, then glanced up. He wasn't looking directly at Paula. He had that faraway look, compounded resignation and defeat. She waited for him to go on; there was a very long silence.

Finally he spoke, and his voice, though low, filled the small room. "I was enraged most of the time I was there. Rage sometimes makes for very bad writing, but it can make for brilliant writing, too. The only problem was, I had a lot of rage left over. I didn't want just to speak out against what I considered to be atrocities, to speak to people thousands of miles away. I wanted to do something there, where everything was happening."

"And?" She wanted him to go on, but she was

afraid that should she break the spell of the moment with questions, he might retreat into secretiveness.

"You know," he said, seeming to change the subject, "there are many brotherhoods in this world. One is the brotherhood of lovers." He laughed softly, taking her hand and kissing her palm, then nestling her fingers in his hands. "Since you've allowed me into your life, I seem to have become adept at spotting other lovers."

She smiled at him. He squeezed her hand tenderly and didn't release it as he went on.

"There is, as you no doubt know, a brotherhood of teachers and of journalists. And of subversives. It's never difficult to find a brother when you're determined. To make a long story short, I got involved in an effort to set up an underground press in the country where I worked most often. It was a technical as well as a journalistic challenge, and the implications would have been far-reaching, because we had plans for a whole network— Anyway, there were rumors that I was the one who had spearheaded the operation. A man is as much a fool to deny such rumors as to confirm them.

"In any case, when the final stages of planning for our project were complete and we were waiting for our first shipment of materials...I was severely injured while covering a quite ordinary gathering of local politicians. Why a government truck should suddenly explode and burst into flame without reason—within two yards of where I stood—was never explained. It just happened. The way such things always 'just happen.' "

Luc turned his face away, and for a moment there was no sound in the room except for the rhythm of their breathing. After a while he resumed, his tone harsher. "I am a man who learns his lesson eventually. I found I had a year and a half to think about matters, a year and a half to learn all that pain can teach a person.

"The first thing I learned is that I seem to have a

strong preference for life as opposed to death. Simple as that lesson appears, there were times when the will to live was quite beyond me, especially when Lise died...." Paula didn't think she could bear to hear anything more about the journalist's death. It wasn't jealousy that made her feel that way, but compassion. She gave Luc's hand a squeeze of comfort and sympathy. He went on with his story.

"In the long empty days of my convalescence, I decided, as well, that those who try to interfere in the affairs of others are fools—dangerous to themselves and others. Those who advise minding one's own business know what they're talking about. I now accept that there are things in this world that no amount of intervention can prevent. Honest men don't run the world. I don't run it. Never again will I make the mistake of thinking I do."

There was such virulent bitterness in his voice that Paula couldn't respond.

"And so," he said, "I became what I am today: a hypocrite."

"Luc! You, a hypocrite? How can you say—"

"Day after day I teach young people to write. I tell them that words have power, that *their* words have power. I imply that they can change the world by means of words. Yet I myself am without faith in the very things I teach. My words change nothing."

"Luc, you're wrong—you're so wrong. You've changed me. I would never have had the courage to tell Bret off. And what about Karel? He's doing better this year than ever before. He'll have a job for sure when he graduates...." Her eager words fell into silence. She knew Luc was talking about more than these incidents of his past. He was talking about his future.

"You can't go on letting this bitterness—this unfinished business—ruin your life, Luc. Your body is

healed, and you'll be healed inside, too.'' She put her
hand to his heart, and his own hand came up to press
her palm more firmly against the warmth of his chest.
Paula trembled, but she went on. ''You can't go on
with this open wound in your soul. You can't fool
yourself into thinking your life will ever be complete
until you solve—''

''Please— Don't you think I live with that fact every
day of my life?'' There was anger in his voice, but
anger directed at himself. Paula couldn't bear to continue this heartrending discussion.

''You say words change nothing, Luc. I know these
words can't change the world—can't even change your
world very much—but they're true, anyway. I love
you.''

''I know.'' Tenderly he took her face between his
hands and kissed her lowered lids before seeking the
softness of her willing mouth. For a moment they sat
in breathless stillness, only their lips touching. But
soon, simultaneously, their arms wound around each
other compassionately. Nearness brought a return of
desire, and with a spasm of longing Paula reached up
to take a handful of Luc's thick black hair, pushing his
head back the little distance necessary for her mouth to
succor his.

Wildly he responded, both his hands buried in her
auburn curls, his mouth coming down on hers again
and again with a thrusting power that answered her invitation, her temptingly parted moist lips.

Deftly Luc reached behind him. He pulled a quilt
from the couch and spread it out on the floor. It was
December, but the usually cool room glowed with their
heat.

At times he was so gentle in his lovemaking that she
could barely feel his exploring fingers, his lips that
knew every surface of her hungry body. She arched

closer, then, urging him without words for the pressure of his touch. And when he granted what she desired, when his strong hands grasped, kneaded, smoothed, then grasped again, her breath came in gasps—when it came at all.

Suddenly there was a rough urgency in Luc that brought out a nearly savage response in her. She knew how to make him moan with a pleasure near to madness. And he knew all the secret places of her desire. His lips, his tongue, his fingers. . . more and more intimately he sought those places and drew a tremulous, thrilling response. Until both of them, mindful only of an all-consuming energy, scaled the heights of ecstasy.

Later, in his bed, she curled against him and went to sleep. Oblivious to the market squares where the vendors were already setting up the stalls of bright fruit, now and then stopping to rub their hands in the early-morning cold. Paula didn't see the café owners sweeping away the last of the long night's debris, or the most junior priests readying the myriad altars of the city for the day's first masses.

Nor did Paula realize that the man who held her so closely, his hand cradling her face against his breast, didn't sleep himself. Luc stared into the slowly intensifying light, contemplating for the thousandth time how to preserve his future with this woman, this woman who he knew could only continue to love him if he found the courage he'd lost.

CHAPTER SEVENTEEN

IT TOOK LUC an impossibly long time to decide what to get Paula for Christmas.

The first thing was the most obvious: emeralds. He knew she wouldn't miss the symbolic significance. Not that he had any right to stake a claim to her; ideas like that were entirely foreign to his notion of love. Paula wasn't a possession, nor was his love for her something one could mark out the way an animal marks out a territory. No, what the emeralds would have symbolized were his feelings: lasting, beautiful, rare. And the gems would have matched the challenging, captivating depths of her eyes.

But he decided against emeralds, not because he couldn't afford them. He just didn't like the idea of giving her something poor men risked their lives to mine for the pleasure of rich women. He realized she wouldn't have liked that idea, either.

Next he considered writing something for her. He didn't doubt he could do it, but he was afraid she would see in such a gift more than he was really able to offer: a promise for the future—his future. He couldn't bear the thought that she might expect him to do something he still didn't think he could do. Moens, Marc Fortin, even Merit the bookseller never let up. Pressure from them was what had driven him to take up the local free-lance assignments. Even those had cost him a good deal of soul-searching. To attempt more, to attempt to finish what he'd started— He was in no way ready to suggest even the possibility of that.

In the end Luc settled on a book. He worried that it wasn't an expensive enough present, though even with the discount Merit allowed him, it still cost a good number of francs. He wasn't worried about the book's appeal. Despite the fact that it had been bound in the eighteenth century, the rose-colored smooth leather binding, the pink satin endpapers, the gilt-edged parchmentlike pages were nearly as fresh, fully as delightful as when new. And the poems, though written by someone Luc had never heard of, were as lovely as the book itself, almost a fraction as lovely as the hand that would hold the book, the eyes that would read it.

The afternoon of Christmas Eve, Paula insisted on going to the Grand'Place to see if the flower vendors were still there. He didn't refuse her, even though it seemed cold to him. He wondered if she guessed that he found it almost impossible to refuse her anything—anything he could honestly give, that was.

Most of the vendors were gone, but she managed to find enough dried flowers and fir boughs to decorate his rooms for the holiday. Seeing her balanced on a chair, her slender body outlined against the window's fading light as she pinned a branch to the lintel, Luc wanted to catch her in his arms, to hold her for the mystical length of time called "forever."

Paula loved the book. And as he had half hoped she would, she read him some of the poems. Her voice was a lilting song in the holiday kitchen. Such an accent she had! As though something of the wild, free spaces of Canada were caught in her speech the way a bird is caught in the wind that carries it far abroad. He loved her. This was the happiest Christmas he'd ever had.

FOR PAULA the festive season had been perfect. Her present to Luc, a writing portfolio in gray leather with black silk lining piped in burgundy, had been ready on time, a minor miracle. She'd only just designed it a month earlier, and it had taken her a week to find a craft teacher willing to make it.

The day before Christmas, she and Luc spent the whole morning and part of the afternoon at the markets. To Paula it seemed remarkably warm for the season, but she hurried because Luc was obviously cold. She loved the way the winter breezes stirred in his black hair, the crisp air adding color to his cheeks. Most of all she loved how his eyes glowed every time she caught them on her.

Late in the afternoon as they made their way to his place, the bells started to peal—all the bells of Brussels, it seemed. The sound of them filled her with such rapture that it hurt. Paula turned to the man beside her and saw that he, too, felt the special happiness of that moment.

She wished then that she could give him the one thing she most longed for him to have: the confidence to finish his work. But that wasn't something one person could give another. Instead she gave him her yuletide joy, her presence, her love.

The next day he gave her a Christmas dinner worthy of any three- or five-star chef: roast duck with all the trimmings.

BEFORE LONG it was January, the beginning of the last term of school for her seniors—Villette, Karel and Margaret among them. It was also the beginning of Paula's second year at Le Berceau.

Part of her training had been vocational, and it stood her in good stead as she began to work with the seniors, helping them develop the various skills necessary to finding jobs. Both Villette and Margaret had always intended to look for work immediately after graduation, but Karel had had to wage a long war with his father to do what he really wanted to do—work at a newspaper instead of going on to university. Aside from serving as a sounding board for his problems, there wasn't a lot Paula could offer the boy in the way of advice, since Luc, as his mentor, was helping him with letters of inquiry, résumés and applications.

Villette, as always, demanded a great deal of Paula's time and attention. "Please come, miss," she begged one afternoon. "You won't be sorry. It'll be great. Imagine—Gallant himself is going to be there!"

"Villette, I'd be delighted to come to your class. But I do think you have to be careful about getting your hopes up too high. In the next little while you're going to be dancing in a lot of auditions, and you can't afford to get so excited about each one. It may take many before an inexperienced dancer even gets a role, let alone a place in a company as prestigious as Gallant's Ballets d'Aujourd'hui."

"I'll get a place; you'll see. Anyway, this is just an open class. The real audition isn't until the spring, and you wouldn't be allowed to go to that—professionals only."

"And you, miss, plan to be a professional by then?"

"I'm a professional already," Villette declared with premature but glowing pride.

On the day of the open class, Paula offered a few words of encouragement to Laurice LePan, the dance teacher, before taking one of the chairs stretched in a row across the front of the studio. Before long Monsieur Josef struck a chord, and ten of the senior ballet students entered in a graceful line.

Paula's eyes went immediately to Villette. Her blond

hair was drawn back somewhat from her face, but it still managed to fall in a golden tumble against her fresh brow and rosy cheeks. Her pale beige, almost skin-colored leotard was not only sleeveless—unlike anybody else's, it was also low cut and practically transparent. Over the leotard she had on a dance skirt, not a tutu, but a scarflike bit of fluff that drew attention to her slender waist and her hips, which were quite curvaceous for a ballerina. Her tights were the same shade as her leotard, and the total effect was quite suggestive.

It took Paula only a minute to figure out what Villette was up to. The girl had obviously decided to draw attention to herself in any way possible. She danced only for Roland Gallant, the distinguished visitor. She never took her eyes from the choreographer the whole hour of the class. She managed to plant herself in front of him whenever possible. She flirted with him; she attempted to cajole him into watching only her. At times she nearly succeeded. Again and again his eyes strayed to her as though he was mesmerized.

Poor Madame LePan didn't seem to know whether to feel proud or embarrassed, Paula judged from the look on her face. Villette's technique couldn't be called flawless—even a less-than-expert viewer like Paula could see that. Yet the girl certainly had stage presence. She had mastered the trick of capturing her audience's attention.

"He loved me!" Villette declared, bursting into Paula's office the next morning.

"I thought I asked you not to come in in the mornings. You know I only see students in the afternoon unless there's an emergency." Paula's voice wasn't really stern. And this wasn't by any means the first time Villette had interrupted her during the hour before lunch that she tried to devote to paperwork.

"This is an emergency—a good emergency, old grouch. Gallant loved me. I'm the only one he picked to audition in the spring. Isn't it wonderful?"

"Yes, Villette," Paula said sincerely. "It *is* wonderful. Yesterday afternoon after class, Madame LePan told me she was fairly sure Gallant would want you to audition. But you know, getting an audition isn't the same thing as getting a job. Not at all. Madame LePan is concerned about your technique. She says you need to spend more time in the studio. You've missed Saturday classes three weeks in a row."

"So I slept in. Big deal!" she said, surprising Paula with her English.

"You sound like a character from an American TV show."

"Video. Karel's father let him get some videocassettes from London and New York," the girl said, resuming in French. "We stayed up almost all night watching them last weekend."

"Don't your parents mind your being out so late?"

"They're in Amsterdam. Granddaddy puts his chauffeur on standby, or whatever you call it. When I'm ready to come home, I just phone...."

"Villette, I worry about you sometimes, you know that?"

"Save it," she said again in English, her voice lively and holding contempt for anything serious. "Want to sit with me at lunch today?"

"How would you like it if I took you out?"

"It's against school rules for students to leave the premises at lunch," Villette declared saucily but without conviction.

"Whenever have you cared about school rules?"

"You've got a point, Paula."

"Mademoiselle Emanuel. Be at the front door in forty-five minutes."

"It's a deal. Thanks, *Mademoiselle* Emanuel." That was Villette's favorite taunt. Paula hoped the girl never learned the antiquated English term, "old maid." She would never hear the end of it.

VILLETTE WASN'T THE ONLY STUDENT to be congratulated that month. Kathelijne de Schutter entered a juried art show and received a prize for the best work. This was so unusual a feat for a student—and a junior student, at that—that she had been interviewed by *Le Soir*, and her photograph had appeared.

Not everyone's work was proceeding so well. A tearful Margaret Johnson sat opposite Paula one afternoon.

"I wanted him to be proud of me, and now he's ashamed...."

"Margaret, Monsieur Josef is an experienced teacher. He's had students fail exams before. I'm sure he understands—"

"Well, *I'm* ashamed. I was awful. I was so awful." Fresh tears fell, and Paula stood up, coming around to put her hand on the student's shoulder.

"All I can say is thank God nobody was there but the adjudicator. She didn't say anything, but I could see by her face that she was going to fail me. She hated me."

"Nobody hates you. You have to stop thinking that way. Look, one of the biggest problems arts students have is that they can't always separate judgments of their work from judgments of themselves. You're a fine girl, Margaret, and soon you're going to be a fine woman. You're intelligent, sensitive and kind. I know you think of others before you think of yourself. You're—"

"I'm a lousy singer."

"No. You are not a bad singer. But you are not a top-notch performer, either. We've talked about that lots of times before, haven't we?"

"It's the same thing."

"Margaret—how much do you want to be a professional singer? How much does singing mean to you?"

"A lot," the girl answered strongly. "Singing means almost everything to me."

"Does it mean you'd be willing to sacrifice something for it?"

"What would I have to sacrifice?"

"A little of your ambition."

"What?"

"Margaret, perhaps to remain a singer, you're going to have to abandon your hopes of being a solo performer."

"But that's the whole purpose of my being here."

"No. The purpose of your being here is to study singing. You hate recitals, Margaret. . . ."

"You're right," she said brokenly. "I *hate* them!" Again she burst into tears. Paula said nothing, merely standing behind the girl and comforting her with the touch of her hand.

After a while the sobbing subsided and Paula was slowly able to resume the conversation. "I can't tell you what's right and what's wrong in your career, Margaret. We can start talking about alternatives, though. Why don't you think about that until our next session?"

"Okay. . . . I guess I can."

"You know, Margaret, the first step toward solving any problem is simply to admit the problem exists. From then on, you can work hard to find a solution."

SOMETIMES PAULA WISHED she could believe in her own advice. She was ready to admit her lack of a plan for her future was a problem, a problem no nearer solution than it had been the night Luc told her about his disillusionment following his injury.

They were both very busy. During the past few weeks Luc had been involved in another municipal issue. It was no secret that he was now spending quite a bit of time working on newspaper articles.

"How do you feel about all this?" Paula casually asked him one night when he had to run off after a quickly shared dinner to attend a municipal meeting.

"About the bylaw? Neutral. In this commune of Brussels, they tend to sit on things until the last minute."

"What I mean is, how do you feel about the reporting, about getting involved again?"

The line of his jaw was taut as he carefully answered. "About the reporting, I feel fine. I see what needs to be said, and I say it. But there's no involvement. This is just exercise. The kids like to think their teacher can actually do the thing he's teaching!" He laughed, but there was a cold edge to his voice.

Standing, he bent to give her a quick kiss. "Thanks for cooking supper, love. Leave the dishes. I'll do them tomorrow...." And he was gone.

As she cleared the table and cleaned up before heading for her own place, Paula decided it pleased her to know he was writing again, but fear accompanied the thought. She still wondered whether he had been in charge of the underground press. If he had, that could mean his work hadn't been carried on by anyone else. Paula had no way of knowing. Everything he'd ever told her about these things, he'd told her in his own good time. She could only wait. Even if he was contemplating something that would part them. Even if he was planning it.

One afternoon not long after, she was passing his

classroom and caught the drift of his lecturing. She was astonished at the change in his methods. All the fire seemed gone from him. He didn't harangue, he didn't scold. When Paula peeked in, she saw boredom on the students' faces. A few looked puzzled and disappointed.

Another day she overheard an argument between Luc and Marie.

"Why now? Why after all this time?" Marie was tender and cajoling, as she often was when she spoke to Luc, but there was an undercurrent of near hysteria in her tone. "It's the middle of the term. The seniors—"

"I'll prepare them as best I can—"

"Prepare them? Then you've decided definitely? I thought we were talking about an idea, a possibility."

"I *would* prepare them."

"Luc. Please."

"Marie, I'm telling you these things so that you can consider making plans in advance. If I had thought it would upset you so much, I would have—"

"Upset me! Of course it upsets me! You're a fool, Luc. You don't know when you're well off. Consider just what you'll be throwing away. You are a complete fool. The waste of it. *Mon Dieu*, the utter waste!"

Paula didn't see Luc for three days after that, not even in class. She couldn't understand his absence or his silence. They hadn't argued. The last time they'd been together, his lovemaking had had about it an undeniable urgency. But he'd acted that way before. And so had she.

The morning of the third day, she awoke with a dull headache that throbbed persistently through an early meeting with a personnel recruiter from an international arts-management corporation. She had to make a conscious effort to pay attention to what the woman was saying, even though under normal circumstances she would have had no difficulty considering the recruiter's needs and matching them with possible candidates. Today her mind couldn't seem to focus on anything.

By lunch she was well aware of the fact that Luc was absent yet again. Villette plunked herself down beside Paula and asked, "Where's your boyfriend?"

"I don't have a boyfriend," Paula answered automatically, her usual way of dealing with Villette's taunts when she didn't have the energy to play games with the girl.

"Are you all right, miss?" Villette asked, touching Paula's arm. The gesture was genuinely compassionate, and it occurred to Paula that maybe Villette was finally growing up. Nonetheless, there was no way she could confide in the student beyond the most superficial disclosures.

"I have a headache, that's all. Want my dessert? I don't think I can handle it."

"No thanks, Paula. I'm on a diet."

"You? Will wonders never cease?"

"I told you I was a professional, and as a professional I have to keep my body in top-notch condition."

"Not to mention your mind," Paula teased.

"Don't you worry about my mind," the girl retorted. "Or my heart, either. Speaking of which, where's Monsieur Luc been?"

"I don't know, Villette," Paula said simply. But the deep concern in her voice must have registered with the student.

"If I can do anything. . ." the girl offered.

Apparently there was nothing anybody could do. By the final hours of work on that third day, Paula was distraught. Luc hadn't shown up. Marie had taken over two of his classes and canceled the rest. She, too, knew nothing of the writing teacher's whereabouts, or so she swore. At a quarter to three in the afternoon, Paula dismissed one of her student clients early and went in search of Karel, hoping he wasn't tied up in class. She found him quickly. He was sitting in the garden, apparently oblivious to the winter cold.

"Karel," Paula said softly as she approached him from behind, "what are you doing out here?"

Despite the gentleness of her voice, the boy jumped. He turned, and Paula could see that strong emotion had taken hold of him, though he struggled to keep his face expressionless. "You scared me, miss," he said. He motioned for her to sit beside him.

"What's wrong, Karel?" she asked. She saw him swallow hard before he answered.

"Nothing. I'm just thinking."

"It's a little cold to be sitting outside, don't you think?"

"I hadn't noticed."

Paula hated to disturb him further, but she knew she had to ask. "Karel, do you know where Luc is?"

He looked down, staring fixedly at the flagstones at his feet. Slowly he shook his head. There was a moment's silence; then he said, "It's been a long time, miss, since Monsieur Luc has missed classes because of illness. I sure hope that's not going to start again!"

Despite her own deep concern, Paula felt the need to reassure Karel. She touched his shoulder. "Don't worry. Whatever Luc's problem is, he'll solve it. Just as he always has. He's a strong man."

"I know he is. But even strong people get sick."

"Try not to worry."

It hadn't even occurred to Paula that Luc might be ill. She convinced Karel to leave the cold garden, while she went back into the building to grab her coat. After throwing it on she ran all the way to Luc's place. If he was sick it would explain why he hadn't answered his phone in days. . . .

"I DON'T BELIEVE he's ill," the woman said, "but I haven't seen him in a day or two. He's a wanderer, that one. . . ."

"Please, if you could just hurry and open the door."

He wasn't there. His rooms were neater than usual, as though he hadn't eaten or slept there for a while. Only his desk showed signs of recent use; it was littered with letters. All of them were in Spanish, and Paula could see that they were recent. But she couldn't have read them even if she had wanted to.

She had no idea where he was or what he was doing, but she doubted that he was sick. Dejected, she carefully locked his door, descended the three flights to the street and walked slowly back to Le Berceau.

"Where have you been?" Angèle Martel asked as soon as she got back to her office. "Margaret was here. I had to send her away. And you're five minutes late for study—"

"Oh, no!" Without even taking off her coat, Paula rushed to the study hall. She could tell by the noise audible through the door that the lack of supervision had had an effect.

The hour flew by because Paula was there in body only. Her mind was with Luc, wherever he was. She wasn't worried. She wasn't angry. She was empty. The students settled down. There was a time of silence, then a bell signaling the end of the session and the day. There was a scuffle of feet as the students left. Wearily she rose to go, too. But she went to the window first. It was February, though there was no snow. No flowers, either, of course. The garden was barren and deserted.

No, it wasn't. He was there.

He didn't notice her. He seemed to notice nothing but the ground at his feet. He looked slightly unkempt, and he hadn't shaved that day. She could see the raven strands of his hair graze the top of the collar of his black raincoat; the wind had tousled the dark tresses. Without moving Paula stared at him.

Luc's hands were clasped behind his back as he paced the flagstone walk. Back and forth—totally lost in thought. Like a lion, she reflected. But whether a lion pacing the jungle fearing impending captivity, or one pacing his cage dreaming of release, she couldn't tell. She watched with a nameless grief.

Twilight settled over the winter garden. The weak light faded. Her window view, so clear when Paula had begun her watch, was marred by the reflection of the lighted room behind her. The man outside seemed not to notice the approach of night. The woman didn't see a member of the cleaning staff enter the study hall, sweep briskly, then leave her alone again in the large room. Paula moved only to breathe, until the man she watched stopped, drew his breath, squared his shoulders and headed for the door.

She lost sight of him, but she knew he would find her. With a heavy heart she sank into one of the chairs beside a long oak table. She hadn't even removed her coat. When she looked up, she saw that he still wore his.

Luc came to her, grabbing her hand in both of his, which were icy. He kissed her with such passion that he stopped her breath, and for that fleeting instant, stopped her fear, as well. He sat beside her, putting his arm around her shoulders. The scent of musk mingled with the coldness of winter air. She would not cry. She would not.

"Paula," he began, "I have to say this before I run out of courage. I love you. Make no mistake about that. The last thing I want is to hurt you. But I'm going to hurt you—at least for a while. I'm no good to you or to myself the way I am now. As long as I'm here in Belgium, as long as I'm staying away from the work I started, I can have no self-respect. You can have no respect for me.

"Please, don't shake your head. Stop crying. You understand. I know you do. Paula, I want the same thing for you as for me. I want us to be all we are capable of being. I want to face life not as a dreamer but a doer. I started something years ago that I have to finish. I fought against that truth for a long time. Now my fighting is over. I have to go, love. I've decided. In fact, this afternoon I sent a telegram that commits me on my honor. I'm returning to Central America as soon as arrangements can be made."

CHAPTER EIGHTEEN

SHE WANTED TO CRY OUT, *What about what you started with me? What about* that *unfinished business?*

She didn't say those words or anything like them. Not in the dining hall, nor on the slow, silent walk to Luc's rooms. Nor at any moment in the long night, while they clung to each other as though for the last time.

By morning she managed to get some conviction into her voice when she swore, "Luc, I know this is for the best. I don't think it's the only way. But if it's the way you have to take— It's just that I'd wished...."

"What, my love? What did you wish?"

"That we had a future."

"Paula, I wish that, too. But I can't talk about the future in the same way you can—not now, not yet. Please try to understand."

"I do understand. I know this has nothing to do with me personally. I know you're not rejecting me."

"No. No, you don't understand. Not if it could even enter your head that I'd reject you." Tenderly he took her hand and held it to his lips. She reached up and captured his fingers, drawing his cool palm to the heat of her cheek. He kissed her forehead and held her more tightly to him. They were in his bed, and she had no way of knowing whether she would ever lie in this room again.

"Nor is it right to say you have nothing to do with this." His eyes burned with tears as he sought hers.

"Paula," he said, "you changed my life. If you hadn't been standing in Marie's office that rainy night last year, I might still be as lost as I was then. I might have spent the rest of my days being nothing but a lonely, frustrated writing teacher."

"Luc, you'll never be able to make me stop believing that you're a fine teacher, that you can do as much good—"

"I know you can't help the vocational counseling," Luc teased, tweaking her chin. But he was deadly serious as he continued. "You can say what you want about my abilities as a teacher, but nobody can deny my loneliness, my sense of failure. I felt it didn't matter what I did with my life anymore. Getting from one day to the next was about all I could manage sometimes, and that seemed good enough. It's true I put on a front for the kids. Maybe I fooled some of them."

"Luc, you're fooling yourself if you think you didn't inspire your students."

"It was a job. It *is* a job, and I'll continue to do what I can for the next few weeks or so—"

"Few weeks? Oh, Luc. So short a time!"

"Paula, you've given me back so much of myself. But this last task is mine alone. It may be more than three weeks; it may be less. If I could I'd spend every minute of that time with you, but I can't. If you don't see me, if I don't call—"

"But why can't you?"

"From today on, my time isn't my own. In a sense, my life isn't my own. The worst of it is, I can't explain. I can only ask you to trust me. I can only ask you to believe that I love you, that I'd stay here with you in my home, in my arms, forever if I could. I can't."

ANOTHER MARCH DESCENDED on Brussels, but unlike the previous one, it wasn't lovely. The garden displayed no early flowers and no errant flautist. Luc was far too busy to visit the garden, to supervise his team of high-school reporters or even to teach all his classes, some of which Marie Légère carried on for him.

As the cold, rainy days continued, Paula saw him less and less. Sometimes the months of their intimacy seemed nothing but a dream. At night, alone in bed, she remembered the warmth of him, his body curled against hers in sleep. In the wakeful darkness of those nights, she feared she was being punished for having loved him so strongly, so openly, without any promise of the future. But her heart was so full of caring that she could find no wrong in what they'd been to each other, what they would always be if Luc should complete his work and come back to her.

And if he didn't come back? He hadn't left yet, but already the fear was rooted in her heart. She would be brave, she convinced herself, as brave as he. She had always thought of love as something that demanded two people should be together. Now she understood that sometimes they must be apart.

Paula was willing to give him the time he needed, even though it meant she had almost no time with him. Still, she did see him at school. Sometimes he looked at her with an expression that hid all feeling not only from her but from the students and fellow teachers who surrounded him. Sometimes when she caught his eye, he looked away, his face tight and grim. And other times she caught him unawares, seeing then in the violet eyes such naked pain, such undisguised longing that she wished she could run to him, convince him to forget his plans, to stay with her, or even—she thought wildly—to take her with him.

She knew that was out of the question. She also knew Luc wasn't just trying to decide what to do about his trip. He was deciding what to do about her.

After a few weeks had passed and he was still there, though they'd had no more intimate evenings, Paula began to get used to seeing him only across crowded corridors, only at meals served with a hundred others present, only in the company of fellow professionals. She almost grew used to hiding her eyes from the accidental scrutiny of his. She tried hard to concentrate on her work, to hide her emotions from others, to speak to Luc the very few times she had the chance in a way that revealed nothing of the searing pain she felt to be near but unable to ask him all the things she longed to know. "I can't explain," he had said. "I can only ask you to trust me."

THE PLACE was a shambles. Luc looked around, however, and saw not all his earthly possessions in total disarray. What he saw was more work, which meant more time; time that was rapidly running out.

How he hated this packing! Once he had considered himself a man who traveled lightly through life. Now here he was, frantically shoving bits and pieces into cardboard cartons as though every item was a treasure just because it was going to be part of the new place. He couldn't help smiling when he thought about that, because despite the fear, the agonizing decision making, and worst of all, the impending separation, he now had something to look forward to, something he'd dreamed of in the days before he'd learned just how long it takes for dreams to come true.

His dreams were of Paula and the surprise. And when he found the pictures of Lise, he carefully packed them away, offering a prayer for her. He winced at the sight of the guns in the background of the candid photo. He offered a prayer for himself.

Books, dishes, clothes, records, tapes, towels. As fast as he could effectively work, he stowed them into the cartons. He wasn't particularly careful, knowing that nothing had very far to travel, nothing, that was, except the contents of the single battered suitcase he had packed first. It sat by the door as if waiting, as he was, for the call. Luc had no idea when that call would come, but time was fleeing. It would come soon.

Growing even more bored with the tedious work, he pulled his cassette player from one of the boxes and dug a few tapes out of another. He'd only just switched the thing on when he had to turn it down before answering the door.

"Karel! Great—I'm glad you could make it," he said heartily. The boy's face was a study in sorrow, but Luc didn't let on that he could see how upset the kid was. "Come on in."

"Luc, I—"

"Before you say anything, Karel, push some junk off a chair and sit down. Can I get you a beer?"

"Beer?"

"Yeah. Wet stuff with foam on top. What do you say?"

"Okay. Thanks."

In the kitchen, Luc opened the fridge. There wasn't any food in it and hadn't been for several days, but there were three beers, and he took two of them back into the living room. Karel was staring off into space. Luc handed him an open bottle and a glass, a nicety he dispensed with as he quaffed his own beer. Clearing off a space on the couch, he sat down.

"I wasn't sure you'd want to come," Luc began.

Karel shrugged his shoulders, not looking at his mentor.

"I'd be really hurt if I thought you considered my going a betrayal, Karel."

"Luc," the boy said, looking directly at the man for the first time, "you've taught me better than that. I'm not worried about missing you. I'm worried about losing you."

The eloquence of the statement caught Luc by surprise, and he had to fight against the catch in the back of his throat. "Then I'll just have to make sure I'm not lost—right?"

"Are you doing this just to prove a point, Luc?" the boy blurted out. "Because if you are, you should know that nobody thinks it's necessary. Everybody thinks you're a hero already."

Luc suppressed a smile at the word "hero." It seemed to be a word teenagers loved. That was fine, except he hoped they would learn it had little place in an adult's vocabulary.

"A person can only be genuinely heroic in his own eyes, Karel, because only he can know when he's lived up to what he's capable of. That's what this trip is about—that and the fact that what I'm about to do will eventually help a lot of people. You understand that."

"Yes, but . . . ."

"But . . . ?"

"But I wish you didn't have to go."

"So do I, Karel. So do I."

STILL PAULA WAITED. It was a strange time of an unusual kind of faith. She knew in her heart that soon secrets would be revealed and real plans would be made, though everything between Luc and her remained unspoken.

One day after lunch she wandered into the teachers' lounge. She had a few minutes to spare and was restless even after having strolled in the garden. She walked over to the table where teachers often left books and magazines for each other. She stood thumbing through a journal, not really paying much attention to anything in it. At the sound of a footstep in the doorway, she turned, eager for a bit of adult company before she had to return to an afternoon of counseling.

She was shocked to see Luc standing there. For a moment he was startled, too. Then he fairly flew to her and swept her into his arms. His lips took hers with a hunger that was achingly familiar. She clung to him, feeling beneath her encircling arms the strength of his body, the fragile joy of his presence, which any day now would be shattered by his leaving.

She longed to hold him, kiss him, talk to him... keep him. But in far too brief a moment they both came to their senses. Realizing that any of the teachers might walk in, they pulled apart.

"Luc?" Paula asked, his name alone sufficient question for all she longed to know.

"Paula, I'm still waiting...."

"Can't we— Couldn't I come over to your place?"

"Not yet. Not— Paula, it's so hard for me. To have you near would—"

"Ah, Luc, there you are!" It was Marie's voice in the open doorway. "Can I see you for a moment?"

Shooting Paula a subtle but promising glance, Luc followed the principal out of the lounge. To have her near would what? Make him change his mind? She thought about that for only a moment before letting out a sigh of frustration that verged on hopelessness. Not only did she long to be with Luc, but she had to put up with Marie's new tendency to monopolize what little time he had. The principal seemed to be calling him away or into her office with increasing frequency.

It soon became common knowledge that Luc was about to resign his teaching position. The grapevine was buzzing long before the formal announcement. When the official word came it was heartbreaking, not only for the students, but for the teachers, who had to listen to Luc deliver an uncharacteristically short, yet still elegant speech in the lounge after lunch. He had decided to give only one day's notice of his departure.

Though she was one of the first to see him enter, and though he pressed a comforting hand into her back as he passed, Paula was stunned when he strolled up to the table where the teachers were gathered—at Marie's express request—and called them to attention.

He took a seat. "Well, my friends," he began, "today I'm about to dispel one rumor and confirm another."

Everyone hung on Luc's words as they so often had during staff meetings.

"The rumor I'm about to lay to rest concerns us all." He hesitated dramatically, still in control of his voice and of the situation. "There are those who are convinced that the bunch of us are just failed artists teaching others to be failed artists."

There was a ripple of laughter around the table. Not waiting for it to subside completely, Luc went on. "As of this afternoon, I am about to leave the ranks of failed artists, thus making that famous rumor untrue in my own case, or at least I hope so. I don't know whether 'artist' is the right word. And I can't say much about what sort of failures the future may make up for—or hold." His voice was becoming a little choked, and the room had grown terribly still.

"The rumor I'm confirming is that I'm leaving the school and the country—for now. I know that doesn't come as a surprise. And I hope that you all know how aware I am that I owe you people a lot. You've been patient colleagues and loyal friends. I'm flying out tomorrow at two, and when I go I'm going to carry with me the memory of your support. And I'm going to look forward avidly to the day when I can see you all again.... "

Hearing his words to the teachers, Paula knew a

shocked grief beyond naming. Though everyone had suspected he was going, no one, including her, had dreamed he'd be among them for only one more day. He must have tried to reach her, but she'd been so tired from several sleepless nights that she'd taken her phone off the hook and gone to bed early the night before. And that morning she'd been tied up in a lengthy session with an upset parent. Paula could only stare now. His eyes met and held hers; there was a message there, but she was in no state to read it. Sensing that, he made for her the moment he concluded his remarks. But several teachers, including Marie, stepped between him and Paula, who couldn't bear to stay one moment longer. She hurried to her office in search of needed privacy.

Before she even got to her door, she heard whispering and weeping. Mustering what little professional poise she could, she walked into her office. Karel, his body racked with sobs, was slumped against Paula's desk. Villette, more sobered than Paula had ever seen her, was comforting the boy.

"What is it?" Paula asked, her effort to control herself making her voice sound hard and cold.

"Karel is— Karel needs help, miss. He just found out Monsieur Luc is leaving tomorrow. I told him he should come here to your office because you... because you're...." Villette's eyes were shiny, but she shed no tears. "I'm sorry for both you and Karel, miss," she said, planting a kiss of pure kindness on Paula's cheek.

Adult thoughtfulness from someone who had almost always seemed a self-absorbed child was nearly Paula's undoing. "Thank you, Villette," she managed. "Will you leave us now?"

Gently Paula made Karel stand up. It was probably against staff regulations, but she held Karel in her arms until he calmed down enough to go home in the taxi Paula called for him.

After he left she sat down, her elbows on her desk, her head in her hands. She sat for a moment in silence before she heard a slight scuffle at her door. Looking up, she was surprised to see Marie.

"I've canceled classes, and I'm sending everyone home until Monday. I haven't done that in years. It's ill-advised, I'm sure, but nothing's going to get done around here for the next day or so, anyway." The principal was as cool and controlled as ever, yet Paula didn't doubt she was as upset as everyone else at Le Berceau. Marie was silent, her lips a grim line, her jaw clenched. When she collected herself to speak again, she said, "I really can't understand why Luc is doing this, Paula. I always knew he wasn't happy here, but everyone respected him so, and his students did well. I thought that with time. . . ."

She sighed, unable or unwilling to finish. She glanced down, and for the first time Paula clearly saw the woman's vulnerability. Whatever Marie's feelings for Luc, genuine concern was among them.

"Marie, the day may come when he's back here driving us all crazy again. Don't give up hope." Though intended as solace for the other woman, Paula's words brought hope to herself. She smiled.

Marie, smiling rather weakly in return, said, "I came to tell you that he's waiting for you in my office. . . ."

As SHE HAD DONE on her first night in Brussels, Paula approached the principal's office feeling she held her whole future in her trembling hands. Luc had announced he was leaving Belgium at two the next afternoon. It was now one o'clock. Twenty-five hours. In twenty-five hours, a war could be won or lost. In twenty-five hours a life could be saved or a person could die. A woman could become a wife, or a widow. It was a matter of courage, of pride, of luck.

Suddenly Paula cared nothing about courage and pride. She didn't care about Luc's commitment to some country thousands of miles away. She didn't care about what he thought he had to do. There was something she had to do: convince him to stay. In the instant before she thrust open the door to Marie's office, she made up her mind that she was going to throw herself into his arms and beg him not to go.

The minute she opened the door, she changed her mind.

She gazed at him. On this most important day of leave-taking, he had dressed in a trim suit. He had got a haircut, too. In the teachers' lounge he had looked distant, professional. Now, for the first time in many weeks, he looked like himself again—like the Luc of old, full of energy, full of his irascible charm, full of the disregard for ordinary courtesy that allowed him to butt into everybody else's business. Because, with his back to Paula, Luc was down on one knee in front of Marie's safe, one hand on the open door. He was rummaging through Marie's papers with abandon, examining various documents with cursory speed, then rejecting each by tossing it to the floor, where a sloppy little pile was growing.

"Luc! What in heaven's name are you doing? Marie will—"

"She forgot to give me back a certain paper," he answered, determined in his search, not turning his head at the sound of Paula's voice. Despite the intense state of her emotions, she was struck by the old desire to laugh at him. Affection flashed in her misty green eyes as a grin spread on her lips, the first true sign of happiness in a long time.

"Luc," she said, walking toward him and putting her hand on his shoulder. "Marie is going to—"

He interrupted her, standing abruptly and seizing her in his strong arms. His lips took hers in a kiss of brief but powerful passion. "Forget Marie," he breathed. "She won't be back until we're gone."

She wanted to ask how he could be so sure, but his breath was a moist heat on her cheek, and the musky fragrance of his skin was sudden intoxication. She moved closer into the circle of his embrace, and teasing his lips with her eager tongue, initiated another searing kiss.

"There's a better place to be doing this," Luc said hoarsely. Thinking she understood what he meant, Paula took a step away, and Luc didn't try to pull her nearer. He went back to his search, but it only took a moment longer to find what he was seeking. "Ah," he said with satisfaction, holding up a legal-looking document; on the outside, a single word in large letters was partially visible.

Titre. Was it a deed? What would he be doing with a deed? Wild hope twisted in her heart. Had he changed his mind about leaving?

"I see a question in your eyes, my love," Luc said, "but the answer is no." Again he kissed her, a gentle, caressing kiss. His tenderness after so many weeks of enforced separation was too much for Paula. Tears sprang to her eyes. "Stop," he cajoled, wiping the saltiness from her cheeks. "You'll have reason and time to cry soon enough, and so will I. But not now, not yet."

He turned from her to the safe, and with a quick shuffle, put the papers he'd strewn on the floor back in order, keeping the one aside. From a little distance Paula stared at that paper as though her future were contained in the folds. Luc swung the door shut, gave the combination device a few turns and slipped the document into his pocket. His eyes expressed what could only be called merriment.

"Luc," Paula said, smiling in spite of herself, "what is going on?"

"What are you willing to do to find out? Are you willing, perhaps, to give me another kiss or two?"

Caught up in his mood, she literally threw herself at him. The kisses she planted on his cheek were girlish in their cheerful enthusiasm, but he held her tightly, his arms around her waist, and the kisses changed.

"You are about to take a little journey with me." His voice was husky and commanding. "Go get your coat."

Paula was back in a flash. She had no idea where they were going, but the ends of the earth would have been okay if he'd asked.

"Are we going to your place?" She ran along behind him as he took a small corridor toward a side exit from the school. The corridor led to the parking lot. Since neither of them had a car, why they were taking that route was just one more mystery in an afternoon of mysteries.

Luc stopped short at her question, turning to her. There was pain in his eyes. "Paula, it never occurred to me that I should have brought you back to the place one last time. It's empty. Someone else is moving in tonight."

It was as though Eden had suddenly been wiped from the map. All the hours they'd shared at Luc's— the talk, the love, the poems, their first Christmas—all of it seemed to pass before Paula's eyes. Never again. For a moment she stood still, feeling that the world was beginning to slow in its spin. Uncertain new gravities were hindering her from taking a step.

"Where are all your things?" she asked weakly.

"You'll see," he said so softly that she almost didn't hear.

"What?"

"Come on," Luc said, taking her hand. "Here's the car."

"The car?" she asked, thoroughly puzzled now. "But you don't have a car!"

"Well, I had to rent one for the past week to get around to handle last-minute details. Come on, get in, miss. We're going for a ride."

"Where?"

"You'll see."

Luc LeBlanc drove with passionate intensity. Before long they had passed the wide busy boulevards ringing the inner city and were headed for the suburbs. Paula gave up trying to get him to tell her what was going on. She concentrated instead on looking at him, on touching him whenever possible. She wanted desperately to save as many memories of him as she could, for whatever this mystery tour was about, Luc hadn't changed his plans. She knew it was useless to hope for that or anything like it.

After a drive of three-quarters of an hour, they entered a suburb of old, stately houses, some in the characteristic crow-stepped Flemish style, and others with architectural features more influenced by Paris than Amsterdam. The house they finally stopped at was the smallest on the street, but one of the loveliest, a whitewashed stucco bungalow with a dark roof and detail in dark wood. Beside the front door, bushes twined their bare branches around a trellis, promising roses to come. There was a little tree-lined drive beside the house, and Luc pulled into it.

"Are we going to visit someone?" Paula asked in disbelief. He couldn't have picked a worse time.

"No," Luc answered cryptically. Again Paula noticed the merriment in his tone, but it was mixed with something else—with unmistakable excitement.

"Come on, Luc, tell me what's going on. And don't say, 'You'll see.'"

"You'll see," he teased, hopping out of the car. By the time he came around to her side she was standing on the drive, waiting, her hands on her hips in mock impatience. Luc grabbed her hand and nearly dragged her to the front door of the little house; he couldn't wait to get inside. Stopping on the flagstone porch, he unlocked the door with a key on the same ring as the car keys—and his crystal pineapple.

"But Luc. . .?" And then Paula understood.

"I lied about the car," he said. "It's ours. So is this house." And he swung open the door for her first view of this, his gift.

CHAPTER NINETEEN

PAULA'S HEART WAS FULL of an unspeakable joy as she walked from room to room. There was a wide entrance hall just beyond the front door. Standing there, Paula saw the kitchen directly ahead through a short corridor. The room was dazzled by sunlight from a huge window, hung with the plants that had been in Luc's old kitchen.

Nothing else in this room was familiar. The table wasn't the old chipped, white-painted one they'd shared so many meals at. The table here was of warm-toned, oiled pine. It looked handmade from an old design, but it was smooth and new, as were the matching chairs and the hutch that Luc now drew Paula to. He opened the glass doors and took out a fine, nearly transparent china plate, putting it into her wondering hands. It was white, but the edge was decorated by a pale green pattern, a repetition of the maple leaf. Looking up, she saw the dish was one of a set—plates, bowls, cups, saucers. "No sharing with your sister," Luc said. "This set is all yours. And so are these—" He opened other drawers and doors. She saw the gleam of crystal and silver, the snowy white of linen and lace.

"Oh, Luc," she whispered. "I don't know what to say."

"Say nothing yet," he answered, leading her into another room, a living room decorated with tapestries and musical instruments that had been in Luc's apartment, along with some other Latin American art objects.

And he showed her the study. His desk was there. His books lined the shelves. She stepped up to gaze again at the familiar volumes, and to her utter amazement she saw a whole row of her own books—every one, in fact, that she'd left in storage space at her apartment.

"How did you know where they were?" It was a silly question considering the many other questions that needed to be asked.

"You once told Marie, and Marie told me," Luc answered. He picked up something from his desk. "This isn't really part of my surprise, but it's something I was thinking about, and I looked into it for you. These are the catalogs of several schools offering advanced courses in psychology. Once you mentioned to me—and to Marie, too—that you were interested in going for another degree. Well, Marie and I feel the board may be moving in the direction of hiring a staff psychologist based on the work you've done so far. It would be a shame for someone else to get a job you paved the way for. Marie feels—and I agree—that the board might be willing to keep you on when your contract expires next January if you were engaged in upgrading your credentials. I mention this now, because you could begin your studies while you're waiting...."

"While I'm waiting for what, Luc?" Paula's voice was steady. Far steadier than her heart. Her eyes had been trained on the catalogs, but now she looked up at him. His eyes were a sea of emotion, the violet of a sea at sunset or at the moment before first light. His gaze locked with hers as he reached into his pocket and took out the folded document. The paper he pressed into her hand was warm from the heat of his body.

"This is the deed to our home," he said, his voice throaty and full of promise. "You will wait for me here, and I will come back." His lips took hers in what seemed an endless kiss, a kiss that robbed her of the breath for protests, questions, thanks. "I *will* come back. It's taken me many long weeks to arrange all this, but now it's settled. I'm going to train a man to finish what I started myself three years ago. I'll have to stay with him out there for six months. But after that, you're going to be stuck with a burnt-out writing teacher again—"

His voice broke, and Paula, holding him closer, could feel a tremor run through him. She clung to him, pressing the whole length of her body against his, as though she could keep him in her arms forever. Wordlessly they stood locked in each other's embrace until he pulled away. "There's one more room," he whispered, "but not yet, my love, not yet."

She knew he meant the bedroom, but she had no idea what the tone of his voice implied, a tone of beguiling mystery.

"Luc?" she questioned. "How did you find this place? How did you furnish it? There are so many things I have to ask...."

"And so little time," he answered. Together they walked back to the kitchen, where Luc produced a bottle of wine. Pouring it into two of their new crystal glasses, he led Paula to the living room and sat beside her on the couch, cradling her in his arms.

"There is so much to explain that I don't know where to start," he said. "Part of the reason I've had so little time is because of this place. Marie helped a lot. She's your ally, Paula. She's family."

Paula nodded. There was too much to try to understand all at once.

"As for the money to buy the house and car and the new things, well...." He hesitated. When he resumed, his tone was tinged with familiar melancholy. "I had a

lot saved from my years as a journalist. Ever since I
left Central America, it's been sitting in an account in
Switzerland. I always meant it to be for my home, but
I couldn't see the use of spending it on myself." He offered her more wine, but she had drunk little of what
he'd given her. He took a sip of his; he didn't raise his
eyes from the glass. "Paula," he said, his voice tightly
controlled, "I'm going to dream about this place; I'm
going to promise myself that the sooner I get my work
done, the sooner I can be here with you. When I finish,
when I come back, I'll never leave again. I want. . . I
want us to be together, then and always. Paula, I want
us to get married."

"Married?"

"I know, the prospect of marrying your old enemy
will take time to get used to. Only there is no time."

"Do you mean— Oh, Luc, what *do* you mean?"

"Marry me today. Now. I love you. I love you more
than I've ever loved anyone, more than anyone else
has loved you. I'm presumptuous, I realize. I presume
you want me and this house and this country. You are
free to say no. But don't. Please don't, Paula. . . ."

She hesitated. She was weighing her whole future
and had only a minute to do so. It didn't take her that
long. "Luc, I'm not free to say no to your offer, just
as you're not free to say no to this trip. Yes, my love,
yes."

PAULA KNEW THAT FOREVER AFTER she would regard it
as one of the most unusual—but nonetheless most
wonderful—weddings ever to have been solemnized.

"The situation is this," Luc explained as he once
more negotiated the city streets, driving them to yet
another mysterious destination. "In this country it's
necessary to have both a civil and a religious ceremony. I would have to have had your cooperation if

I'd wanted to get the necessary papers for the civil wedding—it would have ruined my secret. Far more important, I just couldn't be sure of the time factor. I found out at six o'clock this morning, Paula. I called you, but I put the phone down before it rang. I just couldn't wake you with news like that, though, as it turned out, I guess I broke it to you in a worse way."

"Luc, it's okay."

"And poor Karel. If you can, keep an eye on him for me, will you?"

"Yes, of course. Where are we going, Luc? All this mystery is making me a nervous wreck!"

"We're going to our wedding. Our first wedding."

"First?"

"As I was trying to explain—"

"Before you interrupted yourself...."

"As I was trying to explain, what I intend is for us to make this fully legal when I get back. Sentimental as it sounds, I want us to have the civil ceremony then in the *salle des mariages* at the town hall, because it's at the very center of Brussels, and this city will always be inextricably bound up in my mind and my heart with you. I know you have the right to make a claim for Montreal, but—"

"I'll have to think about what to tell my sister sooner or later, now that you mention Montreal, but there's time for that. Luc, I'd marry you on the moon if it meant you'd come back to me."

"The moon wasn't what I had in mind," he answered, "though I feel the same way." Tenderly he reached for her hand.

"Marc Fortin's brother is a Jesuit," Luc went on. "Father Silas is his name. Given the unusual circumstances, especially the fact that I have to leave tomorrow, he's agreed to dispense with some of the ordinary prerequisites and perform the religious ceremony in a local rectory. He's waiting for us."

The one thing Luc had forgotten in all his planning for this day was that if they were to be married, they needed witnesses. Luckily there were two suitable people close at hand. The first was a cleaning woman who regularly worked at the rectory. She agreed to be Paula's matron of honor, provided the bride and groom were willing to wait for her to go home to change her dress. When she assured Luc that she lived only a few houses away, he agreed. Time, every second of it, was as precious as breath.

The second witness, the best man, was a diocesan auditor who had been looking over the parish books. He graciously put aside pencil and calculator to step into the rectory's small chapel.

As she stood beside Luc, all the unhappiness of the past, all the fear of the future were blessedly suspended. This moment was one frozen instant in the turbulent hours of their lives. The ceremony was brief, only as long as it took for a few prayers and a mutual promise.

"I pledge myself to you, Luc."

"And I to you, Paula."

THE RECEPTION wasn't conducted in the traditional manner, either, for the only guests were the bride and groom. Laughing, Luc carried Paula over the threshold, kicking closed the door and bearing her through the hallway and living room into the bedroom. He urged her to inspect the room's rich decor in shades of peach and white before he came back with a bottle of the finest champagne. He popped the cork and offered a toast. "To our hours together, my love. May they carry us through the months apart."

"To our life together, Luc," Paula toasted.

At his invitation, she tried their new bed, sitting gingerly on the edge. . . but it was only moments before she found herself stretched out beneath him.

The hours were fast fleeing. She hadn't for a single

instant lost track of time that day, despite all that had happened. Already the sun was waning. Soon it would be dark, and when it was light again, Luc would be on his way. She arched her body toward him.

There were no words for the feelings that surged between them, no words as effective as the burning, feverish kisses, the embraces, the sighs of pleasure and promise. Gently he undressed her, his fingers as careful as impatience would allow. She, too, was impatient, her heart a clock ticking away the minutes with cruel swiftness.

Paula lay beneath his hands, rising to his touch as he removed the last of her clothes and began to explore all of her with his mobile lips, his tongue. He kissed her face, her throat, the curve of her shoulder. His mouth on her breast was a warm, moist gift. Lower and lower, more and more insistently his tongue moved until she pressed higher, closer, asking with her whole body for the pleasure only he could give.

He ceased his exploration, drew back a little. He invited her to remove his clothes, which she did more slowly than he had. Her fingers were teasing; her lips followed where her fingers had been until he lay naked and blatantly aroused. Beside the bed a lamp glowed as the outside light faded. By that soft light, Paula looked at Luc. She scarcely noticed his scars anymore, because she loved him so deeply that every inch of him was beautiful to her. He watched her watching him. His eyes glowed their deepest indigo. The strong lines of his jaw and chin were softened by the light and love that seemed to emanate from his whole body.

Tenderly Paula reached down and kissed his cheek with the innocence of a virgin bride. And eagerly Luc turned her so that once again she lay beneath him. The weight of his body, the warm eroticism of his skin along every part of her brought to a pitch the hunger spiraling inside her. She parted her legs, lifting them to encircle his waist, and he responded by slipping deep into her with a shuddering sigh of passion and of need.

With the primal rhythms of nature they moved, two made one by love and desire. Over and over he whispered endearments in French, but she had no word to answer with except his name.

Then even that word left her; she felt the spiral of pleasure widen, engulfing them both. She cried out and heard her cry mingle with his, a trembling song of consummation.

All night they lay in each other's arms, but they slept little. For long hours they talked. Sometimes he told her things about his past and asked her about her childhood, insisting on hearing everything—even things she knew she'd told him before. Luc seemed to want to take with him all of her that he could, every touch, every word.

Once he dozed and when he woke, he found her sobbing. He comforted her back to sleep. Later she woke and felt by the gentle shaking of his shoulder beside her that he was crying. She turned to him, leaned over and kissed away the salty tears. His hands came up, entwining themselves in her hair. The sensation of his strong fingers against her vulnerable scalp set off such a surge of desire that she reached down and caressed him until he responded with a passion to equal hers. Once more they made love.

They lay awake late into the night, she curled in his arms, neither knowing how swiftly the sun grew strong, dissolving the brief hours of their wedding night.

At ten she stirred and woke. At first she panicked, not knowing where she was, then feared she'd be late for school. Until everything came back to her, including the fact that the school was closed.

She looked down on Luc, his face softened by sleep. A poignant sorrow, stinging enough to take away her breath, seized her. She wanted to cry out to him to stay, to stay forever. Instead she touched his cheek. He opened his eyes and stared at her. In the daze of waking he didn't recognize her. Then he lost that blank expression. Swiftly there flitted across his face the look of love, then great sorrow, then fear—naked and plain. He sat up and reached for her; her arms went around his back. And it seemed to her that as strong as she knew Luc to be, he was also immeasurably fragile.

By noon he was gone.

For six months.

Or longer.

Or always.

CHAPTER TWENTY

DURING THE NEXT FEW DAYS Paula moved as though in a dream. She and Luc had agreed to keep their marriage secret until they had the civil ceremony. Marie Légère knew about them, and of course about the house she had helped Luc to furnish. Paula was grateful for Marie's friendship. Having someone to share the burden of Luc's absence with was a blessing.

For the remaining months of the school year, another teacher took Luc's place, a quiet, efficient, thoroughly boring man. Karel and Villette would have little to do with him, declaring their continuing loyalty and their resolution to "keep Monsieur Luc's memory alive." The phrase chilled Paula, but she appreciated the sentiment.

As the end of another school year approached, Paula's work load increased. After much counseling, Margaret Johnson decided to return to Toronto to continue her studies at that university's faculty of music.

"I'm going to give performance one more try," Margaret declared during one session with Paula. "Monsieur Josef has been a wonderful music teacher, but at university I can find teachers who specialize in the kind of problem I'm having."

"The important thing is that you're happy with that decision, Margaret."

"I am. I didn't do well here on auditions and exams, I know, but the exposure to other arts students convinced me I have to do something in music. If I can't solve my performance problems, I can teach in a school like this. A person wouldn't need to be ashamed if they ended up like Monsieur Josef."

"No, I should say not." Paula had begun to talk more often to Luc's brother. His shyness seemed to exacerbate her own, so she knew they would find it difficult to become close, but he was a good man and—though he didn't know it himself—her brother-in-law.

"You've helped me a lot, miss," Margaret said now. "I really appreciate that."

"I'm glad I was able to. It was a pleasure, Margaret. I'm certain that now you've decided on a course that includes at least one alternative, you'll do fine. So—what are you and I going to talk about for the rest of the year?"

"Going home, I guess," the girl said with a genuinely happy smile.

GOING HOME. After giving a month's notice on her apartment, Paula moved into her new home. Officially, that is. She'd never slept anywhere else since her wedding. Her days were full, but no matter how busy she was, she never stopped thinking about Luc for long. His letters were brief and brave, and she cherished each one.

Ma chère, ma belle, Paula, the rainy season is ending, and insect season is about to begin. You who are by now used to the benign drizzle of Brussels would be shocked at the power of the rain in this country. I love the music of it, though it frightens some. The insects frighten me. Nonetheless, the work goes well.

Carlos, the man who taught me panpipes, is here with me. He says my style has deteriorated drastically since I went back to Belgium. According to him, I now sound far too much like Ravel! He says such civilized sounds offend the birds, and that he feels obliged to teach me to "play wild" again.

Paula, I miss you. At night I sleep alone in a dusty little room in Rudolfo's house, the local shoemaker, gasoline vendor and smuggler of cosmetics from Miami! I'm waiting for news of what our next move has to be. And I'm waiting for you.

I picture you waiting, too. Around me I see a newer, rougher, stranger world than the little garden that is Belgium, but you're the flower of both garden and jungle. I love you. I'm coming back to you....

Once, only once, he called. It was late, and Paula was startled by the loud ringing in the echoing stillness of the house. Lifting the receiver, she heard Luc's voice and recognized it at once, though he was speaking not to her but to the operator, and in Spanish.

They talked for an hour. Afterward she could remember little of what he'd said in words, while the caressing tone of his voice filled her with a warmth that stayed with her for days. The only part of his message she had remembered word for word was that he wouldn't be able to call again, and that his letters would be less frequent. He didn't say he was moving on to a more-dangerous stage in his work, only that he was leaving the city and going to a small village farther inland. Paula knew it meant the same thing.

THE MONTHS that Villette had waited for the important Gallant audition had dwindled to weeks; the weeks had dwindled to one. Paula's work with the girl was now designed to keep her confidence up without feeding false pride. Constant harping from both Paula and the ballet teacher had resulted in Villette's being in top shape techniquewise. There was nothing more for Villette to do than to show up, do her best, wait for the results and take it from there. Or so it seemed.

The week before the audition, Villette disappeared from her grandfather's house. She wasn't missed until Saturday afternoon, at which point it occurred to her grandfather to ask the chauffeur whether he'd brought the young lady home the previous evening. On Sunday Paula learned, during a phone call from Marie, that Villette wasn't the only student missing.

"I'm afraid I have to ask you to come down to the school. Karel's parents are here, and so is Villette's grandfather's secretary. We all feel you may be able to give us some clues. I sense there's less here than meets the eye, but of course the relatives are most upset."

Paula was upset, too, but when she arrived at Le Berceau she did her best to explain what she thought might have motivated the two to run off. Pure mischief on the part of the one, she figured, and as for the other....

"As I'm sure you're both aware, Karel has been terribly upset since Luc LeBlanc left," she said, addressing the boy's mother and father. "I must admit, though, that I'm surprised to learn he's gone off again. We've spent a lot of time together lately, Karel and I, and I was under the strong impression that he was coming to grips with Luc's absence."

"Perhaps so," Monsieur Foubert said. "But my son still refuses to listen to reason when it comes to his future. He has managed to miss every deadline for application to the universities."

"*Monsieur*, maybe now isn't the best time to be talking about this, but would it be so very difficult to give Karel a little time in which to, well, to find himself? I realize you have very high hopes for him, well-placed hopes, I'm sure. Karel's an intelligent young man. But he's also an exceptionally talented writer. It's not at all premature for him to be thinking about writing professionally, or at least getting a start in that direction.

"I hesitate to mention it, because he asked me to forget that he told me this, but I know you refused to allow him to use one of your employee's names as a reference on a job application. Karel felt that refusal was a betrayal." Paula believed her mentioning that was a betrayal, as well, but it seemed essential to speak openly.

"Miss Emanuel, Karel and I have had it out about that more than once. I'm not an unreasonable man; I might be willing to relent. All right, I'm willing to apologize and see to it that he gets his reference for his newspaper job. But it isn't only his refusal to go to university that bothers me. Lately he seems to have got it into his head that he has to be some kind of adventurer in order to have things to write about. That's what's worrying me at the moment. Heaven only knows what he's got himself into! My wife feels it's too soon to call the police, considering that he came back on his own the last time, but I don't know. And the fact that Villette is involved. . . ."

"How well do you know Villette, Monsieur Foubert?" Marie Légère asked.

"Well enough to know she's no stranger to just plain mischief, *madame*," Foubert replied.

"If you feel we should call the police," Paula said, nodding at both Marie and Madame Foubert, "then we will, but I think that before too long we'll see that mischief is exactly what we're dealing with."

And within an hour she and Marie were proved

right. The housekeeper at the Foubert home called to say Karel was back, and Villette was with him. The two had been gone for less than forty-eight hours. Monsieur Foubert asked the housekeeper to send Villette to the school in a taxi, while he and his wife headed home to deal with their son. Before he left the banker spoke to Karel on the phone. From the tone of his voice, it seemed to Paula that perhaps Monsieur Foubert was finally starting to realize his son was ready to begin to live his own life.

Paula asked to speak to Karel before his father hung up. "Are you all right?" she asked.

"Paula," he answered, his voice subdued, "I'm so sorry. I have no excuse. It seemed as though it would be fun to fool everybody by disappearing for a day or two. I guess I just needed to get everybody off my back. I didn't think about how upset you'd all be until we were on our way home."

"You had us all worried, Karel. I promised Luc I'd keep my eye on you...."

"It's not your fault, miss...Paula. You know, I promised Luc I'd keep my eye on *you*. I won't disappoint you again. My father and I are going to settle this thing between us. I can't keep running away."

"I'm glad you realize that, Karel. I'll see you tomorrow."

"I'm sorry."

"I know."

As for Villette, she appeared triumphant when she arrived at the school. Her grandfather's secretary had no authority to reprimand, apparently. He politely inquired as to whether *mademoiselle* was ready to go home, and she smirked her cocky acquiescence, only a little subdued when her eye caught Marie's stony glance that promised later punishment.

"I SHOULD PUNISH both of them severely," Marie confided to Paula the next day when classes were over and they were enjoying tea in Marie's office. "They actually made it all the way to Paris!"

"How did they get the tickets and the money?"

"The plane reservations were no problem. The Foubert home has more than one personal computer, I'm told. As for the money, Karel had some cash, while Villette had wrangled a credit card out of her father as an advance eighteenth-birthday present. If she were my daughter...." Marie's face wrinkled into what would have been called a scowl on a less-dignified person. Then she relaxed. "But, *Dieu merci*, she is not my daughter. I haven't the slightest doubt that she instigated this whole thing and dragged Karel along just for the added fun of getting someone else in trouble."

Paula felt Marie was too harsh. "So are you going to punish her?" she asked. Despite the fact that she realized Villette's actions had been wrong—not to mention dangerous—Paula sensed that like any other student facing an important audition, Villette was under a lot of pressure. It wouldn't be fair to come down hard on her now.

Marie was too good an administrator not to have realized that herself. "Before classes this morning I had a talk with her. I told her exactly what I thought of her behavior and her lack of concern for her own welfare and Karel's. I wouldn't be surprised if it all went in one pretty ear and out the other, but she was quite quiet and still the whole time, almost as though she was really listening to what I had to say. I told her I'd spare her any punishment because of the audition, but after that was over she and I would have to have another talk. By then she might have a few suggestions as to how she could avoid such mischief in the future."

As it turned out, Marie changed her mind about even the talk with the girl. Villette did very poorly in the audition and was eliminated after the first round. Marie told Paula she actually pitied the young woman, and that her humiliation was probably sufficient punishment.

Paula felt awful for Villette, but she discovered her sympathy was completely wasted. "Don't feel sorry for me, miss," Villette advised during their final session. "Karel and I had such a lark in Paris! Next time I'll stay there. Daddy will pay until I get a job. Let's face it—who'd dance here if they could dance there?"

"You can't expect just to go there and get a job. It's a huge place, and you don't know anybody."

"I'll meet somebody. Look, Paula—"

"Don't call me by my first name."

"Look, Paula," Villette repeated with the effrontery she'd always shown, "let me give you a bit of advice. The school year's almost over. You've been here for a long time—"

"Not even two years."

"That's ages. And you're not getting any younger. I know you and Monsieur Luc had a thing for each other, but he's gone now. You might not have a lot of chances left. You should go somewhere exciting, do something exciting—like me. You're really okay, miss. You're just a little timid, that's all. You can still find someone else. Maybe even get married finally. Who knows?"

"It's too late."

"Because you're too old? Don't be silly. Lots—" The light dawned in Villette's mischievous eyes. "You don't mean it's true? It is true, isn't it—the rumor that you and Luc got married? Oh, is that ever romantic—secretly and everything! Good for you, miss. Did you have a honeymoon? Does he write every day?"

"Villette, I'm going to tell you this one last time. Mind your own business." Paula made her voice as stern as she could, but she couldn't hide from herself, or from the girl, the grudging but real affection she felt.

"Oh, miss," Villette gushed, jumping up and coming around Paula's desk to plant a kiss on her cheek. "You're all right, you know that? I used to think you were just a mouse, but I know better now. I'm going to miss you."

"I'm going to miss you, too."

"Oh, not for long. Before you know it, there'll be some other student as talented as me for you to help. Life goes on...."

CHAPTER TWENTY-ONE

IT AMAZED HIM how quickly he had been overwhelmed by the heat. And not just climactic heat, either. His own Liègeois background might make him a little emotional at times, but he didn't hold a candle to some of the men and women he now worked with. Luc hated stereotypes, so he was willing to admit that the unusual circumstances would have put anyone on edge, but he had seen a frightening anger in Carlos that morning.

They'd argued—for at least the tenth time—about security. Luc thought they were being lax, Carlos thought Luc was paranoid. The few others involved were divided half-and-half on the issue. Nothing had been settled. But at the end of the argument—that particular segment of it, anyway—Carlos had put his hand on Luc's shoulder with his usual open affection and said, "You are too hotheaded, my friend, and too cautious. But without you...." Luc turned away from thoughts of the man's praise, looking across the small room to Carlos himself.

His hands on the guitar, one of several instruments he played, moved so quickly they became a blur. Though he didn't often play Spanish music, preferring the folk music of his own country, tonight Carlos was treating them to flamenco. It made Luc uneasy because it stirred in him a hunger he didn't know when he could satisfy. A hunger for his wife. Unbidden images of Paula came to him, not to his eyes, but to his hands. He remembered the smooth feel of the curves of her beneath his fingers, the soft silkiness of her skin against his palms, the slide of her satiny hair on his shoulder when she lay with her head upon his chest.

"Carlos! *Amigo*, change your tune," he demanded. "You're driving me crazy with that stuff!"

The others laughed at Luc. They knew he was pining for someone, and they joked about it with him often during the evenings when they congregated at the little tavern in the village. "Get your pipes and play us something yourself, then!" someone shouted. Shaking away thoughts of home, Luc took up his instrument and complied.

ALL SUMMER LONG Paula studied, not only psychology, but Belgian history and Dutch, as well. Her job at Le Berceau shielded her somewhat from the language problem when school was in session, but she was convinced the two languages were necessary to a full enjoyment of life in Brussels, just as two languages had been essential in Montreal.

According to Luc's original estimate—and she'd heard nothing to the contrary since—she could expect him home around the end of September. She often had dinner with Marie and Josef and sometimes lunched with other teachers from the school. She even accepted an invitation to another musical soiree at the van Becks. It amused her that this time when she told Dr. Pieter that she wasn't available, he believed her at once and immediately turned away to press his charms on somebody else.

Time spent with friends helped to pass the lonely hours, but nothing took her mind off Luc for very long. His letters, now far more infrequent, were a lifeline to her. She eagerly awaited the postman, and when a letter did arrive, she opened it before she even went back into the house. They were often short, but Paula could tell from the carefully worded messages that he was moving toward finishing his work, setting up the press and gathering writers and printers to work for it.

By the first of September she was registered in a part-time university course, and she had mapped out much of her program for the first few months' work at Le Berceau. She soon found that Luc, too, had been even busier than she'd thought.

He had had his subscription to his favorite paper, *Les Gens*, transferred from his old apartment to the house. Paula generally took a glance at it but seldom read all the articles in an issue. One day as she was scanning the headlines, she noticed a piece relevant to Luc. Looking more closely, she was amazed to see it was a special dispatch from Luc himself! The article was a scathing indictment of an allegedly planned foreign intervention in the Central American country. There were many who would strongly disagree with Luc—especially those fighting for power where he was now. It frightened Paula to read his words, because she understood the risk he was taking. Yet she was enormously proud of his courage and of the reasoned eloquence of his writing.

Day followed day, and she waited. She carried her love for him and her knowledge of his love like a precious object that for now was hidden but that would soon know the light of full sun. She waited with utter faith that he would return, that the promised homecoming was growing near. Often she studied his words, the ones addressed to her alone and the ones she saw over his by-line more and more often.

Across the miles he thought of her. Constantly when he wasn't working. He was thinking of her, in a sense, the night they came for him. He was dreaming. They were home in their house, but it looked a little like Luc's old rooms. As at Christmas, Paula was decorating the windows, not with fir boughs this time, but with the bright flowers of spring. As then, too, her form was outlined, a silhouette against the sun streaming in.

Luc took a step, reached for her. But before his hand touched her, he heard a scuffle at the door—argument, shouting, knocking, and then a sound that made him realize he was no longer dreaming, a sound a man couldn't fail to recognize if he'd ever heard it before, and Luc had. The sound of the butt of a gun against wood that was cracking under force.

ONE DAY, going directly to the page where Luc's articles usually appeared, Paula found not an article, but a notice. It said that the paper regretted to inform its readers that Luc LeBlanc and a fellow Belgian journalist had recently been jailed on charges of sedition and espionage.

The paper fell from her shaking fingers. For a moment she merely stood, waiting for some thought of what she should do to come to her. Finally, as if in a daze, she stumbled toward the study. In the top drawer of his desk she found a card with a phone number on it, which Luc had told her to call in case anything came up that she couldn't handle. She'd shoved it in the drawer the day he left and hadn't thought about it since. Now, her hand trembling, she dialed. After many attempts, all of which netted a busy signal, she nearly gave up. But she tried once more, and the phone was answered by someone whose voice she was surprised to recognize: Monsieur Merit's, the bookseller.

He came to her house at once and offered what comfort he could. "There's no reason for alarm yet, Paula," he assured her. "We have to wait and see. Luc has been arrested before. Sometimes it's only a matter of a few hours in these cases—sometimes longer. We can only be patient until word arrives."

Word hadn't arrived by the end of the week, nor by the beginning of the next week, when she began her psychology course. She had to fight strong feelings of futility. Studying, working, waiting—nothing made sense without the promise of Luc's return. She kept up a good front at Le Berceau, but the effort cost her dearly. Many nights she fell exhausted into bed and awoke in the morning no less tired.

For eight weeks Paula went without word of him or from him. Sometimes Monsieur Merit phoned, but his calls only scared her. The kindly gentleman had no news, simply called to see how she was holding up. But every time she heard his voice, she was so afraid of what he might be about to tell her that she finally asked him not to call unless there was new information.

THE FIRST DAY of November was a day off. In that Catholic country, All Saints' Day was an official holiday. Paula slept very late at least in part because it was such a dark, lowering day. She woke up at ten, thinking it was closer to seven or eight. From the moment she awoke she had such a feeling of foreboding that she felt like weeping. She resisted that urge and the urge to remain in bed. Getting up, she dressed and was headed for the kitchen when the doorbell rang. With a nervous start she ran to answer it.

"Goedemorgen. Bonjour, madame!" Standing on Paula's flagstone porch was a very blond neighborhood girl of six or seven. In her hand she held a basket covered with a sparkling-white linen cloth.

"Goedemorgen, Bertrande," Paula answered, mustering a smile and accepting the basket. "What have you brought me?"

"Zielekoekjes—soul cakes. For you."

"Dank u," Paula said politely, but she had to hide a

spasm of fear and distaste. The little girl noticed nothing amiss. She curtsied with old-fashioned charm and was soon skipping down the street toward her own house not far away.

Paula discarded the cakes immediately. At any other time she would have welcomed such a gift, but her nerves were reaching the breaking point. She knew the cakes commemorated the next day, All Souls' Day, on which Catholics worldwide gave special thought to the dead. The cakes were in keeping with a tradition ingrained in her, too. She couldn't stand to think about death. Not while Luc was in prison.

As it progressed, the day brightened not at all. Paula did some chores around the house, but by noon she had run out of things to do. She was far too restless to read or sew. The feeling of foreboding would not be shaken off; she decided to go out for a run despite the weather.

It was Luc who had introduced her to running, and as her feet hit the damp pavement, their rhythm seemed to match the rhythm of her unsteady heart, heightening her anxiety.

Still, she ran and ran, losing track of time, distance, direction. She ran in a huge circle that brought her home. And she was no less tense when she finished than when she'd begun. Paula showered, put on jeans and a T-shirt and was headed for the kitchen to make a cup of tea when the doorbell rang.

It sounded like a death knell in the cool still air of the house. Her heart was in her throat as she grabbed the knob and yanked open the door.

Monsieur Merit was standing with his hat in his hand. He was pale, and he was looking at her with an expression she didn't want to see. His lined face was full of pity. "Paula, may I come in?" His tone was grave and gentle, but the sight of him terrified her. She could find no words to greet him, to invite him into the house. Stepping forward, he took her arm, led her back into the hallway and closed the door.

"I have to talk to you, dear. There's news." At his words she began to tremble. Her legs seemed to lose their strength, and she reached out, leaning her hand against the wall. Monsieur Merit, clearly alarmed, urged her toward the living room, but she shook off his hand.

There was a ceiling light in the hallway, on today because it was so dark. By its light Paula's face was like a white porcelain mask as she demanded, "Tell me. Whatever it is, just tell me now."

"Come and sit down—"

"No." Her voice was barely a whisper. "Just tell me."

Monsieur Merit cleared his throat. Again both his hands gripped his hat. With the eye for detail that seems to grow keenest in the most desperate of moments, Paula noticed that his hands looked old, that his knuckles were white with the gripping.

"The news is this," he said, his voice breaking a little despite his attempt to steady it. "Of the two Belgian journalists who were incarcerated, one has been released and given twenty-four hours to get out of the country. . . ."

Paula's pain-filled eyes shot up, forcing Monsieur Merit to look directly at her. She had no way of knowing whether he saw the hope in her eyes; she saw little in his. Her face registered puzzlement, then something approaching horror. Monsieur Merit's hand came up to her shoulder to support her. "The other journalist," he said, finishing his sentence in a single breath, "the other journalist has been executed. And so help me God, Paula, I don't know which one was Luc!"

The hallway reeled. She felt herself sinking. She felt his arm beneath her knees. . . .

When she came to, he was mopping her face with great sweeping motions. It took her several minutes to collect herself, but when she did she said, "Monsieur Merit, I know how difficult this is for you, too. I'm okay now. I was just making some tea. Would you like some?"

He accepted gratefully. He waited in silence for the tea to be ready, and he drank it in silence. Both were lost in their own thoughts, even though they were thinking about the same person. After a while he rose to go, saying, "We must still wait. There's still hope." His voice was weary and no consolation to Paula. "I'll return as soon as I can find out. In the meantime. . . ."

In the meantime, nothing, Paula thought.

"I'll see myself out," the man offered, but she found the strength to show him to the door. At the threshold he stopped and turned. He leaned down and kissed her forehead the way an old man kisses a much-younger woman. His eyes were eloquent, but there were no words equal to that message, so Paula was silent. Sadly he sighed and turned to go.

She had to lean against the wall again, but after what seemed a very long while she was able to move back through the living-room door. She took from beneath a small writing desk a straight-back chair and set it beside the west window. She sat with her back to the door to wait some more. To wait for something she dared not name.

As though in a trance she sat for hours. Scenes of her days with Luc flashed before her eyes. Luc the stranger. Luc the helper. The pest, the friend, the teacher, the tyrant. Luc the lover. The lost.

How could she face the future without him? *A fifty-fifty chance, that's what you've got,* she thought. And she knew, too, that if she won, someone else would lose. Someone else whose loved one would not come home.

How could I have come so far, loved him for so short a time. How can I. . . .

Paula's tears fell and dried and fell again. The day that was dark with clouds grew darker with the approach of night. And after a while the darkness, broken only by the single light from the hallway, became a kind of comfort. So did the utter immobility of sitting as she was with no motion except for her breathing and the beating of her heart. No other sounds, either. Maybe she would sit like that forever, enveloped in her complete aloneness.

Suddenly, there was another sound, the noise of a car approaching, stopping, a door closing before the car pulled away again. Listening intently, Paula could make out muffled steps coming up the front walk. Then silence again. Then a slight scraping sound, a brushing against the wood of the door.

A key turned in the lock. Of all the world's billion keys, there were only two that fit that door. One was in the pocket of her jeans.

Electrified, she salt bolt upright. She could not move, could not cry out.

After an eternity of seconds, the door opened. Then it slammed shut, echoing like gunshot into every corner of the house. Silence. Then sharp footsteps crossed the entrance hall toward the study. No. Away from the study. Toward the living room, where she sat.

With shaking but determined legs Paula stood. She turned. She saw him standing in a pool of light from the hallway fixture.

His shoes were wet. His dark coat was rumpled. His full beard glinted a little in the soft light. He was wearing his glasses, but they didn't hide his violet eyes shining now at the sight of her coming out of the dimness toward his outstretched arms.

She ran the last few steps; she had to. In a rush of sensation she felt the taut hardness of his body, the pulsating warmth of him. She smelled rain and musk and clean hair and his skin. And she clung to him as strongly as one person could cling to another. As strongly as he clung to her.

After endless moments he pulled away. His voice was a caressing whisper in her ear. "Paula, I know I'm late. A whole month. You have every reason to complain—"

"Luc, oh, please, not now—don't tease me now," she said with a laugh.

"I have a very good excuse for my lateness," he went on. "It's finished."

"The work?"

"Yes. They caught me when I had already returned to the city, to Rudolfo's. They have no idea where the press is, nor who is running it."

"The other journalist?"

"He wasn't one of us. He was a man who'd spent his entire life in the field. He died as he wanted to die, Paula, and he left nobody behind."

They were both silent as a sign of respect. Then, tentatively, Paula breathed, "And now you're here to stay?"

"You bet!" he said in English, teasing her again, but his voice caught in his throat. "Oh, Paula, to stay. For good, forever."

"Forever is a long time, Luc."

"I hope so, my love," he answered. "I certainly hope it is."

ABOUT THE AUTHOR

Lucy Snow moved to Canada from the States in the early seventies. Since then, as a novelist, editor and poet, she has enjoyed both "real" travel and armchair excursions from her Toronto home. *Garden of Lions* is Lucy's third Superromance.

Books by Lucy Snow

HARLEQUIN SUPERROMANCE

83–SONG OF EDEN
115–A RED BIRD IN WINTER
155–GARDEN OF LIONS

These books may be available at your local bookseller.

Don't miss any of our special offers. Write to us at the following address for information on our newest releases.

Harlequin Reader Service
P.O. Box 52040, Phoenix, AZ 85072-2040
Canadian address: P.O. Box 2800, Postal Station A,
5170 Yonge St., Willowdale, Ont. M2N 6J3

Readers rave about Harlequin American Romance!

" ...the best series of modern romances
I have read...great, exciting, stupendous,
wonderful."
—S.E.,* Coweta, Oklahoma

" ...they are absolutely fantastic...going to be
a smash hit and hard to keep on the
bookshelves."
—P.D., Easton, Pennsylvania

"The American line is great. I've enjoyed
every one I've read so far."
—W.M.K., Lansing, Illinois

" ...the best stories I have read in a long
time."
—R.H., Northport, New York

*Names available on request.